The King's Angels

By Anne Stevens

High Treason in Henry's Court

Foreword

It is 1532, and Will Draper is back from Italy. He returns home to England, to find it a subtly different place from the country he left, but the year before. Henry now realises, thanks to Thomas Cromwell's machinations, that Pope Clement will never grant his freedom from Queen Katherine, and is disposed to gain his desires by any means open to him, as king.

He is hedged in, on all sides, by men willing to offer him advice. Those closest to the king are Cromwell, Norfolk, Charles Brandon, the dissolute Duke of Suffolk, George Boleyn, Stephen Gardiner, the Bishop of Winchester, and Sir Thomas More, Lord Chancellor of England.

These men are like the king's 'guardian angels', drawn together to provide help and support to the increasingly wayward monarch. He uses them, instead, like birds of prey; each, in turn must fly, stoop, and hunt for him. Each man moves in, and out of favour on a seemingly weekly basis, and each must look to their own devices, if they are to survive these turbulent times

Thomas Cromwell, the son of a blacksmith, is the least privileged of Henry's band of angels, and must fight hard for his place at the high table. He is, at heart, more of a Protestant reformer, and he wishes the church, and the state, to change for the better.

Norfolk, and the Boleyn family support Cromwell, but for their own ends, and Suffolk is deep in his debt. Stephen Gardiner and Thomas More are his two oldest, and dearest friends, yet pose a terrible threat to his grand design.

Since being declared the 'Head of the Church in England ~ for as far as the law of Christ allows' in 1531, Henry's deep distrust, and hatred of the Papacy has grown apace, and he sees, quite rightly, intrigue and treason around every corner.

The king can be a generous master to his guardian angels, but demands, in return, their unwavering loyalty. Sometimes, however, they must remember their own limitations and, deep in their hearts, they know one stark truth.

Even angels may fall.

.

1   A New Task

Will Draper opens one eye, and groans. The sounds of the house on the river are reminding him that he is back home, and that he must conform toMiriam's way of life with a goodwill born out of his love for her. She is, after all is said and done, the true head of the household, and runs it with a passion and dedication unusual in so young a woman.

He works, when required, for Master Thomas Cromwell, the Privy Councillor, and earns a good, though sporadic income from his adventures. Just a few months before, he returned from Venice with over seven hundred pounds in gold ducats, only to find that Miriam has outdone him. She has increased her market business two fold, and opened a large new warehouse in Putney, from where she distributes an ever widening list of goods.

He rolls over, and stands. His clothes are laid out on a nearby chair, and a good breakfast will be waiting for him below. On a working day, his wife is up at five, and about her business by six, at the latest. She runs market stalls, and imports both Dutch and North Country cheeses, rope from Derbyshire, lamp oil from Bristol, salted herrings from Lowestoft's fish markets, fresh eels from the Thames, and casks of mace from Venice.

Their combined income is well above fifteen hundred pounds a year, which is close to the two thousand a year that Norfolk's estates bring him in. Folk in the neighbourhood have taken to calling their ever growing household, Draper's Hall, much to the amusement of Tom Cromwell, who admires their thrift, and hard work.

"The girl is an angel, sent from Heaven above," he tells Will, when they meet, later in the morning. "She will make a lord of you inside ten years."

"I do not wish to be a lord, Master Thomas … as neither do you. How often do you tell me to keep to the shadows, else we attract greedy, dangerous men to us?"

"True enough." Cromwell sighs. He sighs a lot these days, and is more prone to introspection than he once was. It is his age, he suspects. "Let the girl make you rich, Will, and I will keep you from under her feet."

"Ah, you have a task for me?" Will Draper tries to sound as if he is annoyed, but in truth, is happy for something to do. His wife is making him look like an indolent oaf, and he needs to be employed. "Not another trip to Italy, I hope?"

"The Doge wrote to me but the other day, Will," Thomas Cromwell replies. "He still speaks glowingly of how you smashed the condottiero's army … with but thirty men at your back. I would pay a thousand pounds in gold to have been alongside you that day, my boy. A man is never so much alive, as when he faces death and danger at every turn. Oh, to be that young again."

Will believes him. Cromwell has always longed for the far off days when he was a freebooting mercenary, fighting on the wrong side of every battle, and escaping scrapes by the skin of his teeth. The fight, outside San Gemini, in Umbria had been no more than a skirmish, with scarcely a thousand men under arms. Still, it was a close run thing, with a desperate last charge turning the affair.

The forces of Malatesta Baglioni, the infamous

condottiero, had been on the brink of breaking the Doge's Swiss guards and the young gentlemen of Venice, when he and Mush had charged into the enemy's rear, with but thirty men. So violently had they struck home, that the condottiero's men had believed them to be a relieving army, and scattered to the four winds.

With hundreds dead on each side, Will could hardly call it a great victory - more a pyrrhic one. Still, the Doge of Venice had been most grateful, sending him and his friends home laden with sacks of gold, and a valuable import licence for mace, which Miriam has taken up with great gusto. London is now buying her imported spice at a good price, and all is going well.

"What would you have me do?" Will asks, in a not unkindly voice. Thomas Cromwell is a good, and fair minded master, and seldom leaves him unrewarded. Though, sometimes, his demands border on the unpalatable, and Will has to test his own moral code to the limit.

"I need you to go to Calais, and find a man for me," Tom Cromwell says.

"Is he in hiding?" Will understands this kind of a job, and slips into the right frame of mind. He is to seek out that which is hidden, and to do it with sensitivity, and guile.

"Not from us," Cromwell replies, evasively.

"Please, define 'us', master." Will Draper knows Thomas Cromwell has a foot in many camps, and does not want to make a fundamental mistake. He must know which colours he is riding under for this particular mission.

"I mean, not from me," Cromwell says. "He has been in a place called Augsburg for many months past, on the king's diplomatic business. Then he was called home at the end of his mission. In Bruges, he was waylaid by several villains, who tried to kill him. He fought them off, made good his escape, and is now hiding out in Calais. The fellow is one of ours, Will, as well as a dear friend to me, personally. I want him safely home again, and under my roof. There is some danger, I believe. Can you do it?"

"I shall need some help. Mush will come, of course."

"Take Tom Wyatt too."

"I cannot. He is still in Portugal." Will is on thin ice now, as he does not wish to speak of why Wyatt was knocked out, and put on a Lisbon bound cargo vessel.

"I cannot imagine why the boy would want to go there," Tom Cromwell says, rubbing his chin. "He has no family over there, or any business interests. Did he not give any clue to you?"

"None," Will replies. He does not like lying to Cromwell, but the truth, that Wyatt needed to be kept away from England, is too dangerous to know. The handsome poet is wildly infatuated with Anne Boleyn, and cannot be trusted to keep his mouth shut, and his head on his shoulders. King Henry is a powder keg where his future wife is concerned, and Tom Wyatt's lovelorn poetry is the tinder that might well light the fuse. A hint of illicit love, and the poet's handsome head would be on a spike, high above the Tower of London's gate.

"I fear that I worry about the fellow far too much," says Cromwell. It is only a few weeks since an inflammatory pamphlet about a French trained whore, and a poet named as Tom Whatnot has come to the attention of the king, and the matter is still being investigated by Sir Thomas Audley, leader of the House of Commons, and a close friend of Austin Friars' master. "For 'tis only that I know his father, and did make a foolish promise to the old man, that I will keep him safe. My word is my bond though, and I am saddled with the young reprobate for evermore."

"God looks after all his fools," Will tells his master, and smiles. "Now, who is it I must find for you?"

"Stephen Vaughan. When not abroad, on the king's secret business, he is a merchant … of sorts."

"Sweet Christ, sir, but you know some choice fellows, and no mistake." Will Draper exclaims. "On my return from Italy, I heard some tale around your breakfast table, concerning the man. Was he not almost taken up as a heretic, and burnt at the stake?"

"That would be that wicked business with the priest, George Constantine," Tom Cromwell replies. "Sir Thomas More took the cowardly fellow up, and accused him of being a heretic. The man broke, as soon as the Lord Chancellor's men started to stretch his bones. He named two of his friends, and another priest, as conspirators in the distribution of certain texts by William Tyndale."

"It was only a matter of time before Sir Thomas retaliated, sir. You have dealt him one or two blows, of late." Will knows that, for his betrayal, Constantine was allowed to flee to France, and save himself from the fire. His comrades had fared worse, and were quickly condemned, and burnt at the stake, before Cromwell could sway the king to show some mercy. "Those men will become martyrs to the greater cause."

"That will console their widows, and their five fatherless children," Cromwell says, sarcastically. "I have made provision for them, but cannot keep everyone whose husband goes to the stake for their beliefs. Our Father Constantine will burn in Hell for his treachery. It was after naming his friends, that More played him false, saying that he must name the greatest culprit … Stephen Vaughan. Though the two have never met, Constantine denounced him, as a friend of Tyndale, and a known heretic."

"I see." Will Draper wonders why the man is still alive, and asks the question.

"Because of me." Cromwell rings a bell, and orders wine. He is taking more these days, and usually un-watered. "I went to the king, and showed him that this cowardly priest, Constantine must have lied. Henry accepted my word, but demanded that Stephen be removed from court, until the Lord Chancellor's men had ceased searching for him."

"So, you sent him to Augsburg," Will says, "where, no doubt, you found a number of very useful things for him to do for you."

"So young, and so cynical." Cromwell pours two glasses of rich red wine for them. "And so right. The king has exhausted his banker friends, across Europe. He drives away the rich Jews with his bigotry, threatens the Lombards, and upsets the Medici houses. That leaves only the Fuggers of Augsburg."

"They are bankers?" Will has little experience of the world of high finance, and thinks of bankers as men who stroll around with sacks of money tied to their belts, which they lend out at exorbitant rates of interest.

"Perhaps the richest in the world," Thomas Cromwell explains. "They have the contract with Emperor Charles to handle all the gold and silver that comes out of the New World mines, and have been quietly absorbing the Medici business, piece by piece. Anton Fugger is a year younger than I, and worth more than a thousand Thomas Cromwells."

"Was Master Vaughan successful in his mission?" Will Draper asks, knowing that had he been, he would even now be drinking wine with them in England.

"Partially." Cromwell likes to win, and the thought that the Fugger clan have the best of the deal so far, disquiets him greatly. "Stephen Vaughan has negotiated a loan of two hundred and fifty thousand pounds for the realm, providing we can present them with favourable accounts. Herr Anton Fugger, like any real banker, wishes to know his money is safe."

"And is it?"

"It is. Our current national income is just over one million, and the income from the coming church reformation will double that, but we do not have it yet. In the meantime, we are looking at the possibility of a costly war with France. Once that starts, the Scots will eagerly join in, and we will need two armies."

"Then let us ride on the Scots at once, and so stop their threat," Will says, speaking like a true soldier. "With ten thousand men, and a few cannon, a good general will take Stirling in a week, and bring them to their senses. Once they are beaten, François will think twice before he raises his banner. He will remember his history …. For Agincourt and Crecy still scare them."

"Ah, the military mind at work," Thomas Cromwell replies. "We cannot simply attack the Scots, Will. There must be a valid reason for it, or the world, and all its armies, might turn on us. No, we must wait, and prepare. The king is building war ships, but too few, and too slowly."

"So, Henry must have his loan," Will says. "Then

we can raise our army, and arm our ships well, the better to withstand a war that might never happen?"

"You begin to see, my boy." Thomas Cromwell pours a second glass of wine, and offers the jug to Draper, who refuses. "We must show that we can easily afford the Fugger loan. Master Vaughan was forced to agree to these terms, and their people will visit in a couple of months to take a look at us."

"Is that a problem?"

"Until a few hours ago, I'd have said not," Cromwell tells his agent, "but there are complications. Vaughan's secondary mission was to call in to visit William Tyndale, and ask him to cease printing his English bible. The king thought the idea up, and thinks Tyndale will listen to Vaughan, because they were once friends."

"I wager that did not go down any too well," Will says, smiling at the naïvety of the plan. "Master Tyndale is a Protestant fanatic, and nothing will stop him preaching the new faith, except death. What then?"

"William refused, of course, and Vaughan continued on his way. A message came, just this morning, from Calais. It was in code, and hurriedly written. Stephen writes that he is in hiding, and that he has become aware of a great secret that might ruin our plans."

"What?"

"He would not commit it to paper," Cromwell concludes. "Whatever it is, it is far too dangerous to be put down in any message. You must travel at once, and find Stephen Vaughan, even if you must tear Calais apart."

"For that, I must have a giant," Will replies. "May I take your nephew with me?"

"You may, but I implore you not to get him killed, Will, lest his mother descends on me in a fury. My sister is a most fearsome woman, and I fear her more than any Scottish army!"

*

"We have enough to take our own house now," Gwen Draper says, happily, and Mush's face clouds over. She is almost sixteen years old, and eager to start a family with her new husband. Since coming out of Wales, the girl and her man have been lodging with Mush's sister, and brother-in-law, Will.

"Don't you like living here?" he asks.

"Yes, but Miriam and Will might wish us gone, so that they might have some privacy." Gwen has seen a small house, less than a hundred yards further down towards the estuary, and longs to become a home maker. "Master Gough, the boat maker, says we can have it for six pounds a year."

"Six pounds!" Mush cannot believe how the price of leasing a house has gone up these last twelve months.

"It is always dearer in London, my love," she says, soothingly. "Or we might buy it outright, for sixty pounds."

"The bloody thief, I ought to slit his throat." Mush ben Mordecai, who is now known as Draper, can scarcely believe what he hears. "I risk my life to earn gold, and these fellows make it by sitting at home, building houses."

"Mush, we have almost a thousand pounds invested by Master Cromwell, at four percent a year. I asked him what that means, and he tells me we have a yearly income of thirty nine pounds eight shillings. Add that to what Miriam pays me, and we can afford it with ease."

"Miriam pays you?" Mush still thinks of himself as a single man in many ways, and has yet to learn that he must take an interest in the doings of his wife. "What for?"

"I help with her market stalls," Gwen replies. "I told you I would keep busy whilst you were in Venice, did I not?"

"Well … yes."

"What did you take it to mean?" Gwen asks, becoming irritated with his casual approach to life. "Did I sit at home sewing, or take a lover? No, I did not. I work for Miriam. She pays me two shillings a week."

"What?" Mush is surprised at his wife's revelation. "A brick maker only earns sixpence a day. My sister is generous indeed!"

"She must have about her those she can trust," Gwen explains. "Miriam is going to be a great lady one day, and I think it meet that her family are drawn along with her. I shall help her to the best of my ability."

"Then you must have the trappings of a fine lady," Mush replies. He adores his new Welsh wife, and shall deny her nothing he can afford. "Tell Master Gough that we will buy his house, for fifty pounds. If he accepts, explain to him that he may call on my services, if ever he has need of them."

"How will that help?" Gwen asks. She is new to the Cromwell way of doing things, and cannot see how a favour from Mush might influence a Thames boat builder.

"He will see that I am an Austin Friars man, and

that I have Thomas Cromwell behind me." Mush does not mean this as a threat, but a promise. If the boat builder ever has a problem with the law courts, or from some violent competitor, it will be sorted out for him, the Cromwell way.

"Then I shall speak with him at once," Gwen Draper says. She neglects to mention that Miriam is guiding her hand, and that her sister-in-law has promised them a new bed, and some choice pieces of furniture. "For who can tell when we will need the extra space?"

Mush is slow to pick up the inference, but suddenly pales with a mixture of surprise, and mild shock.

"You don't mean …?" he stutters.

"No, not yet," Gwen replies. "But now you are home, we have much time to catch up. If you have the inclination."

Mush is more than inclined, he is eager. Though any children born from their union will not, in the strict sense, be Jewish, he wants nothing more than to sire a brood of olive skinned children in the heart of London. He slips an arm about Gwen's slim waist, and pulls her close to him. Gwen kisses him, and wonders at her good fortune. A few months before, and she was a wild thing, surviving in a welsh forest, on her wits alone.

"Plenty of time for that later!" Will Draper appears in the doorway, and spoils the moment. "Master Cromwell wishes us to go to Calais."

"Again?" Mush well recalls his last visit to the stinking, sink hole of England. "Can he not send someone he doesn't like?"

"Therein lies the problem," Will replies, laughing. "For Cromwell likes everyone, even his enemies!"

"Of which I may become one," Gwen mutters, and stamps off to seek out Miriam. She finds her by the new jetty, supervising the loading of her barge, which she has had built to suit her purposes. Once loaded the craft, under the command of an ageing boatman, called Hal Petty, will deliver fresh produce to various points along the Thames.

"There you are, Gwen," Miriam says. "I thought you might miss today's trip."

"Not I, mistress," Gwen replies. "For I have little else to do, now your husband has stolen my Mush away again."

"What?" Miriam's heart sinks. The last time Will went away, it was to Venice, and she had to cope alone for six months without him. "They are scarcely home, and Cromwell beckons again. I swear, did we not all owe him so much, I would set up a ringing in his ears!"

"They seem pleased enough to go," Gwen bemoans. "Mush almost leaped for his sword."

"Pray tell me, girl. Where to, and for how long?"

"Calais, your husband says." The girl is upset, and wishes to show her anger. "Why can he not take Master Rafe, or that big ox, Richard Cromwell instead? Mush has his duties at home too."

"Be happy our men are in such great demand," Miriam Draper replies. "For they bring home good money, and help us live so well. Take heart, Gwen and, in the meantime, we shall get on with our own business. Once you have your own house, you will want Mush out from under your feet more times than not!"

"What you say may well come to pass," the petite Welsh girl replies, "but for now, I would as fain have him here to pester me, and want me home."

"I doubt they will be more than a few days," Miriam tells the girl. "Then you can play housewife as much as you wish."

"God keep them safe," Gwen says, "for each time they go forth, they face the chance of death."

"Enough," Miriam concludes. "We must all do our best, and trust to fate. Come, perhaps old Master Petty will let you steer as far as the bridge!"

"Might we stop at Master Gough's yard?" Gwen asks. "Mush says I am to offer him fifty pounds for the new house."

"Offer forty, and let him force you up to fifty," Miriam advises her friend. "Men love to think they have the upper hand, and it will make him more pliable when you ask for the land next door."

"What, that piece of scrub?" Gwen is surprised. "What ever would I want that for?"

"Offer him ten pounds," Miriam explains. "If I ask him, he'll think he can push the price up. I will buy it from you for twenty, and build a house on it."

"Then I will make ten pounds for nothing," Gwen says, smiling.

"And I will build a grand house on the river bank, and lease it out to the Earl of Surrey. He wants a new town house, and will pay a pretty rental."

"The Duke of Norfolk's son is a scoundrel, Mistress Miriam," Gwen replies, frowning. "Are you sure he will pay on time?"

"Norfolk will stand as guarantor for him." Miriam has done her sums, and knows such an arrangement will bring her in a forty pound a year profit. "When the boy tires of the place, I can sell it on, for a tidy sum."

"Then I should buy the land, and sell you half, should I not?" Gwen asks.

"You learn fast," Miriam says. "Very well, let us do it your way. Why, I could use you to buy up half the riverbank, on the quiet, and fill it with houses."

"Then I am a partner?"

"In this matter, yes," Miriam agrees. "I will fund the buying and building, and you will act as my buyer, for a fifth part of the profit."

"A fourth."

"Then you must put in some capital."

"I can find five hundred within the week," Gwen says, and watches Miriam's look of surprise. "Master Cromwell keeps it safe for us, and Mush earns gold in mysterious ways."

"The price of cutting throats for Master Thomas must have risen," Miriam says, and regrets the jest at once. Gwen's face drains of colour as she understands what her friend means to imply about her brother.

"Mush only kills when he must," she says, apologetically.

"Of course," Miriam replies, squeezing the girl's cold hand with her own. "As does Will. He often says the world is a better place for those he and my brother send from it."

"Ah, here is Master Gough's landing," Gwen says. "Let me go ashore, and finish our business with him. Ten pounds, you say, for the scrub?"

"Twelve, if pushed."

"Pushed?" Gwen grins. "Who would dare push the wife of a Cromwell man?"

No, Miriam thinks, that would be decidedly unhealthy.

2   A Council of War

Eustace Chapuys' hand is trembling again. He notes that it is something which only happens when he is in the presence of the Boleyn woman. She smiles, and makes delightful small talk, but hovers over him like a hungry bird of prey. One day, she will stoop, and rip out his heart.

"I hear that the emperor prays six times a day, *M'sieu* Chapuys," she says. "One can only hope his knees are up to the task!" The ladies of her court giggle at the lame jest, and admire how the little Savoyard diplomat keeps his composure.

"Emperor Charles is a robust man, Lady Anne," he replies, smiling to hide his disgust of the woman. "As can be attested to by his great fecundity. To date, he has sired four healthy, living children."

"Including his bastards?" Lady Mary Boleyn asks of the Imperial ambassador, playfully. "For if that is the case, he will soon be overtaken by another."

"Watch your tongue, sister," Anne snaps. "When my time comes to give Henry sons, all others will be illegitimate. The emperor will come to understand that a strong England must take precedence over a mere family tie."

"Queen Katherine is the emperor's very much loved aunt,   Lady Anne," Chapuys says, and immediately regrets his words.

"The Dowager Princess of Wales," Anne says, her voice growing cold, and hard. "In France, they know how to handle these matters better."

"Take care, madam," Chapuys replies, throwing caution to the wind. "For what befell the French queen those many years ago, can befall any man's wife, with enough money to pay the assassin!"

"You tire me, Chapuys," Anne says, turning away. "I meant to introduce you to one of my ladies, but fear you might bore her to death … in quite the wrong way. Good day."

Eustace Chapuys is diplomat enough to know it is time to depart. He bows to her back, and leaves the chamber, accompanied by Lady Mary Boleyn, who plucks, urgently, at his sleeve, so that he steps into an alcove with her.

"My lady?" he asks, stiffly.

"Do not scowl at me, sir," she says, with a smile. "For I am the other Boleyn girl. The nice one. My sister wants only for you to tell your precious master, Charles, how futile his opposition to her is. The king will have his way, despite all. You might be better employed trying to get the best of things for your mistress. If Henry wishes a quiet transition, make him pay for it, dearly."

"Why tell me this?" Chapuys asks, suspiciously. He knows that Mary is an ex lover of Henry's, and has born him a child. Perhaps it is her way of gaining a subtle kind of revenge?

"Ask Katherine's lady-in-waiting, Maria de Salinas whether I am a friend, or a foe," Mary persists. "Implore the queen to step aside gracefully, and demand lands, and titles, in recompense. Henry will agree, if it is done well. Thomas Cromwell would know how to ask for her. Seek his advice, sir."

"I am the emperor's ambassador at the king's court, Lady Mary, not the queen's, though I love her well enough." Chapuys means this, and respects Katherine's stubborn adherence to the marriage.

"Then speak to Cromwell," Lady Mary insists. "He has an audience with the more wicked Boleyn girl soon. Wait about, and take him to one side."

"Our friendship is hard tested, of late," the little man confesses.

"God above!" Mary takes his hand, and places it over her left breast. "Think with this, Señor Chapuys, rather than with your head."

Eustace Chapuys is so surprised that he does not remove his hand, and they look into one another's eyes for long moments. At length, Mary takes the hand, raises it to her lips, and kisses the fingers, one by one.

"Should you ever wish to consummate our friendship," she whispers, "I will be waiting."

"My Lady!" Eustace Chapuys is only human, and Mary's blonde good looks are a sharp counterpoint to her sister's darker, thinner self. "What are you saying? If I were ever to visit you, it must be in secret, for such a liaison would ruin both of us."

"Not if I return to Spain with you," Mary Boleyn replies, huskily. "You might marry me, and we can live in Madrid, or even back in your dear Savoy."

"Mistress, you make me sound like a desperate last measure," the little man tells her. "You are a very fine looking woman, and I am an ageing diplomat. Find yourself a worthy young buck, and give yourself to him."

"If only Henry would let me," Mary confides. "Master Cromwell will find me an estate, and a young husband in an instant, were he allowed, but the king does not want to lose his stand by."

"Dear God, I have heard, of course, but did not believe the king could treat a lady with so little gallantry. Is not your sister upset by this sordid *arrangement?"*

"Were she to know, I would end up like the French queen, dear Master Chapuys."

"My heart goes out to you, my dear Lady Mary, and were circumstances otherwise, I would take you home, without a single regret."

"Oh, you are so gallant, my dear Eustace," she replies, softly. "Forget my foolishness, and speak with Cromwell!"

*

Thomas Cromwell does not like being summoned to court, because it means he is at a disadvantage. He is seldom caught out by Henry, because he knows his character so well, but a visit with Lady Anne Boleyn can be akin to walking on an acrobats high rope.

"*Mon cher Croh-mewl,* but this is *plus charmante,*" the lady says, using the childish mixture of French and English which the king finds so fascinating. The Privy Councillor bows, and kisses the proffered hand. She is wearing the huge yellow stone, with which he effected his introduction, almost two years before.

"The ring adds charm to the already charming," he says, thanking his poet friend, Tom Wyatt, for the useful lines he once penned for just such an occasion.

"Flatter them, Master Cromwell," he had advised. "Tell a mare it is a filly, and swear their beauty blinds you, and most women will swive with you all night."

"Yes, it reminds me of you, constantly, my good friend," Anne says. Cromwell is minded of the old saying about over egging the pudding, and smiles benignly into her cold, calculating eyes. He wonders when she became so dangerous.

"My old heart beats faster at the prospect of being of some service to you, my dear lady." Cromwell strains for another compliment, but does not wish to be too giving, too soon. "How can I help you today?"

"Master Cromwell," she says, slipping back into her normal, soft Norfolk accent, "I thought only to meet with you, for an amiable chat. I hear the king's matter is going very well."

"It is, Lady Anne," Thomas Cromwell says, feeling on safer ground. "Pope Clement has been confounded. He has refused my master's request for an annulment, and put it in writing to the Doge of Venice, who has, very kindly, agreed with him. This means we can proceed with our plans, without losing any more time. What is more, the marriage I was to arrange between the French princess, and Alessandro Medici, the Pope's illegitimate son, has been rejected by the young duke."

"How does that benefit us?" Lady Anne asks.

"The bribe of one hundred thousand pounds is still locked in our vaults, My Lady," Cromwell explains. "Perhaps you might remind the king of this windfall, and share in his joy?"

"How so?"

"I hear that the Duke of Saxony is selling a very fine necklace, to raise money for his fight against Lutheranism. I could procure it, for about five thousand."

"That might damage the Lutherans in Saxony," Lady Anne says. "All for a string of pearls?"

"Yellow diamonds, set in the most beautifully filigreed silver," Thomas Cromwell replies. "Besides, Duke George limits his actions to confiscating those books that offend his Catholic doctrine. He takes the books, burns them, and compensates the owners by paying the full market value."

"Seriously?" Lady Anne is beginning to laugh. "Are all these German fellows as mad?"

"They are certainly not good business men," Cromwell tells her. "Why, I've a mind to buy up all the Lutheran tracts I can, at a low price, and let Duke George confiscate them, and pay well over the odds for their sad loss."

"That is why I like you, Thomas," Anne says. She calls me Thomas, he thinks, which means the unpleasant part is about to commence. Cromwell takes a deep breath.

"So, My Lady, what is it you want of me?"

"The Lord Chancellor tries to insult me, at every turn," she replies. "Thomas More has taken to staying away from court when I am there."

"That is just how the king wants it," Thomas Cromwell tells her. "He feels the man should be kept away from you."

"Where he can spread his poison, unhindered?"

"No, My Lady, that is not so." Cromwell wonders how best to explain matters to the woman. She bears a grudge for ever, and keeps lists of those whom she believes has slighted her. There is going to be a day of reckoning, and the Privy Councillor fears the consequences. "I have spoken to Sir Thomas, and we have an understanding. He has failed the king badly, and knows he is now out of favour. Though the king, graciously allows him to keep his title, he is confined to Utopia, and advised to read books, rather than write them."

"There are pamphlets, concerning my honour."

"Not of his doing, My Lady."

"He opposes my marriage."

"Not so, Lady Anne. He opposes nothing, but has an opinion, like most men. As his opinion in this matter does not coincide with the king's, he must hold his tongue."

"I want rid of him."

"Lady, he is already gone." Thomas Cromwell wants her to stop talking now, and accept what he says, but she cannot. She hates, far better than she loves.

"I mean, really gone," Anne Boleyn snaps. "Like Wolsey!"

"The Cardinal was a great man," Cromwell says, carefully, "and he died in his bed. The king has often spoken of how he was going to forgive him, and restore him to his rightful place. We must have a care that you do not remind the king of Wolsey, My Lady, lest he turns me out, and brings More back in. For then, madam, your position would be a dangerous one."

"Then he should die, for both our sakes."

"Enough!" Lady Anne steps back, startled, and Cromwell shakes his head, wondering how he can possibly deal with this vicious woman. "The man is disgraced, and sitting by his fire, with a bible on his knee. He can do no more harm to you."

"Have him gone," Anne says, doggedly. "Then we will know peace, Cromwell."

"Can you not understand?" The Privy Councillor makes a final effort. "If I do this, and Sir Thomas dies, the whole of Europe will call him a saint, and say his blood is on *your* hands. Not mine, and not Henry's. Yours. For they see you as the king's mistress, and the one who most benefits from his murder."

"By then, I will be queen," Anne replies, stubbornly. "Who then could hurt me?"

"The king will let you kill More," Cromwell concludes, "but it will weigh on his conscience, as Wolsey's death does, and he will seek out those who caused the mischief. Once it is in his mind, he will not rest until he expunges the guilt. Think, My Lady. Who else can he blame, but your family?"

"I cannot allow him to sit at home, laughing at me," she tells Cromwell, who sighs, and nods his understanding. It is a simple matter of revenge, and Anne must have a full measure… short of death.

"Very well, I will make it so he must resign his Lord Chancellorship, and forgo his pensions." Cromwell can always make arrangements so that the man and his family do not starve to death. "Will that be enough?"

"I suppose it must, for now, Cromwell," she says, but she feels as if she has been cheated of her real wish. "I think you are making a serious mistake."

"Let it be on my head, Lady Anne," Cromwell replies with finality, "for I will not do murder for you!"

"Then go," Anne Boleyn tells him. "I see you do not wish to keep my friendship, Master Cromwell."

"My friendship is a valuable asset, My Lady," Cromwell says. "Do you really wish to discard it over so trivial a matter?"

"You have made it so that I will be queen before this coming Christmas, Master Cromwell. Within the next year, I will have borne the king's son, and be in an unassailable position. Then, I will not ask you for More's head, I will *demand* it!"

"Perhaps you might do well to remember the French queen, My Lady," Cromwell says, bowing. "Her only crime was to displease the king."

"You threaten me, Cromwell?"

"No, I warn you, for your own sake," the Privy Councillor says. "Now, are we to continue as allies, if not friends?"

"How can you serve me now, stable lad?"

"My father was a blacksmith, My Lady," Thomas Cromwell explains. "As yours was a petty farmer, who managed to wed well. I can make your father rich, and keep your brother from ruining things. I can stop the Duchess of Norfolk blackening your name at every turn, and I might even be able to find another husband for your sister, and have her moved from court."

"I will whip Mary if she still harbours thoughts of love for Henry, Uncle Norfolk's wife can go hang, and my brother can mind his own business."

"Can he mind his wife's?" Cromwell enjoys the look of shock on her face, but it quickly goes.

"What is Lady Rochford complaining of?" Anne asks. "Does she want to ruin her husband?"

"As he has ruined her?" says Cromwell. "There are rumours going about court, which, if believed, can destroy George. I can stop those idle tongues from wagging."

"You speak in riddles," Anne snaps at him. "Speak plainly."

"Very well. The king wishes to keep Mary close by. It is almost time to give in to his desires, lest you lose him. The Duchess hates you, because you seek to be higher than she. A queen precedes a mere duchess, after all. She spreads rumours about Henry and another lady, which might ruin your chances. Lady Rochford has confessed to me that your brother was not happy to wed her. On the wedding night, he became very drunk, and forced himself upon her, in a most disgusting, and unnatural, way."

"Dear Christ, Cromwell, what is it you do not know?"

"After that night, he has never touched her again," Cromwell says, pressing home his advantage. "I can only assume he finds his pleasures in other ways, and in other places. Your brother does not love women, I fear."

"Do you know what you say?" Anne asks. She is shocked by the depth of Cromwell's knowledge. "Such a rumour might get my brother … punished."

"Impalement, whilst still alive," Cromwell says, brutally. "I cannot imagine a more horrific death. Now, madam, for one last time… are we to be allies, or enemies?"

"*Mon cher Croh-mewl,*" Lady Anne Boleyn says, slipping back into her sibilant French accent, "*Nous sommes amis, jusqu'à ce que la mort nous sépare.*"

It is not the best French, but Thomas Cromwell understands that the deal is struck. Sir Thomas More will be allowed to fade away, sister Mary will be married off, and Norfolk's wife told to mind her manners. George will be warned to keep his codpiece out of strange places, and Lady Anne will content herself to be guided by her faithful old friend … Thomas Cromwell.

Friends, she agrees, until death us do part. Cromwell takes his leave, but wonders how long it will be before the Boleyn family overstep the mark once more. A dark, half hidden shape steps from a shadowy alcove, and resolves itself into Eustace Chapuys.

"A chance meeting, Ambassador Chapuys?" Cromwell says.

"You must return to calling me Eustace," Chapuys says, as he hurries to keep pace with the taller man. "For, though we fell out over your Venetian adventure, I never really stopped being your dearest friend."

"Nor I yours," Thomas Cromwell replies. "Will you come to dinner tonight?"

"With pleasure," says Chapuys, "for my cook knows only how to boil beef. I am wasting away to nothing!"

"We cannot have that, my friend." Cromwell steps out into the fresh air. "Shall we say about eight?"

"Shall I bring anything?" Chapuys must ask, but in truth, his salary is three months behind, and his credit is almost used up. He cannot even afford a few bottles of cheap wine.

"Just your good self," Cromwell replies. "I need to speak with you about your share of the venture. Your letters to Pope Clement, and the Doge of Venice, in which you so castigated the king, and demanded they refuse my emissaries, worked well."

"I did not write those letters to …" Chapuys stops, and frowns. "How did you know about them? I wrote in code, and sent them by the most circuitous routs."

"No matter. I have a fiftieth part of the profit held in your name, and only need to know when you want it."

"I have made money from your outrageous enterprise?" Chapuys is mystified at how such a thing can have happened.

"Yes, by mere happenstance, we won a famous battle, and there was much gold taken from the fallen. The Pope also sent gifts, as did Andrea Gritti, the Doge of Venice. Your share is a fiftieth part, which comes to seven hundred Venetian Ducati … or four hundred and ninety eight pounds."

"Seven hundred Ducati," Chapuys says. He is aware that he is being consoled, for losing the battle to keep Henry and Katherine together, "That is a lot of money, my friend."

"A paltry sum," Cromwell replies. "Will Draper, Tom Wyatt, Mush Draper, and my nephew each gained two fiftieths. For my part, which was mostly sitting at home, drinking wine, I receive twelve fiftieths. Nine fiftieths went on expenses, and bribes, and the remaining twenty fiftieths went into the royal coffers, where it will be turned into a new man o' war, or a thousand new muskets."

"But seven hundred ducats…"

"Less outgoings, of course."

"Outgoings?"

"Yes. I deducted the six months rent you owe me."

"Then we are financially even, my friend," Eustace Chapuys says. "Though I am unable to accept this money. The emperor might see it as a bribe."

"For what?" Cromwell asks. "We have not spoken for almost three months, and you seek to undo me at every turn. I advise the king, and you argue against it. I speak to Lady Anne about you, and she says what good company you are. I try to force through the separation, and you denounce me, in writing, and pay for rude pamphlets to be sent about London."

"Not those that concern Master Whatnot, my friend."

"I know that, Eustace," Cromwell says. "That is another, more poisonous hand. No, I mean the one that draws a picture of me as a fat, penny pinching, Tyndale lover."

"Ah, you have seen that one?"

"Seen it?" Cromwell slaps his friend's back, and they set off walking back towards Austin Friars. "I own the printer who ran it off for you."

"You sly dog!"

"Just so. I will also deduct the printer's eleven silver *angels* charge from your seven hundred ducats," Cromwell tells his friend. "Now, what is it that you wish to tell me?"

"The matter is ... rather delicate," Chapuys says, colouring slightly. He is a pious sort of man, and not given to wanton lewdness.

"I am a man of the world, my friend. Speak."

"Firstly, Lady Mary Boleyn, still a most handsome looking woman, has expressed an unexpected, and explicit desire to have ... carnal relations with me."

"Dear God, I hope you kept your hand on your codpiece, old friend," Tom Cromwell says, laughing. "For, if you did, we are the only two men in London she has not swived. My doctor tells me it is because of an inflammation of the womb, which excites ladies to excessive lust. She will lay down for any man who wishes it."

"Yet the king still seems enamoured," Chapuys says.

"Even His Majesty can enjoy indulging himself in low tastes," Cromwell replies. "I am told that the lady was French trained in the art of seduction, and knows well how to please any man."

"And Lady Anne?" Eustace Chapuys cannot help but point out the obvious inference. "Was she not also at this same French court, my friend?"

"Have a care, Master Ambassador," Cromwell

says. "Your high position might keep you from execution, but you are not above being casually poisoned. The Boleyn clan would have your tongue out for saying such a thing in public."

"Henry must be blind," Chapuys chuckles. "In that respect he, and love, have something in common."

"The king will have his way, no matter what," Tom Cromwell replies. "Though I confess, I would rather he married a solid, reliable Lutheran girl."

"You will advise this to him?" Chapuys asks, but he already knows the answer.

"I am not so foolish, old friend," says Cromwell. "The lamb might lie down with the lion… but he does not have to place his head in the beast's mouth!"

3   **A Night in Calais**

Mush Draper is suffering before the small cog has even left Dover's harbour, and by the time they reach Calais, he wants nothing but a soft bed for the night. His brother-in-law, Will Draper, and Richard Cromwell, have no wish to carry their ailing friend all about the town, so take lodgings in the first inn they come to, once off the small boat.

"He smells like a pigsty," Richard complains, hoisting Mush into one of the three narrow bunks in their room. "Stale vomit, and sweat are a poor mix."

"The streets smell just as badly," Will replies, kicking off his boots. "Calais is the only part of France we still rule, but it is the backside of England, my friend. Our man is either in the town, or the English *Calaisis* countryside beyond. We need not linger, once we have found the damned troublesome fellow."

"Stephen Vaughan is not the sort to bring us on a wild goose chase," the big man says. "He is a dour sort of a fellow, and not prone to scare mongering. If he says there is some great danger coming our way, I am readily inclined to believe him."

"Your uncle has said much the same," Will replies. "Though what it might be is beyond my understanding. Master Vaughan is a merchant, and spends his days with bankers, and other wool merchants. He does not normally mix with desperate men."

"Someone wishes him dead," Richard says, testing the comfort of his straw filled mattress. "He is in fear for his life. Once he is found, we will know all, no doubt. How do we start?"

"I suggest we get a night's sleep, then start our

search of the town tomorrow." Will yawns, and unbuckles his sword. "There cannot be too many places for our friend to hide. I suspect he will be lodged with one of the English wool merchants who run the place."

"And if not?"

"Then we spread out net wider," Will explains. "The English *Calaisis* stretches beyond the town walls, for a few miles. He might be in one of the two dozen outlying villages."

Richard grunts, and rolls over onto his side. He is a simple soul, and seldom has any trouble sleeping. Will lies awake for a while longer, wondering what calamity Stephen Vaughan believes is coming at them, and who the enemy might turn out to be.

He ponders if the threat might be from the Fugger family, who are wealthy friends of the Holy Roman Emperor, or some powerful Catholic faction who wish to stop England's coming church reformation. It is midnight when he finally falls asleep, still not knowing from whence the threat is coming.

*

"Father George Constantine?" The wiry, middle aged preacher looks up, nervously into the eyes of a swarthy, Spanish looking fellow. "My name is Don Alessandro Gomes, and I am here to help you, my friend."

"Help me?" the man asks. "Do I know you, sir?"

"We have mutual friends," the tough looking Spaniard explains. "Master William sends his best wishes, and begs that you listen to my proposition. It will be to your liking."

"How so?" Constantine asks. He has been living

in a small, but prosperous, village outside Bruges, since fleeing England the previous Christmas, and his funds are dwindling fast. "Do you have money for me?"

"If you need it," Gomes replies. "My master wishes you to undertake a mission for him, and you will be well rewarded. We wish you to return to England."

"Impossible," Constantine says. "I have too many enemies there, these days."

"You also have friends, sir," the dangerous looking Spaniard tells him. "Your denunciation of the heretics to Sir Thomas More made you many powerful friends. Those friends offer to protect your life, if you return, and work for them."

"In what capacity?"

"As an agent."

"A spy?"

"No, an agent. My master wants you to meet with certain well placed gentlemen, and further his designs for him." Gomes takes a purse from his belt, and drops it on the table. "There is plenty more gold to come, my dear Father George. Will you accept the commission I am commanded to offer to you?"

"And do what?" Constantine asks. "You speak in riddles. I am a country preacher. How can I serve your master?"

"By arranging for a certain package to leave England, and come to Bruges." Gomes calls for wine. "Once delivered into my hands, you will be rewarded."

"How much?"

"Two hundred English pounds."

Father George Constantine does not need much persuasion to accept the offer. Having once betrayed his friends, he will find it increasingly easier, from now on.

His only concern is his own personal safety. Having tasted the rack once, he has no wish to fall into More's hands again, and says so.

"The Lord Chancellor has fallen from grace," Allesandro Gomes says. "The king turns more and more to Thomas Cromwell, who is little more than a filthy heretic himself. He will turn a blind eye to you."

"Whilst I do what?" Constantine asks, again. "For two hundred pounds, you could wish me to murder the king."

"We mean no harm to Henry," the Spaniard replies, smiling at the very notion. "You will cross the channel, meet some people in London, and return here to us."

"With a package."

"Yes."

"For two hundred pounds?"

"Yes. Then you can disappear." Gomes considers for a moment. "You might buy a small estate, in France, or become a silk merchant. We do not really care."

"Who is your master?"

"The name will mean nothing to you."

"I believe you wish to involve me in a criminal act, rather than a political one," the preacher says.

"Think what you wish. Will you do it?"

"I cannot fall into More's hands again," Constantine says. "He threatened me with death, if I ever return to England."

"You will travel under a Flanders passport, and with a false name," Gomes tells him. "Once in London, you will send word to a certain person, who will then arrange a meeting. This person will give you a package for us. Return to Flanders, and you are a wealthy man."

"And if I decline?"

"Can you afford to?" The preacher frowns. He has a few shillings in his purse, and does not know how he will continue, without financial support.

"No, I cannot. I am your man, sir."

"Good. Then let us drink on it." Gomes is pleased with the outcome, for the alternative was not to his liking. Had the preacher declined his offer, he was to have the man killed, and his body concealed.

*

The dinner lives up to Eustace Chapuys' expectations, and the new Italian wine, brought home by Will Draper, is light, and refreshing on the palate. The little Savoyard is so content, that he almost forgets why he is back at Austin Friars. He and Cromwell find themselves to be mutually beneficial, and Chapuys owes his friend at least one good favour.

"I had a communication from home the other morning," he says, casually. "It came by unusual means."

"What, I must uncover another of your mysterious postal methods, Eustace?" Cromwell says, pouring more wine. "Do you do it just to keep my agents on their tip toes?"

"A monk came to me."

"A monk?" Cromwell sighs heavily. "The Bishop of Rome is getting intrusive, my friend."

"Brother Gustav is some sort of German."

"From Saxony?" Cromwell's mind jumps back to his flippant conversation about the Saxon Duke's necklace.

"Hessen, I believe, which is not too distant from there," Eustace Chapuys replies. "Why do you ask?"

"Oh, 'tis probably nothing," Cromwell says. "Do go on. This monk brought you a letter, you say?"

"No, he brought me a message from the emperor, which he had committed to memory." Chapuys is a little uneasy. He has something to say, but does not want to divulge the whole message.

"Which part do you think concerns me, Eustace?"

"He used a phrase, to confirm the veracity of the message," the Savoyard diplomat explains. "Then he spoke of several things that must remain private. At the last, he told me that I might be approached by '*a great personage*' soon, and must render them any help I can."

"I see." Cromwell can sniff out a conspiracy like a pig finds truffles, and the news annoys him. "You are an ambassador, and should be held above such petty intrigues, my friend. Think of your personal honour, and how such pettiness might hurt it."

"Would that it were so very petty," Eustace Chapuys responds. "Brother Gustav, who is a dour sort of a man, intimates that I am to be part of a great undertaking, that will bring about the downfall of England."

"A plot against Henry?" Cromwell is vexed, as he runs the best string of agents in Europe, and has heard nothing of any planned assassination, or uprising.

"No, I don't think so," Chapuys replies. "Though the monk is but a messenger, he actually means the end of England, not its king. I am worried, Thomas. How do you destroy a whole kingdom, without laying it waste, from end to end?"

"You cannot," says Cromwell. "It would take the combined armies of France and Spain, and two thousand ships to transport them. Then you must continue to supply your men with fresh horses, food, and reinforcements … for we would fight to the death."

"But it *could* happen," the ambassador says.

"Imagine it, Eustace. Norfolk, Suffolk, and Percy, can field sixty thousand men within a week. Then we have the Welsh army, numbering another fifteen thousand. Add to that every land owner, and free Englishman who can raise a pike, or swing an axe, and the odds are nearer even."

"The monk seems confident." Chapuys is not, and thus seeks to put his friend on guard. "It is my duty to encourage friendship between our two masters, Thomas, yet I am being recruited into something that can only do harm to that friendship."

"Who is this great personage the monk talks about?" Thomas Cromwell asks. "I cannot believe any man would raise his standard against Henry. The king is too well loved by his people, and he is protected by my own agents."

"How many Will Drapers do you possess?" Chapuys means it as a jest, but Cromwell understands well enough what he means. One determined man is all it takes to kill even a king. He remembers how, once, only the knife of Mush ben Mordecai stood between Henry, and a cruel death.

"I take it that you do not wish to become embroiled in this scheme?" Cromwell knows Chapuys wishes a quiet life, but cannot be seen to disobey his master, Charles V, the Holy Roman Emperor.

"I must obey instructions."

"I expect nothing less, Eustace. You are the most loyal of men, and have served Katherine well. Any move against the king now, might seriously affect her future position. I do not threaten, my friend … I merely warn you."

"I come to you openly, Thomas, in the hope that you can see a way out of it for all of us," Chapuys explains. "I must obey, and my master must not feel betrayed. Nor can we allow Europe to become embroiled in a terrible war, which will ruin us all."

"Tell me true, Eustace, is Charles behind this?"

"I think not. He might have endorsed Brother Gustav's strange visit, but I wonder if the last part of the message was not added later, by some person, intent on mischief."

"We think alike." Cromwell calls for a hot poker, and mulls two mugs of honeyed mead for them. "A warmer, to send us comfortably to bed, my friend. You will stay tonight."

"I cannot, for I have to…"

"No, you misunderstand me, Eustace. You *will* stay here tonight. I fear for you. This dark monk you talk of sounds to be… dangerous, and I must have him taken up, at once."

"Good luck with that, my friend," Chapuys says, quite agreeable to stopping over. The beds are more comfortable, and the breakfast is quite sumptuous. "The fellow seems to be a wily rogue, and well able to disappear into the river mist."

"You make him sound like a spirit," Cromwell replies, chuckling, but he too is well aware of how hard it can be to find a single soul in a city the size of London. Especially when they do not wish to be found. "My young men will try to find him, and stop him from making any more mischief. Now, let me show you the wonderful manuscript Bishop Gardiner has sent me as a gift."

"You are on friendly terms with him again?" Chapuys marvels at how simple Cromwell makes it all seem. Stephen Gardiner, now Bishop of Winchester, and a confidant of the king, has been a friend, become an enemy, and is now a friend again.

"He sees that we are of a like mind," Cromwell replies. "He has no taste for burning heretics, and wishes only for a quiet life, in a stable realm. Together, we will stand firm against the king's enemies, and guide him onto the right path."

"The Cromwell road?" Chapuys snipes. "You know that Anne Boleyn dislikes him, of course?"

"All the more reason to cherish his friendship, old friend," Cromwell explains. "For if Henry makes her his queen, we will all need such well placed allies."

"If?" The ambassador smiles broadly. "Is there some doubt?"

Cromwell shrugs, as if to indicate that it is all in the lap of the gods. He links the Savoyard diplomat, and strolls out into the chill late afternoon sun, where several young men are loitering; waiting for their benefactor's orders.

"Master Christian!" Cromwell calls, and a stocky, square jawed ruffian steps forward. "There is a troublesome monk on the loose. Señor Chapuys will give you a good description. I want him found, and brought to me, alive."

"Alive, sir?"

"Dead men tell no tales," Cromwell replies. "Have the boys search every ship out of the harbours, and look into every inn. Best check the whore houses too, seeing as how he is a monk!"

*

Mush is not sure how long he has been awake,

but the sickness from the rough boat crossing has started to subside, and his mouth is dry. He realises that he is lying on a low, hard bed, and the noises from below suggest he is in some sort of inn, or wayside tavern. He is fully clothed, and does not smell too good. He is about to try and sit up, when he hears a latch scrape, close by.

Someone is coming into the room, with as much stealth as they can muster. Mush moves is right hand down towards the knife which he has concealed in his right boot, and holds his breath. If there is more than one visitor, he must be quick. Once on his feet, he will have but a moment to kill one, and turn to face the other. Any more than two, and he must rely on the others waking up to save the situation.

The bedroom door opens, but the evening is so dark that Mush must rely on his ears, rather than his eyesight. The intruder is little more than a darker shape within the dark, and seems to be of a middling size. He touches the knife hilt with his finger tips, and draws it into the palm of his hand. The shape shifts, and looms over one of the other beds in the room.

Mush senses the man's position, rather than sees it, and springs from his bed. The figure turns, and starts to cry out, as Mush grasps him about the neck. One wrench, and the man is down. The young Jew pulls the head back, and raises his blade, ready to slash it down, across the exposed throat. From out of the dark, a big hand grabs his wrist, and stays the blow.

A candle flares into life, and Richard Cromwell holds Mush back from his would be victim. Will Draper, candle in one hand, and sword in the other, steps forward, allowing a pool of light to illuminate the scene. Mush is hanging onto the intruders neck for all he is worth, and cursing his big friend, who is laughing, and shaking the knife from his grip.

"Let him go, Mush," Will says. "I don't think we have anything to fear from Master Vaughan." The newcomer gasps for air, and staggers to his feet, rubbing his neck.

"You expected me?" Stephen Vaughan asks.

"Calais is a small town, sir," Will tells him. "Once news of our arrival went abroad, I suspected you might come calling. Forgive my friend, he was laid up with sea sickness, and did not know of my suspicion."

"I thought myself to be in the wrong room, and a dead man, for sure," Vaughan tells them. "Good evening, Richard, I see you are as strong as ever."

"Stephen," Richard says, nodding a greeting. They are of a similar age, and have both been in Cromwell's service for the past ten years. "It is good to see you alive."

"Just so," Vaughan replies. "The rogues have tried to silence me twice. My information must be truly important."

"Your note spoke of great danger," Will says. "To whom?"

"I have no idea." Stephen Vaughan is unused to the rough and tumble that comes with being one of Cromwell's more active agents. He is a more subtle type of spy, often spending days trying to catch a wrong word, or unravel a partly deciphered message. "I was supposed to be on a transparent errand to the bankers of Augsburg."

"Perhaps you might tell us what you *do* know?" Will prefers action to intrigue, but cannot fight an invisible enemy. "How came you to be amongst these bankers?"

"I had need of a safe haven," Stephen replies. "Old Tom More was after my blood in England. It seems that some preacher called Constantine has denounced me as a heretic, and I must needs be abroad for a few months. The king wishes to borrow a large amount of money from somewhere, and I was to be the conduit, between Henry, and the German banking houses."

"The Fuggers?"

"Exactly. Anton Mugger is a delightful fellow," Vaughan explains. "I think he must sleep with an abacus under his pillow. My task was to try and raise a loan, with almost no collateral. He has taken over from the Medici family, and is as rich as the ancient king of Lydia, Croesus."

"I don't know him," says Richard. "Perhaps he could lend to Henry?" Mush, who is now fully recovered, smirks at his friend's lack of wit, and slips his knife away.

"You are under our protection now," he tells the man whose throat he was so lately trying to slit. "Who is after you?"

"As I say, I am not sure." Stephen Vaughan martial's his thoughts. "All I saw was a part of a document. It purports to be from the Emperor Charles to Anton Fugger, and speaks of a 'great plan' that is to be set against England."

"Not Henry?"

"No, which is odd, for Charles has a dislike of the king, because of his relationship to Queen Katherine. The emperor supports her, and has a morbid hatred of any protestant feelings."

"Then he must hate Henry, and Anne Boleyn, as much as Martin Luther, and William Tyndale." Will can understand this, but does not see how one can wish to harm a whole country, without going to war. "What else did you see?"

"Nothing then. The document was on Fugger's desk, half covered with other documents. As he was in the room with me, I could hardly pick it up and have a good read, could I?"

"Then how is it he wants you dead?" Richard asks. He is a good man in a scrap, and faithful to his uncle, but slow on the uptake. "Did he see you looking at the document?"

"No, I was discreet, and carried on my negotiations as if nothing was amiss." Stephen Vaughan is tired, and finds it hard to keep his tale in order. "It was later, when the household was asleep that I went in search of more information."

To tell of how he crept from his bed, and made his way down long, silent corridors, with only the light of the moon to guide him, and of how he had to make his way past a dozing guard by the main hall's great door, would have taken too long. Nor did he explain how he came to Anton Fugger's study, and slipped inside. It was a moment of great satisfaction, but also of rising fear to see the heaps of correspondence on the banker's huge desk.

"What did you find?" Mush asks.

"The same letter, which rambled on about the pervasive sickness of protestant heresy, then concluded with Charles writing: *'It is clear that we are of a like mind in this, and I consider it God's Work that we shall proceed with this great plan, and utterly confound England, unto its final ruin.'* I memorised it, word for word."

"Anything else?" Will Draper can only see war

being any nation's ruin, and wonders where the troops and supplies will come from. The only safe place to launch an invasion from is Flanders, he thinks, and the Holy Roman domain must be flooding with men, even as they speak.

"A second letter, in draft form, from Fugger to someone unknown. There are many crossings out, and alterations, and it seems he was struggling to disguise his true intent. He speaks of 'going to take account of his holdings in Flanders', and of 'seeking out our good father' who will 'convey our wishes to that great personage, whom we hold dear, in England.' Then he closes with a line about 'restoring the faith, once our enemies are confounded.' Which leads me to believe that Anton Fugger is using some secret agent to further his plot."

"Do we have no clue to this man's identity?" Will asks.

"Not really. Save that he writes in Spanish."

"There we have it, my friends," Mush says. "We know who sets the plot in motion, and that a Spaniard might be involved, alongside some priest, and a great person in England. All that is left for us to find out is, what do they mean to do, where, and when."

"The intent is clear," Richard says, echoing all their thoughts. "The emperor means to invade England, and destroy it."

"Then he must have vast armies," Will says. "Where are they, and why does the emperor use a banker to head the plot? Surely, would he not put his greatest generals in charge?"

"True enough, and why would they need some great personage in England?" Mush asks. "I can only think of three or four with enough power to upset the military balance. My money is on that toad Harry Percy. The Duke of Northumberland is out of favour with Henry, and he is always looking to gain revenge."

"Then he might raise the north, and join up with the Scottish king." Will Draper considers this, but thinks it is too wild a card to play. "He can march south with, perhaps twenty five thousand men. Chester will stay loyal, as will Warwick and Worcester. That will be enough to halt their advance. Then Percy's only hope will be a huge invasion across the channel. Taken from two sides, we will be hard pressed."

"Yes, I agree, but not so as to be utterly destroyed," Stephen Vaughan says. "They must capture at least one port. Dover is too strong, and Sandwich, along with the other Cinque Ports, are too well garrisoned. The plan is doomed to failure, even if they manage to land troops."

"That is what I cannot understand," Will concludes. "Any general, worth his salt, will confirm these facts. An invasion on so large a scale will cost a half million pounds, at least, and cost twenty thousand dead, just to establish a toe hold on our shores."

"Then what are we missing?" Richard asks. "How do you spirit eighty or a hundred thousand men across the channel, and get them into England, without us knowing?"

"Perhaps they are already there?" Stephen Vaughan says, softly. "Dear Christ, what if this great person they speak of has the men under his command already?"

"But who has that kind of power?" Will says, shaking his head. "Even Suffolk must have a month to raise his yeomen, and then they number only fifteen or twenty thousand. Besides, he loves Henry too well to betray him."

"What if he and Norfolk combine?" Mush sees a traitor around every corner, and dislikes both men.

"Then why involve Charles and this Anton Fugger fellow?" says Will Draper. "Why not just raise their armies, and march on London? The king might have enough to withstand them, but they will hold the rest of England. No, we are on the wrong tack, my friends. Tomorrow, we must ride out into the *Calaisis*… the rural hinterland, and see what we might find out."

"A sound idea, sir," Stephen Vaughan says. "For no one can hide so many men … not even in all of Flanders."

"Unless Richard is right, of course … and we are up against invisible spirits," Mush says. "Now, can we get back to sleep?"

4   **Domini Canes**

"Hold hard, sir!" The mounted sergeant reins in his mount and bars the rutted track. "What is your business?"

"I am, as you, an Englishman, good fellow," the mud spattered traveller replies. "From your livery I see you are from the Calais garrison. Am I far away from the town?"

"This is good English soil you ride on," the man tells him, proudly. "Though it do be stuck on France, like a boil festering upon its hairy arse. Again sir, what is your business?"

"I am a poet, sir."

"A poet?" the soldier grins, and notes the fine sword, at the man's waist, and the heavy saddle pistol in its holster. "If you are a poet, prove it, for I have a fancy that you are a spy, sir."

Thomas Wyatt, who is on the last leg of his return from Portugal smiles, and clears his throat.

> *"The soldiers' endless tales of triumphs won,*
> *Then the day that doth refute their lies,*
> *I see the wounded wailing in the hot noon's sun,*
> *Those dead, the dust, and blood gorged flies."*

"A soldiers tale indeed, sir," the man says, admiringly. "Not a poets lying words. You must come with me. My commander is a half mile behind, and will have words with you."

Tom Wyatt shrugs. Now he is within the English *Calaisis*, he is no longer under threat. He pulls his horses head about, and canters after the big English sergeant. A minute later, and the following band come into sight. The poet is astounded, and spurs his mount forward to meet old friends.

"Will Draper," he cries, "you treacherous bastard! I have a mind to pull you from your horse, and run you through."

"We are well met, Tom Wyatt," Draper replies, subduing a smile. "How was your trip to Portugal?"

"Too damned hot," says Wyatt. "I was forced to leave Lisbon after I misjudged the temperament of a local magistrate. It seems he was the jealous sort, and I had to flee into Spain. Since then, I have been borrowing from every banker between Madrid and Paris. I used Cromwell as my surety."

"Then I take it our meeting is a coincidence," Will Draper says. "See, old friend, Mush and Richard are with me, and the fourth is Master Stephen Vaughan. Sergeant Buffery you have met."

"Well?" Tom Wyatt asks, still somewhat petulantly. "What deviousness are you about now, Master Draper? "

"Please, call me Will," his friend asks of him. "Anyone might think it was I, and not Richard, who knocked you out, and put you on a boat to Portugal."

"True enough," Mush puts in, with an impish grin. "Will and I merely stood by, and watched the fun." They cannot all help but laugh at this, and the awkward moment is forgotten. The poet is fully aware of what would have befallen him, had he continued on to England. Since then, he has learned to mind his tongue better when it comes to talking about Anne Boleyn.

"Then let bygones be bygones," Tom Wyatt says, holding out a hand to Richard, who, fool that he is, takes it. The poet, kicks his friend's horse, and grips the proffered hand. Richard Cromwell's own great weight works against him, and he tumbles to the ground.

"Why, you..." Richard surges to his feet, but cannot help roar with laughter at his own gullibility. "That will teach me, I suppose."

"Perhaps, my big friend, but from now on, I suggest you salute, rather than shake hands," Tom Wyatt says. "Now, what is afoot?"

"We are scouting the land, for hoards of Holy Roman soldiers," Mush says, sarcastically. "Will thinks there are about eighty thousand hiding in the villages here about."

"Then they are well hidden," the poet replies. "I have ridden all the way from Paris, and lodged in a half dozen villages, without seeing a single armed man."

"Not a single troop?" Will is dismayed, and wonders what is going on. "Can they be thinking of coming from Spain, by sea?"

"You would need five hundred galleons," Stephen Vaughan says. "There are not that many ships in the Christian world, Will."

"Then we are wrong footed," Mush concludes. "If Charles has an army, it must be hidden in far off Muscovy, or Sweden. We are missing something, my friends."

"The only armed men I have seen all morning, are the *Domini Canes* from the Friary in Artois."

"They are far from home," Stephen says. "They call them that ... God's Hounds ... because of the way they doggedly track down victims for the Inquisition. Since it spilled out of Spain, the Inquisition has reached far and wide."

"They are not allowed to set foot on English soil, sir," Sergeant Buffery advises. "Black Friars, we call them, and it's a good name, for never was any so black hearted as the Dominicans."

"Not on English soil, you say?" Tom Wyatt gestures down the road, where about twenty men are riding towards them. They are all dressed in the familiar white cassocks, and black cowls, except their leader, who is wearing a steel breastplate, and helmet.

"It seems that the Inquisition has come to England, gentlemen," Will says, coldly. "These fellows are coming on like they wish to do us harm. Spread out, and prepare to defend yourselves."

"Fighting with priests?" Richard scowls. "Uncle Thomas will never believe it!" He draws his sword with the right hand, and a long handled axe with the other. His intention is to control his mount with his knees, and so be able to deal out twice as much in blows.

The group slow to a trot, then a walk. At last, they stop about fifty paces away from Will Draper and his friends. The leader, a muscular, dark skinned man, calls to them, in Spanish. Tom Wyatt answers in Italian, before they find French to be a mutual language.

"Might I name myself, sir, as Don Alessandro Gomes, a member of the Emperor Charles' household. These men are Dominican friars, about their business as holy Inquisitors."

"Your business with us, sir?" Wyatt asks.

"None, my dear friends," Gomes replies. "We seek only to take into custody the heretic, *Esteban Vann*, who is in league with William Tyndale. I see he is in your company. Does he ride with you?"

"You have no jurisdiction, Don Alessandro," the poet informs the Spaniard. "If Master Vaughan is, truly a heretic, we shall return him to London, where he will receive a fair trial."

"I cannot let you have the man," Gomes snaps. "He has eluded my agents twice, and is a fugitive from the empire."

"This is, according to the sergeant with us, English soil, sir, and that means that it is you who are now in the wrong. God's Hounds have no place in a civilised country."

"You mock God?" The Spaniard makes a slight movement of his left hand, and the Dominican friars all produce weapons from beneath their garments. "The brothers will be most displeased."

"If they love God so much, perhaps we can send a few of them to meet Him today?" Tom Wyatt drops a hand to the heavy pistol hanging on his saddle. "Perhaps you should go?"

The Spaniard looks as though he wants to throw himself at Wyatt, but instead, he turns his horse, and trots back towards his dour looking *Domini Canes*. They have been listening, and await but one word from their leader.

"Do they mean to fight?" Will asks, in English. Tom Wyatt nods, and drops his hand down onto his pistol. The single shot will not stop a concerted rush, but he intends to shoot Gomes from his horse at the first sign of trouble. Will also reaches for his saddle pistol, a gun invented for use on horseback. Once discharged, it has a stabbing blade under the thick barrel, or it can be used as a very effective club.

"Do we draw on the foreign bastards, sir?" Sergeant Buffery asks, and as if in answer, the mounted friars come at them, at the gallop. Will is first to react. He raises, aims, and discharges his pistol, in the blink of an eye. The leading man topples from his horse, and Tom Wyatt fires at Gomes. The one inch lead ball whistles past the Spaniard's shoulder, and hit's a horse behind him.

The beast goes down in a great flailing of legs, and surprised friar. Two more horses balk at the loud noises, and sheer away from the charge. Mush throws one of his perfectly balanced knives, and is rewarded with a scream of pain, then he is forced to duck under a swinging sword. All about them steel clashes against steel, as the Dominicans try to take Stephen Vaughan, dead, or alive.

Vaughan is no fighter, but manages to get his sword above his head, to parry a savage swipe. Richard Cromwell, who has just unhorsed one man, turns, and chops his axe into the unguarded thigh of Vaughan's assailant. The man cries out, and Stephen, seeing his chance, thrusts his own blade into the man's chest. It hits a rib, but the strike is enough to unhorse his opponent.

Sergeant Buffery, either offended at having to fight mere priests, or scared of killing a man of God, turns his heavy military sabre side on, and uses it like a hammer to knock three Dominicans from their saddles. Two of the friars wheel about, and attack Richard from behind, His horse is slashed, and it goes down in a welter of blood. Richard rolls clear, and comes up like a demon from Hell.

The two Dominicans make the mistake of thinking him easier prey now, and spur their horses to the kill. Richard blocks one blow with his axe, and thrusts upwards with his sword, into an unguarded chest. The man topples backwards, spewing blood from his mouth. The second man is almost past, when Richard turns, and throws the axe. It strikes the man's mount, and they both tumble down.

Richard strides forward, to finish his man, but the Dominican is up, and running for his life. Behind him, he leaves seven dead comrades, and three more battered into a stupor. The Spaniard is furious, and demanding the survivors return to the fray.

"You do God's work!" he cries. The head of the surviving friars shakes his head.

"Not today, brother Gomes," the man says. "You must employ soldiers for this sort of a task. My friars have been found wanting. Come!"

Will watches as the Dominicans canter away from the battle arena. The Spaniard, Gomes, stays at a distance, then follows his defeated troops. Mush and Richard are disappointed to find that the friars have nothing to steal, except for a motley collection of weapons.

"Thank God they were not armed with muskets," Stephen Vaughan says. "I killed my first man today ... and it has to be a bloody monk!"

"They are friars, my friend, not monks" Tom Wyatt replies. "Though reports of your man's death are greatly exaggerated, I fear. He is up, and staggering after his comrades."

"Thank God, for I would do no man harm," Vaughan says, as if he has spared the friar on purpose. "What of these others?"

"Seven of them dead, and three battered senseless by our picky sergeant. He turns his nose up at a fight, unless they are the emperor's bodyguard, or the finest Muscovite infantry!" Tom Wyatt stoops, and pulls one of the men to his feet. "Now, my dear *Domini Canes*, you and I shall talk. What tongue do you favour ... Spanish, German, Italian, or French. Ah, I see your eyes light up. Let us speak French, brother."

"I am an Inquisitor, and as such, inviolate." The man, little more than a youth must be disabused of his belief quickly.

"You are a brigand, and an outlaw, brother," Tom Wyatt tells him, sharply. "My leader - the man reloading his pistol - has a mind to hang you for a rogue. Now, who is this Gomes man?"

"I know not, sir," the young friar replies, dabbing at the blood on his cheek. "He came to us, with letters from above, and said we must search for an Englishman."

"Well, you found several," Tom Wyatt says, grinning. "So, you simply took up arms, and followed him?"

"It is the will of our master," the friar replies, earnestly. "I saw the Holy Seal with my own eyes!"

"Holy Seal?" The poet curses beneath his breath. "Gomes had orders from the Pope?" The friar nods. With such an authority, they were forced to help out.

"The Spaniard spoke of only one man. A spy, who has stolen a treasure, and must be taken, or killed." The friar seems to see the carnage about him for the first time, and shudders. "I must help my comrade's souls to rest, sir."

"You may take your dead, and your wounded away," Wyatt tells him, "but first, you must tell me whatever you know about Gomes."

"Nothing, I swear," the friar tells the poet. "He and his companion came to us out of a stormy night, and demanded our help."

"You say Gomes had a companion?"

"Yes, he did."

"Do you know who the man was, or what he looks like?"

"A tall, spare man, who spoke very poor French," the friar replies. "At our evening meal, Brother Raoul took pity on him, and spoke in English."

"The man was English?"

"Why, yes. He was an English priest, I think," the friar says.

"Why do you think that?"

"His French was poor, but his Latin was that of a man in Holy Orders."

*

"Not a silver penny amongst the lot of them," Richard Cromwell curses, and spits on the ground at his feet. "Nor could they fight well. I understand now why the sergeant disdains them, and refuses to bloody his blade."

"Still, five against twenty," Mush replies. "It will make a fine tale around Austin Friars breakfast table."

"We were six," Richard says.

"I do not count poor Stephen," Mush tells his friend. "He was more like to cut off his own leg, as hurt one of them. Thank goodness there are no spoils to divide, else he would have an empty pocket."

Will Draper smiles over his friends, who are discussing a bounty they have not got. He takes a look at the other two men, who are suffering from nothing more than sore heads, and dented pride.

"Richard, help the sergeant load the dead onto four horses, and set them on their way with their wounded. Then we will take the remaining six horses, and sell them off in Calais. What price there for a decent mount, Sergeant Buffery?"

"The Quartermaster's office pay six pounds each,

if they be sound," the sergeant informs Will. "Though you might wish to ship them back to England, where you'll get a little more."

"And if they do not manage the voyage well, some crimping bastard will try to beggar us," Will tells him. Some years before, he was a quartermaster for the army in Ireland, and he knows most of their tricks. "Let us do our sums, Sergeant Buffery. Six horses at six pounds a piece is …"

"Thirty six pounds," Mush says, eagerly. "Then we will make something from this little scuffle."

"Equal shares?" Will asks, and watches their faces for any dissent. "Then that is six pounds each man. We Cromwell men will put a cut into the Austin Friars kitty, as usual, and still come out with four pounds each."

"Six pounds!" Sergeant Buffery is shocked by his sudden wealth. As a garrison soldier, the sergeant usually earns seven pounds twelve shillings a year, less the cost of his food, and the maintenance of his uniform and arms, which means he is lucky to clear four pounds in a good year. "That is enough for me to throw over soldiering, and go home to Cambridgeshire."

"And do what?" Tom Wyatt asks. "Is not soldiering in your blood?"

"Not in mine, sir," the man replies, happily. "Tap mine, and you will taste wine. A good wine shop in the market town, run by your servant, Rob Buffery, will make a tidy living."

"You must speak with my wife," Will says. "She has a regular supply of Italian and Portuguese wine shipped in, and is ever looking for new customers."

"I bless the day you settled on me as an escort, Captain Draper," the big soldier tells Will. "For my life is changed from this day forth. Why, I might even bethink to take a wife."

"Not your own, I hope," Tom Wyatt says. "The best wine is often sipped from another man's cask!"

*

"You swore that it was safe!" The preacher, Father George Constantine, can scarcely keep his hands from trembling. "How can I go to England, knowing that Vaughan still draws breath?"

"It was ill luck that the man has fallen in with a gang of mercenaries," Gomes says. "The Dominicans were no match for them. I dare say that he will be on a boat from Calais within the day."

"But, he knows!" Constantine whines.

"He knows nothing for a certainty," Gomes snaps back. "Only that he has had sight of a half written letter, proposing some sort of venture against the English. He does not know of your involvement, and he does not know of whom we speak when the 'great personage' is mentioned. You must keep your nerve, and carry out your part of the plot."

"I cannot," the preacher confesses, "for I am too frightened of what will become of me. The Lord Chancellor promised to burn me, if I ever crossed his path again, and there are others who wish me harm. Tom Cromwell never forgets a grudge, and I wronged him when I falsely accused Vaughan."

"If you wish to withdraw, I fully understand," Gomes says, with a heavy sigh. "Though others will not. Herr Fugger has invested several thousand ducats in the scheme, so far, and will want some form of return. If I cannot persuade you to your duty, I must send him your head."

"Oh, dear God above!" Constantine is now shaking with terror. "You would kill me, sir?"

"Eventually." Allesandro Gomes toys with the dagger at his belt. "Though first it would be remiss of me not to exact some further retribution on the man who seeks to betray us. I might slice off an ear, or sever a few of your fingers. The Dominican Inquisitors have a way with red hot irons, which they press into a man's privy parts, until he screams his guilt."

"I have not the courage to face you," the preacher replies. He is becoming used to betraying those about him, and prefers losing his honour, rather than his manhood, or even the odd thumb. "Tell me what I must do, and I will obey."

"Your part is a simple one, Father," Gomes explains. "A fishing boat will land you on the English coast, close by to where our ally lives. Your task is easy. Go to our friend, and say that the plot is approved, and that they are to send word to the Keeper of the Angels. Once that is done, our plan will run its course."

"And no more from me?" The treacherous preacher hopes that his part in the plot is thus limited, and he can slip away, with his generous fee.

"There is always more, my friend," Gomes says. "You will stay close by our great ally, and act as messenger. It might be that you have to roam the West Country with secrets to tell."

"Then I must go in disguise, for I am from Suffolk, and my face is known from Norwich and Ipswich, and across to Cambridge."

"Then grow a beard, and change your demeanour," Gomes snaps. "For mark me well, sir …

you must do all that is bid of you."

"I cannot kill."

"I know that. Though you can send men to their deaths, it seems," the Spaniard tells the frightened preacher. "Do as you are bid, and your life will be spared. Fail me, and you die. Is that plain enough, sir?"

"Would that I did not fear death so easily," Constantine curses. "For then many men would still be alive, and my honour intact, even though I did burn on the heretic's pyre!"

"Talk is cheaply bought, Master Preacher." Gomes touches the hilt of his sword. "I am sworn to do, or die, and will not rest until the race is run."

*

"I fear we are returning to Master Cromwell empty handed," Stephen Vaughan says, as they climb the gangplank of their waiting boat. "I return with a sorry tale of a half read letter, and a mysterious Spaniard who can command churchmen to fight for him."

"What about this English priest?" Will asks. "Perhaps that might lead us to some other thing?" He cannot think of anything else to add, and throws his leather bag down onto the deck.

The others, including the now retired Sergeant Buffery, do the same, and look about for a comfortable place to lay their heads, whilst traversing the Channel. Mush, like Richard, cannot go below decks, without fearing some calamity. The boat seems frail to them, and they cannot understand how it manages to beat its way back and forth between Calais and Dover without mishap.

In truth, the Cog is a reliable workhorse of a boat, designed to shift cargo, and people with relative ease, and some comfort. The flush laid flat bottom at midships gradually curves out, thanks to ingeniously laid overlapping strakes of timber. Each oak plank is secured with double-clenched iron nails, and tightly caulked with tarred moss.

The single decked vessel is controlled by a single rectangular sail, and a stern-mounted central rudder which, the ship's master assures them, is little different from the Norse craft of centuries past. The twelve man crew are a dubious mix of English and Flemish rascals, who go about their business fully armed.

"French pirates breed like fleas," the ship's master explains.

"Would they risk attacking us?" Mush asks.

"Unlikely, but why take the chance?" he replies, unlashing the rudder bar. "Sometimes, two or more ships join forces, and fall on any stray cog as comes their way. My lads are all good fellows, though, and always ready for a fight. The king pays well for captured pirate ships."

"Does he, by God!" Tom Wyatt says. "It almost makes you wish for one to come our way, sir!"

"Be careful what you pray for," the ship's master replies, grinning. "For these Frenchies eat babies, and shit lightening for breakfast."

"Did I hear the mention of breakfast?" Richard Cromwell appears at the first mention of food. "A piece of well salted pork will do nicely!"

The cog slips anchor, and is rowed out of the confines of Calais harbour, before the single sail is hoisted. Will and his party remain on deck, scouring the horizon for any sign of pirates, but see nothing but the grey expanse of water that keeps England and France apart. A favourable breeze springs up, and the small craft is blown, serenely on its way to Dover. After an hour, the wind increases, and veers about, pushing them further south.

"We'll not be able to make Dover with this blow," the master informs his passengers. "I must stand off, and run south, for Sandwich. Does that upset your plans, Captain Draper?"

"Not by much," Will replies, turning his face from the increasing spray. "We are on the king's business, so can pick up post horses there, and ride to London. What of you … does it affect your trade?"

"Not a wit, sir," says the cog's captain. "My cargo of salt will sell in any coastal market. It is in cakes, and comes from the famous Istrian salt pans."

"You expect a good return?" Will asks.

"I do, but it will take the merchants a week to bicker over the price, and then I must sell it piece meal."

"What return will you make?"

"On the whole cargo?" the man calculates for a moment. "I will be first to market, so should clear about thirty five pounds on the shipment."

"I will take the entire cargo from you, for thirty pounds," Will tells him. Miriam is always looking for good deals, and Istrian salt will sell well. "Though you must deliver it to my warehouse in London."

"Thirty one, and we have a deal." The man spits into his palm, and they shake hands on it. "Though I will need a cargo for the return journey."

"Speak to my wife in London," Will says, "and she will find you one … at a price."

"Your wife?" the sailing master scowls at the very

idea of such a thing. "I cannot deal with a woman, sir!"

"Then you must forgo your thirty one pounds, and struggle to find a return cargo, for 'tis her business, and her money."

"God's teeth... they'll be sailing ships next!" the man curses, but nods his head in acceptance. "What does your woman usually deal in?"

"Whatever there is that might turn an honest coin, sir," Will says. "She has a way about her for making a profit."

"Aye, my sister can turn silver into gold, right enough," Mush says, "and without resorting to witchcraft."

"God forbid," the ship's master says, laughing, a little uneasily. "Though 'tis clear she has you under her spell well enough, Captain Draper. Now, lend a hand, and help my lads lash a canvas over the hold, lest your newly bought cargo gets a salty soaking!"

"Amen to that," Will tells the seaman. "For my Miriam will turn every grain into a profit, and lament every grain lost to the elements. Pull hard, lads, or my wife will curse us all."

"Do not smile," Richard says, seeing the sailors smile, "for I would rather face a hundred Spaniards, than Mistress Draper in a rage!"

"So much salt," Mush mutters. "I wonder what use even my clever sister will put it to?"

"The gentry will pay well for it," the cog's master says, "but only by the half pound. The merchants usually buy my cargo, and break it into smaller lots."

"Which pushes up the price," Tom Wyatt says to them. "For they hide it away in their warehouses, and pretend to there being a shortage, every year."

"Miriam will not be so tricky," Will says. "It will

go for a fair price, and even common folk will be able to buy a penny bag from one of her stalls."

"Cheap salt for all," Mush declares, with mock sincerity. "Except for that old fool Thomas More."

"But my friend," Wyatt replies, "what will he sprinkle on his eggs each morning?"

"God will provide," Richard Cromwell says, crossing himself. "For all is perfect in Utopia."

"Does he still vex Master Cromwell then?" Tom Wyatt has been away, and is out of touch.

"Nothing he cannot handle," Richard replies. "Though he is loath to do the man any lasting damage. Friendship is a sacred thing with my uncle, and he loves the man for his wit, and past deeds."

"Then the king lets him live?" the poet says. "Henry is mellowing. What says Lady Anne?"

"Too much. She would, like Salome of old, have More's head." Richard frowns. "It causes much strain between the two of them. Boleyns' are not renowned for their forgiving natures."

"Then Master Thomas is between two stools," Wyatt concludes. "I pray he does not let his love of a friend overcome his caution, for Anne can hate with the ardent fervour that a lover loves."

"Well, I suppose you are the man who would know," Mush mutters, and receives a dirty look from the poet. He is resolved to forget the lady, and wishes only for everyone else, including the king, to leave him be.

5   **Marital Disharmony**

"How is My Lady, Master Bowles?" The Duke of Norfolk is barely out of his saddle, and is shaking his steward's shoulder, as if to wring the truth from him.

"Sorely vexed, My Lord," he replies.

"Vexed, you say?"

"Sorely."

"Sorely vexed?" Norfolk clenches his fists in the big, leather riding gloves. "By Holy Christ's Immortal Crucifixion, I'll give the bloody woman 'sorely vexed', and no mistake!" He stomps into the great hall, and bellows out her name. There is silence in return, and Tom Howard, Third Duke of Norfolk, taking it for a show of dumb insolence, is further enraged. "Where is the bitch?"

"Lady Elizabeth is in her chambers, sir," Bowles says, cowering. "She will not come forth, or even eat. She says she will starve herself, unless…"

"Unless?" Norfolk's rage is monumental. "She dares to make demands of her husband? I *am* her husband, am I not, Master Bowles?"

"Yes, My Lord."

"And did she not swear to obey me, in the eyes of God?"

"Yes, Your Lordship."

"Then why does she disobey me?" Norfolk simply cannot understand how, as the most pre-eminent noble in England, he is not immediately given what he wants. "Have I made an onerous demand of her?"

"Not at all, sire," Bowles replies. He does not add anything, as he is unsure quite how the Duchess of Norfolk has displeased his master. She leaves him be, to gamble, drink, and whore entirely as he wishes, and asks nothing in return, but a quiet, comfortable life.

"God's festering bollocks, must I do everything myself?" Norfolk storms up the long staircase, and hammers on the third door along from the landing area. Then he thinks to try it, and it swings open at his touch. He is relieved that his wife, Elizabeth has not thought to lock him out, which would necessitate her swift, and brutal punishment. Inside, he can see her, sitting by candle light, and reading her bible. Norfolk is irritated by her actions, because her Latin is superior to his, and he struggles to read the good book with any fluency.

"I see you, madam!" he cries.

"You want me, My Lord?" she asks.

"No, I see you, but I do not want you, madam," Norfolk snaps. He enters, and slams the door behind himself. "When the fruit withers, a man must look for fresher delights. What have you done with Mistress Holland? I gave strict orders that she was to be accommodated on the estate."

"And so she has been, my dear husband," Elizabeth Howard retorts. "I offered her either a stall in the stables, or some room in one of the pig sties. She declines either, and chooses to stay in her father's cottage."

"Bess Holland is to be given her own rooms, here," Norfolk says, coldly. "She will have adjoining rooms to mine, and she will be given a place of honour at my table."

"Is she to be honoured in our bed also?"

"Be damned to you, bitch," Norfolk says. "I have done with you. Bess will warm my bed, and be my loving wife, in all but name. You will pack up your belongings, and be ready to move out, within the hour."

"Move?" Elizabeth Howard is surprised. She

understands that her husband is taking a new mistress, but losing her place is almost too much to bear. "You want me to leave because of … a cheap, pox ridden whore?"

"I care not where you go, but go you must," Norfolk replies, disdainfully. He is a man of action, and seldom ever plans, or considers any after effects of what he does.

"Then I may take one of the other castles?" Elizabeth asks.

"No, that will not do. You may have a house … a small house, close by." Norfolk cannot understand what the fuss is about. His wife has borne him children, and is now in her late thirties. Bess is nineteen years old, and a willing replacement. In fact, he has been swiving her these past two years, but in some secrecy. "I will settle a couple of hundred on you."

"We have been here before," Elizabeth says. "You cast me out two years ago, but my friends at court made you relent. They will do so again, My Lord, and you will be made to look the fool once more."

"Not so, you evil vixen," Norfolk tells her. "Back then, Thomas Cromwell took pity on you, and asked me to relent. I was soft hearted, and did not wish to offend the Blacksmith's boy. Now, your friend has changed his tune. He wants me to stop you spreading wicked gossip about my niece, and accept that Anne Boleyn must take priority."

"Never!" the Duchess cries. "The Boleyn family are a crew of filthy, debauched peasants, and not fit to sit at the same table as nobility. You should tell Henry to swive the bitch at once, and have done with her."

"I am given leave to stop your mouth … in any way I see fit, madam," Norfolk says. It is a lie. Thomas

Cromwell merely suggests that he speak to her, and urge restraint, but he is in a foul mood, and wishes to break his wife's stiff necked opposition to him taking a new mistress. The girl is nubile, and most willing, which the old duke finds much to his liking. "Defy me, and I will horsewhip you, naked, through the village."

"Then I will have that in common with your slatternly new whore," Elizabeth rejoins. "For many men have seen her bare body around these parts!"

"Enough!" Norfolk does not have the wit to verbally joust with the duchess, who is a learned woman, and possesses a sharp tongue. "I command it. You will leave, and keep your mouth shut."

"That I will, Tom Howard," she replies. "For I have no wish to share you with a poxed up trollop."

"The girl is clean," the duke snaps, and immediately regrets it. "She is a sweet, and..."

"Has the king seen her?"

"What do you imply, madam?"

"Nothing, sir, but that Henry does like to sample all the wares. Ask your sister, and your nieces. God knows, but I have had cause to avoid him around court."

"You seek to anger me, wife."

"I seek to open your eyes," the duchess tells him. "Henry looks to throw off Katherine, as you seek to throw me aside. Then the king will throw off the Boleyn whore. History does have a habit of coming around again, and again, sir. Take care you are not thrown aside with your precious niece, Anne."

"I must be rid of you, madam," Norfolk says, his voice becoming softer. "Lady Bess demands it of me ... as a sign of good faith."

"Good faith? God's teeth, Tom, but she is the

daughter of one of our stewards. The girl is a drab. She was fiddling with the stable lads when she was twelve, and can ride a pintle as well as any half crown jade."

"Have a care," Norfolk mutters. "For I shall strangle you, with my own hands, My Lady. Take your pension, and be gone. It is best for us all this way."

"Indeed?" Elizabeth, Duchess of Norfolk smiles. "I shall have my revenge, sir. Make no mistake. If every hand is now against me, then I shall be against every hand. Turn me out, and I will be left with no other choice, but to strike back at you."

"You tire me, woman," Norfolk says. "I'll send up a couple of your ladies in waiting, who will help you pack up your belongings, My Lady. Mind now, the jewels are mine, and stay under my care."

"To adorn your whore's throat?" Norfolk turns, and stalks out of the room. He considers that he is done with his wife, and that all will now go well. In his arrogance, he does not realise that his wife, the daughter of the great Buckingham, and a descendant of kings, will keep her word.

Come hell or high water, she will exact her revenge, and endeavour to ruin the conceited duke, once and for all time.

*

March slides into April, and Easter comes, and goes without the young men of Austin Friars being able find the mysterious German monk. Nor are they able to unravel the plot, half discovered by Stephen Vaughan. The merchant is back in London, and is re-establishing his links with the local wool traders, who used to use him as a go-between with the Flanders weavers. He spends his evenings telling dinner guests of how he helped to stand off fifty fearsome Inquisitors, and of how he laid many of them low, with his trusty sword arm.

Miriam Draper, after wondering, briefly, what to do with almost two tons of fine Istrian sea salt, is now trading it all over England, and Wales, in small packages, within the price range of common households. She is also making a reasonable return by supplying it to her cheese maker partner in Cheshire. The bulk of each new shipment goes directly to the busy tanneries of the southern counties, where it is used in hide curing.

In return, the sceptical sea farer, who can hardly bring himself to deal with a mere woman, grows fat on the profits made from return cargoes. Miriam fills his cog with every kind of article, from horse shoes, to iron nails, or bales of wool and tanned hides, which find a ready market in France, Flanders, and even further a field. Captain Stubbs becomes so much of an acolyte that he even approaches Miriam with a fine business idea.

"Mistress Draper, you do well from my cog, do you not?" he asks.

"Well enough," Miriam replies, warily. She likes the ageing sea captain, but does not wish to yield too much of her profit to make him rich. "Why do you ask?"

"My cousin wishes to retire," Stubbs says. "He has a cog every bit as fine as mine. Why not buy it, and let me crew it with trusted men for the Draper Company?"

"How will you profit?" Miriam wants to know, but she is interested.

"I put a young fellow in charge of her, and see he keeps busy. You pay him a wage, and a small share for me. Say ten points. Then, as other cogs come available…"

"The Draper Fleet," Miriam says. "Three points per hundred, and you must pay all harbour costs, if no cargo is available. Well, Captain Stubbs?"

"I agree," Stubbs replies. "Though we must have a legal paper, and licenses for all the coastal ports."

"I shall see Master Tom," Miriam says, and they shake hands on the deal.

Thomas Cromwell helps where he can, ensuring that the right licences and legal contracts are always in place. In return, Miriam allows him to infiltrate his agents into her spreading net of business contacts, where they carry out a steady, but unobtrusive, gathering of interesting information.

Richard Cromwell and Rafe Sadler return to the mundane world of the law courts, and Mush Draper settles into the life of a comfortably off town gentleman. He hunts during the day, entertains of an evening, and fulfils his husbandly duties each night, with a steady vigour.

Will Draper seems to be the only one of their group with nothing to really occupy his time. Each morning, he dresses, buckles on his sword, and pays attendance at Austin Friars, where he is told that Master Cromwell has no need of his services that day. With his wife usually away on some business or another, the ex soldier has little to do during daylight hours, save hunt a little, or sit about in taverns, trading tales with other unemployed soldiers of fortune.

It is during one such lazy afternoon that he visits the Old Cock, in East Cheap. They serve a decent ale,

and sell wines supplied by his wife. The inn keeper's
wife keeps a cauldron of stew constantly on the boil,
and her pies come to the table hot, and smothered in
rich gravies. He comes in search of a tasty meal, when
he hears a familiar voice, declaiming from the ill lit
back room.

> *"Though only a diplomat's daughter, she*
> *Is wont to dance 'neath the linden tree,*
> *And gambol away,*
> *With gallants all day,*
> *And no king's pintle 'ere see."*

Draper almost joins in with the roar of approval
from the various drunks and bawd masters, but
understands, only too well who is being referred to in
Tom Wyatt's crude doggerel. He pushes his way into
the room, and finds the poet balanced on a low stool,
with a pot of ale balanced on his head.

"Good day, Master Wyatt," he says, tugging his
friend down from his precarious perch. "I see you have
chosen your company wisely once more."

"Ah, Master Cromwell's personal assassin!" Tom
Wyatt says, through a drunken stupor. The other
customers recognise the black livery often worn by the
Privy Councillor's men, and know of Will Draper's
fierce reputation. They turn away their faces, and
pretend never to have heard a word of the treasonable
ditty.

"Your deafness suits you well, good fellows,"
Will says, and drops a few silver coins on the counter.
"Landlord, drinks are on Thomas Cromwell, until that
runs out!" There is a grateful cheer, and they crowd to
the bar, eager to sup at the great man's expense.

"I'll have another pot," Wyatt mumbles. *"For if ever a man did lose his heart, to lady fair, but far apart...* arghh!"

Will Draper's heavy leather gloved hand crashes against the poet's cheek, and he staggers sideways. The drinkers ignore the little byplay, and continue to swill their free ale. The poet raises his fists, but Will slaps them down contemptuously, and takes Thomas Wyatt by his ale-stained ruff. He shakes him like a rag.

"How many times must I pull your neck from under the axe, Thomas?" Will demands, angrily. "I might just save the king the trouble, and slit your throat now."

"Forgive me, old friend. I only get this way when I drink, and I only drink when I … get this way. No, stay your hand please, I suddenly, am sobered up enough to keep my aching love to myself, if only so as not to irritate you. If only Henry would send me abroad on an embassy, or find me work in far off France, Ireland, or Scotland. Well, perhaps not Scotland. That would be too much of a trial. I am bored, Will."

"As am I," Will replies. "Why, I have half a mind to board a boat for the continent, and see what comes my way. I would rather fight for the Spanish than sit around England growing fat."

"You have a wife," Wyatt says, softly. "Were she married to any man, other than you, I would be singing ballads under her window."

"I doubt you would find her in," Will says. "She is abroad, about her business from sun up to sun down. Then she invites people to dinner. I doubt she would miss my going for a moment."

"Then let us seek adventure," the poet says, staggering to his feet. "Let us ride to Paris, and enlist where we may, dear friend. For the French are a quarrelsome lot, and are always fighting somebody, somewhere!"

"Are you Master Thomas Wyatt?" The big Sergeant at Arms asks from the door. He is flanked by another six men, all as fearsome looking.

"Not I, good fellow," Thomas Wyatt replies quickly. For one never knows when a creditor might turn nasty. "Though I hear he was here anon. There was talk of him sailing to Cathay." The big soldier sighs, and turns to Will Draper, who he recognises from his visits to Whitehall Palace.

"Captain Draper, you are also wanted," he says. "I have orders to take you into custody, and transport you both to the Tower of London. We already have Moshe Draper, and Richard Cromwell, and have a barge waiting for your immediate conveyance."

"Are we under arrest?" Will asks.

"I must suppose so," the sergeant replies. "My captain is not one to discuss the niceties with me."

"Might I have time to send a message to my wife?" Will touches his purse with his fingertips, and the big soldier understands that there is a shilling or two to be earned.

"I dare not, sir," the man says. "Though she will know soon enough. Men are detailed to guard several houses about the city, and yours is one of them. Those inside are to be held, in protective custody."

"Then let me send word to my master, at Austin Friars," Will says, unclasping his purse. "Here, five shillings for your trouble."

"Sir, I have men there already," the sergeant admits. "They are ordered to close the place off, and deny all access … or egress."

"Then this is a sorry mess," Will says. "Take the money, for your honesty, and have a drink on we poor souls. The Tower is a daunting prospect, but Master Wyatt is not a Cromwell man."

"Enough of that," the poet snaps. "I'll not weasel out of this, and will come along with you, my friend. I hear the food is somewhat improved, these days, and that the dungeons often have a window, though it takes a *very* tall man to appreciate the view. Let us join our friends, and await our fate."

"Spoken like a poet," Will replies. The sergeant and his men are heavily armed, and will be difficult to overcome without bloodshed. Besides, he reasons, the law, thanks to Cromwell, is more open of late, and he might get a fair hearing. "Come then, to the Tower … and let things fall as they must."

*

It is a short walk to the river, but with guards hemming them both in tightly, there is no chance of flight. Will sees the waiting barge, and its occupants, and wonders what it is that has caused so catastrophic an upset. As he climbs aboard, he catches Richard Cromwell's eye, who merely shrugs back at him.

"We are all Jews now, Will," Mush mutters, as his brother in law sits beside him. "Eight men, and the sergeant. We can take them, once out on the river. Then we can…"

"What, Mush … row to France?" Tom Wyatt says, as he sits opposite. "I cannot believe we are all so stupid that we did not see this coming. Some enemy has played us false, and we are too blind to see whom it is."

"Thomas More," Richard says, as the big barge is

poled away from the landing. "God curse the Roman Catholic bastard. Uncle is ever too soft with him."

"Sir Thomas is out of favour at court," Will replies. "I doubt he has enough power to effect all of our arrests. This smacks of careful planning, and by a master hand."

"The king then?" Richard persists. Tom Wyatt laughs at the very idea. The king is too besotted with Lady Anne Boleyn to think about court intrigue. His only plan is to get her wed, and into his bed, for which he needs the help of Thomas Cromwell.

"Not Henry," the poet says. "He would strike hard at one or two, perhaps, but why upset the whole of Austin Friars?"

"True enough," Will Draper agrees. "For who might then run England for him?"

"Norfolk," Richard says, harshly. "It must be old Norfolk's doing. He is the only one close enough to Henry who might risk taking us on. What think you, Will?"

"Never mind what Will thinks," Tom Wyatt replies. "I have it on good authority that Tom Howard has finally made a move against his wife. He has thrown her over for young Bess Holland, once and for all. He is now living openly at Kenninghall with the trollop, as if they were married. Poor Elizabeth is farmed out to some small house, and given two hundred a year to stay away, as if she were never a duchess at all. No, My Lord Norfolk is too busy with his new love to meddle with us."

"Then who is against us?" Will Draper asks. He has just started to enjoy his new found wealth, and position, and resents the possibility of losing either so soon. "Can we have been brought down by Stephen

Gardiner, or even that coward Suffolk?"

"Now Gardiner is Bishop of Winchester, he is too careful of offending anyone, and Charles Brandon, though Earl of Suffolk is mortgaged up to the hilt with our master." Richard knows enough to understand that Suffolk's debts will not vanish, just because Cromwell falls. He will simply devolve to another, more demanding lender. "Beside's he is not a coward… at least, not in battle. His cowardice is merely moral, and which of us can fault him for that?"

"Pray, calm yourselves, gentlemen," the big sergeant calls across to them. "I find it best in such matters that you resign yourself to whatever lies ahead. Why, the Duke of Buckingham was as calm as can be when I rowed him down river, some years back. He jested with us, and even passed the journey playing at dice with one of my men. He lost four shillings, as I recall."

"That is most reassuring," Tom Wyatt returns, "considering that he was then beheaded, and his body torn into four pieces. Are you saying we are taken up as traitors, fellow?"

"Well, when all is said and done, sir," the man replies, spitting into the river, "you must all have done something. It stands to reason that all men are guilty of some crime or other, for it is our nature. These days, there are a hundred or more ways to offend His Majesty. I dare say, as gentlemen, they will give you a very fair trial before taking your heads. It is then you will know your crime, I dare say."

"Then you already judge us?" Mush asks.

"As guilty … yes, sir, or how else do I come to have the pleasure of your fine company?"

"Tell me, sergeant," Tom Wyatt asks, by way of

passing the trip, "how many have you escorted to the Tower, and how many back?"

"Nigh on a hundred and fifty, sir," the talkative sergeant replies. "Though I can give a far more exact figure as to them as comes back from there. For that number is a low one, and easy to count ... needing but two fingers. I recall taking up a gentleman who had the misfortune of being named for his father. How we laughed about it, when we realised the mistake, and how relieved the poor fellow was to know 'twas his father whose life was forfeit instead. I had the pleasure of escorting the older man back myself, and did jest with him over the mistake. He laughed, all the way to the block, I believe, sir."

"And the other fellow?" Mush asks.

"Oh, a real, murdering rascal," the sergeant explains to his charges. "We arrested him up river, and brought him to the Tower, only to find him to be stone cold dead as we arrived at Traitor's Gate. It seems the fear of his coming fate stopped his heart. We rowed him out to the deeper part of the river, and consigned him to Father Thames, with a rock in his pants. Now see, here we are. Sit still, whilst we tie up securely, gentlemen, for I do not want anyone drowning on me, at this late juncture!"

"Your sense of humour will be the death of us," says Richard.

The barge is made fast, for and aft, and the guards are joined by another half dozen. Richard, Will, Mush and Tom Wyatt step ashore on the quayside, close by the daunting gate built by Edward 1st, and now used to gain entrance to the inner walls. A small door swings open in the wall, and the sergeant ushers them inside, one by one. As each man passes within, he counts them off, in a stentorian voice, and checks their names off a list he has on a roll of parchment.

The gloom is intense, until someone appears, carrying a firebrand. Another is lit, and the small room is suddenly ablaze with smoke and light. Will can make out two figures hovering like harbingers of doom, and wonders who is sent to lay charges against them, and what those crimes might be.

"Ah, there you are, at last," Thomas Cromwell says from behind the second torch. "I was worried that my men might find you too late!"

6   The Tower of London

Will Draper is far too relieved to vent his anger on Thomas Cromwell, and is, instead, disproportionately pleased to see him, without either iron fetters, or any other sign of constraint.

"I must apologise for this secretive way of assembling you all," Cromwell explains, "but I am unsure who I can trust, other than you four, and am in need of some faithful allies. The business in Calais has come back to haunt me, my friends."

"Calais?" Will asks.

"Yes. Come, I have a comfortable room prepared. It is warm, and there will be some food laid out for us."

He leads the way, followed by the second torch bearer, who turns out to be a rather subdued Rafe Sadler. They pass through cold stone corridors, and Will is reminded of the time he was last within the Tower. On that occasion he was in charge, and given the task of silencing loose tongues that threatened to undermine Thomas Cromwell's plans. The place seems as menacing now, as it did back then, and they all feel their spirits being crushed under the weight of the thick, inescapable walls.

At length, they come upon an iron bound door, which Rafe pushes back on well oiled hinges. He leads them into a well lit chamber, with a table, chairs, and food and ale, all set out for them. The six men each pour a mug of strong ale, and take food from the plank, laid across two barrels. Thomas Cromwell takes the chair at the head of this makeshift oak table, and beckons for them to draw close about him, and also be seated.

"To business, gentlemen. One of my agents came

to me this morning, with strange news." Cromwell rubs one finger against his chin, as if it will help him concentrate on the matter under discussion. "It seems that since that peculiar escapade, which concerned the emperor's phantom army, Charles' spies have been busy. They have been preparing the way for a rather special visitor to our shores. Do you recall talk of an 'English priest', Will?"

"We all do. It mystified us then, and still has us wondering now." Will cannot think why this warrants so peculiar a meeting, away from Austin Friars, and why it has to happen in such a speedy manner. "Why would an English priest be involved with any enemy of the realm, other than the Pope."

"Do you recall a fellow by the name of George Constantine?" Tom Cromwell asks, and Will Draper begins to understand.

"The preacher who betrayed Stephen Vaughan to the Lord Chancellor's office," he says, nodding. "He fled to France, just ahead of our vengeance."

"Yes. You were in Italy at the time, else we might have taken him, and gained some justice for those he condemned to death. I thank God I was able to save Stephen Vaughan from his fate, but the others perished in the flames."

"Then it was he who aided the Spaniard, Gomes?"

"And he still does," Cromwell says. "Yesterday, he was smuggled aboard a Flemish cog in Calais, by the agents of Anton Fugger. I regret that it was not one of Miriam's boats, or things would have gone better for us. My own man found out about it, but just too late. He could do nothing but take the next available ship , and hope to gain England, before the preacher did.

Alas, the winds proved unfavourable, and George Constantine landed at Deal, six hours ahead of my man."

"I take it he has now vanished?" Tom Wyatt asks.

"He has. As soon as the cog berthed, he was taken away, on horseback. My man was able to find out that he was met by a dozen, heavily armed men. He sent a fast messenger to me at Austin Friars, warning us to be on the lookout for Constantine. I had to act speedily, so set some men to round up those I can most readily trust. The sergeant knows only that you were to be found, and brought here."

"Why here?" Richard Cromwell asks. "Austin Friars would be a better choice, Uncle."

"Known to all," Cromwell explains. "Think it through, as I did, gentlemen. Constantine is the agent of Gomes, who works for the wealthy Fugger clan. The head of the family, Anton Fugger, is the emperor's banker. In fact, he funds most of the monarchs in Europe, even Henry to some extent. There is a direct link to Emperor Charles. The plot to destroy England is still afoot, and Constantine is the tinder that will light the fuse. I can only think of two ways to bring this country low. Either kill Henry, or destroy his best councillors."

"You think he intends to murder you, or the king?" Will asks.

"Why not? He has a dozen armed men with him. They cannot get to the king, whom I have sent out of London, and hemmed in with reliable men, but they can descend on Austin Friars, and hope to strike me down."

"Then you have locked yourself in the safest place in England," says Tom Wyatt. "You have set men to guard your house, and that of others?"

"Yes. Miriam will be safe, in case they seek to remove my strong right arm, Will." Cromwell stands, and places his knuckles on the table. "I have increased the guard at Whitehall, and Westminster Palace, and put men secretly around the Lord Chancellor's house in Chelsea. Should political murder be their aim, they will be rebuffed. Then, we will hunt them all down, and kill them. How they could hope to succeed is beyond imagining. Will, I rely on you to root out this Constantine and his band of assassins."

"Of course, master," Will Draper replies. He is back on firm ground again. His believes, modestly, that his only true skill is fighting, and he is very good at it. "I will throw a net over London, and draw it in, until we have our catch. Whom might I use?"

"For the searching, you can use all of my agents. I have about a hundred and fifty men, and women, in my pay, and they can search in all the likely places. When the miscreants are found, I am not sure whom you might trust, outside Austin Friars. Mush, Richard, Master Wyatt, Rafe and yourself must suffice, for now. Barnaby Fowler is needed to defend our homes. He has a couple of dozen roughs, ready to break heads, where ever they are needed most. As for the rest of my young men … they are willing enough, and loyal to a man … but few can fight. Regrettably, I have turned them all into clever lawyers."

""What about Richard Rich?" Tom Wyatt asks. "He can wave a sword around, and he has a good few friends about the court. Might he not raise a troop of gentlemen to protect their king?"

"These young bucks are all allied, in one form or another, to Norfolk, Suffolk, or Northumberland," Cromwell says. "They cannot be trusted. Remember the talk of a '*great personage*' in England, ready to bring the country down? It might be any one of them. Besides, I do not trust Master Rich. One day, he will be a thorn in our sides."

"What of Sir Thomas More?"

"No, not More," Tom Cromwell says. "His time is almost done, and his power is all but drained away. Whilst you track down this very real danger, I will be taking some final steps to nullify the Lord Chancellor."

"A pity," Tom Wyatt says. "Utopia was never as pleasant as Austin Friars, Master Thomas, but More was ever kind to me, as a boy. It is only lately that he did misuse me, and I cannot blame him for that. It was for political ends, not personal. Can you ever truly hate a man who is so true to his own beliefs?"

"I never hated him," Thomas Cromwell replies, wistfully. "Even now, I long for him to take my hand in friendship, and step onto the same path I have chosen."

"Perhaps, now the break with the Church of Rome is almost here…" Wyatt says, but he is not convinced. After all, he thinks, can a mortal man, even if a king, sweep aside fifteen hundred years of Christianity?

"England may break with Rome, and Henry might break with Clement, but More will never break with More." Cromwell's remark sounds enigmatic, but he means what he says. More is More, and exists only for his own ideals. What does it matter to him, if the world changes? More will not.

"Will you stay in the Tower, until this plot is unravelled, Master Cromwell?" Mush asks.

"Why not?" Cromwell says. "It is as safe as anywhere in London. I will keep a few good fellows close to hand, and try to continue with the business of state. Now, eat up, and prepare yourselves for the task ahead. Though I do not believe that one preacher and a dozen men can ruin England, they might have enough about them to cause a little mayhem along the way."

"Shall I bring Constantine to you here?"

"If he can be taken alive," Cromwell tells Will. "There is a great power behind all this, apart from the emperor. Some English lord seeks to bring ruin on us all, and so benefit by it. A live priest might betray his trust, once again."

"Then you shall have him, alive," Will promises. If the scoundrel is in London, he will be cornered, and hemmed in by useful men, who will cut down his bodyguard. Then it is a simple matter to drag the treacherous preacher to the Tower, and stretch his bones, until he confesses all, and unveils the name of the 'great lord' behind the plot.

Rafe Sadler has been busy, and he has already put out the word to look out for Constantine, and his well armed gang. Thirteen men on horseback, with muskets and swords, intent on some mischief, cannot be that hard to find. There will be some low inn, or cheap bawdy house, catering to their needs, and one of Cromwell's agents will pick up the scent.

He informs Will Draper what he has done, and they make arrangements as to which part of the city they will police. Will is for splitting London into five smaller areas, and for each man to look to his portion.

"Let each man command where he is given, and ensure that any search is carried out thoroughly," Will says. "Every house, inn, stable or tavern is to be searched by our agents. Every whore on our payroll is to question any stranger they lay with, and every landlord is to search his own property, even unto the very cellars beneath their businesses. Let both palaces in the city be searched, from privies to gardens, and up into the roof, if need be. Does any man here disagree with that?"

"It makes good sense," Tom Wyatt says. "Shall we each have a few boys with us, to use like *Pheidippides* of old?"

"A good idea, Tom. We will select the best runners amongst the urchins who pay court to us. If any one of us find our prey, we will send word to the rest."

"Fi…" Richard starts, but Mush raises a finger to his lips.

"Hush, Master Genius," he says. "I will explain, as we return to the city."

*

Thomas Cromwell's outward show of calm, belays many real worries that nag at him. How can one cowardly preacher bring down a nation? Why would Charles, ruler of over half of the world, believe Constantine could do such a thing? Why would Anton Fugger, the world's richest banker, and financier of the emperor's New World conquests, become involved?

The Fuggers are an enormously rich family, and are replacing the wealthy Medici of Italy, as financiers to the great and good. Cromwell knows that the Bishop of Rome is in debt to them, to the tune of almost a half million Ducati, and that Charles V is overrunning the Americas with troops and ships, paid for with Fugger money.

The financier, Anton Fugger, is the richest man alive, and has a deep reverence for the Roman church. He lends to Rome, with little expectation of making any return, and he detests the new Protestant movement, which is springing up all about him in the various German principalities. This does not, however, explain to Thomas Cromwell why he is involved in a plot to destroy England.

Destruction means conquest, and for that, the Privy Councillor reasons, you need soldiers. Not thousands, but tens of thousands, in great ships. You need generals, cannon, and vast amounts of weaponry. Like Will Draper, Cromwell cannot see where such a destructive force is hidden.

Then there was the matter of the traitor within. Which great Lord of England would think himself strong enough to bend the country to his will? No matter how he looks at it, there is only one solution that makes any sense. The 'great personage' concerned must have entered into a secret plot with others. A conspiracy of great men?

The combinations were endless, of course. Individually, no duke, or earl, was quite strong enough, and they all deeply mistrust, and hate one another. The only logical combination would be for Harry Percy, the discontented Duke of Northumberland, to ally himself with his cousin by marriage, the devious King of Scotland.

Seumas Stiùbhairt, the fifth King James Stuart of Scotland, is just turned twenty, and has long wished to prove his military acumen. Perhaps, Cromwell muses, the young lion is tired of border raids, and inconclusive treaties with the French. The northern king is Henry's nephew, by virtue of being the son of Margaret Tudor, Henry's much beloved sister.

Should the English king fall, without a legitimate male heir, then James V will have a strong claim to the vacant throne. The possibility must be very tempting for an ambitious young man, and with his highlanders supporting Harry Percy's twenty thousand Northumbrians, there is a strong chance of success. Together, they might just manage to take much of the north, and tip Henry from his golden throne.

Then what? Norfolk and Suffolk will rally to Henry, and a civil war will have to settle the matter. The two great lords, together with the Welsh, and loyal Irish armies, would be enough to drive the Scots back over the border, and overcome Percy. His head would adorn the Tower of London's high walls. No, he decides, it is far too mad a scheme to think about.

"Damn it to Hell's Inferno, and back!" Thomas Cromwell curses. "What *is* going on?"

*

Sir Thomas More does not stray far from his Chelsea home these days, and feels much comforted by Utopia's solid walls. So it is with annoyance that he finds himself asked to visit the house of a city merchant, who claims he has important knowledge of a 'known heretic'. It is something he cannot ignore, as the king still fears the full horror of Lutheranism, and any related topic.

If the king's superstitious fears push him back into the arms of Mother Church, Sir Thomas reasons, then he must exploit the opportunity. It might be the right time to uncover a few witches, or expose some Satanic rite or other, and drum up some good, honest religious hysteria amongst the populace. After all, what matters a couple of wayward souls going to the pyre, if it steers England back into the arms of the Pope?

"Shall I fetch a palanquin, master?" his faithful steward asks. "It might be better not to show yourself in public." Wilfred Boscombe has been with his master for over twelve years, and knows that Sir Thomas does not inspire warmth and love amongst the common herd. "The mob favour your enemies, who scatter pennies amongst them, to buy their low favours."

"I do not fear the people of England, Wilfred," More replies, softly. "I fear only their masters. Have a boy lead me, for I do not know the way."

"I will fetch Isaac Gilbey to join us, and we will go armed, to ensure you are not misused, master," the steward persists. "Mistress Alice will roundly scold us for doing any less for you."

"Pray do not upset my wife, dear friend," Sir Thomas says, smiling thinly. "For her short temper is uneven enough as it is. Yes, do fetch young Gilbey, and let us be on our way. I want to be back in time for dinner, as my daughter, Margaret, promises us a nice lamb stew."

The early evening air is pleasant for the middle of May, and Sir Thomas does not bother to don one of his heavy fur capes. Instead, he wraps a light, woven garment about his narrow shoulders, and sets off, on foot. The walk from Utopia, down to the river, and onto a waiting boat is completed at a steady stroll, and several locals call greetings, or a kind word to him.

"See how the people still think of me?" he says, waving back to the passing Londoners. "They have no love for heresy, and the king might do well to listen to them, now and then. They might think they want their preaching in English, but deep down, they know only Latin will drive away the Devil, and his denizens of evil."

"Have a care, Sir Thomas," Boscombe says, taking his master's elbow. "The riverbank is muddy here, and I would not have you fall for all the world!"

"Nor I, Wilfred," the Lord Chancellor of England replies, smiling wryly. "Nor I."

"Gor' bless, your lordship," the boatman says, taking up his oars. "Is it beyond the bridge you want? Only that will be an extra ha'penny, good sir."

"Cheeky fellow!" More replies, handing over a single penny piece. "As Lord Chancellor, I still set the rates on this river. Take your penny, and be thankful I don't have the skin off your back."

"Your pardon, master," the boatman says, "but I heard you were gone, and another in your place."

"Then let me educate you," Sir Thomas says. "I am Lord Chancellor, and nothing can be put into law without my hand set to it. If you speak of Thomas Cromwell, he is but a lawyer. He writes law, but I, and the king *make* it."

"God save the king," the boatman mutters, and poles his craft out into the middle of the river, where the current catches at them, and sweeps them down, under the great bridge. As they clear the structure, the boat swings towards the bank.

"Watch out for the shallows just here," Thomas More warns. "There is a bank of sand just off your left side."

"Have no fear, sir," the boatman says. "I will land you safely at the Tower, as I was hired to do."

"Not the Tower, you fool," the steward snaps.

"I have my orders, sir," the boatman says.

"And I have my cudgel," Boscombe replies, raising his club above his head. "Do as you are instructed, or we will dash out your brains!"

"Do not offer me violence, sir," the man replies, dropping a hand to the knife in his boot. "Your master is for the Tower, and I am to hear no more about it."

"Then we will throw you into the river, and steer our own way, you saucy knave," young Gilby growls, and edges towards the boatman. "Come, Master Boscombe, let us man handle the rogue into the Thames!"

"Stay your hand, sirs. I have my orders, I say, and should Sir Thomas complain, I am to tell him this … that '*God moves in mysterious ways*'."

Sir Thomas More sighs, and waves his servant back onto his bench. In his younger days, he recalls his first meeting with a young man who used to run errands for the lawyers at Lincoln's, Inn and the Inner and Middle Temples of the law courts. The young fellow has something about him. He hints of having travelled abroad, and seems to know more than one so callow ought. Despite himself, More likes him, and employs him for small errands. After a while, he finds their friendly chats have grown into full blown discussions on politics, religion, and financial matters. The scholar has acquired that rarest of all commodities, a true friend.

One day, the young man had ceased being a runner, and appears dressed in expensive black robes. He has, by some strange alchemy, become a qualified lawyer, and also become attached to the household of Cardinal Wolsey, Lord Chancellor of England. When More asks how this comes to be, the young man smiles, and tells him how '*God moves in mysterious ways*'.

"Then let us make haste to the Tower, fellow," the Lord Chancellor says. "For Master Cromwell is not a patient man."

7   A Meeting of Minds

The boat grounds close to where Will Draper stepped ashore, but a couple of hours before, and Sir Thomas More steps from the craft, helped by his concerned steward. There is a small knot of men waiting to greet him. They are all dressed in a familiar black livery, and remind the Lord Chancellor of crows, brooding in a graveyard.

He tries to shake off thoughts of death, but the slime covered walls of the Tower, look like the cold walls of a mausoleum, and the flock of black cloaked crows seem like harbingers of some coming tragedy. He feels the familiar twist of pain under his heart that has become like a friend to him of late; visiting in the night, and making him wince with hurt.

The crows suddenly flutter about him, and Sir Thomas recognises the familiar embroidered '*C*' adorning their sleeves, and breasts. One steps forward, and offers the Lord Chancellor a slight bow.

"Welcome, Sir Thomas."

"Cromwell." Thomas More returns the cursory nod, and sets his mouth into a tight frown of the deepest disapproval. "How long have you been kidnapping Ministers of State?"

"I stand reproved," Thomas Cromwell replies, taking the Lord Chancellor by the elbow. He steers him towards the small, oak door, set in the great stone wall of the Tower. It does not seem large enough for even a small man to pass through. "Come, we must speak of important matters."

"In secret, Master Cromwell?"

"Needs must... "

"When Satan drives?" The Lord Chancellor

concludes the old saying. "What Devil's work are you about now then?"

"Call me Thomas." Cromwell wishes for the old days, when they discoursed on first name terms, and each held a great regard for the other. He remembers how they would discourse in Latin, stray into Italian, and end up in English, each arguing his own particular point of view. "I am the same man, as always."

"That is for friends. Come then, Master Cromwell, let us talk." More dips his head under the low door's lintel, and enters the forbidding Tower. It is well lit inside, and he is taken to the prepared room, where wine and some cold food awaits. The fare is plain enough, as suit's a man who still wears a hair shirt beneath his outer clothing, as a permanent form of penance to his god.

"I know your simple tastes," Cromwell says, gesturing to the bread and cold lamb laid out for them. "Would that the rest of you were as easy to understand."

"I am not hungry. Though my men, lingering without, might wish a cup of ale whilst they wait for me." Sir Thomas More ignores the table, sits, and places his hands, neatly folded, in his lap. There follows a short, uncomfortable silence, whilst each man composes what to say, in his own mind. At last, the Lord Chancellor speaks. "Well?"

"We must talk about the king."

"Have you a man hiding behind a curtain, writing this down?" More sees the look of hurt on Thomas Cromwell's face, and almost feels a stab of pity for the man. It was a cheap jibe, More thinks, and he regrets it.

"There are no curtains in this room, Thomas," Cromwell replies. He spreads his hands wide, to encompass the bare, stone walls, and closed door. "We are quite alone, and I swear our conversation will remain absolutely private, unless you choose to set it down in print, and have it broadcast about the realm. Come, take out that little bible you always carry in your cloak pocket, and I will put my hand upon it."

For a moment, the Lord Chancellor considers just such an act, but forebears, convinced that his old friend would not keep even an oath sworn on the bible, if it suits his purpose to break it. For their conversation not to be recorded, it must be of a most dangerous, and secretive nature.

"Then speak." More will not unbend an inch. "Though I will not listen to any word of treason. Neither will I hear anything against His Eminence, Pope Clement."

"Last year, my friend, you tried to resign your high office." Thomas Cromwell is only stating what is known about the court, as the conversation was witnessed by several highly placed nobles.

"I did, and King Henry refused my offer, saying that he believed me to be somewhat overworked." Thomas More says. "Instead of letting me go, he lifted some of the workload from my shoulders, and gave it to *inferiors*."

"You seek to belittle me, Thomas, but I have done your duties well, and much as you would have done them yourself. It was my suggestion that the king refused your resignation. I told him you were worn out, and must needs rest for a while."

"Must I thank you for this?" More's sarcasm is cuttingly obvious. He sees only that a man who was once his friend has undermined him, for his own personal gain.

"You should." Cromwell sees that harsher words are needed to make his old friend listen. "I did not want your position, but Lady Anne Boleyn wanted your head."

"It is not hers to take," More replies. "That is the king's prerogative. Let him put me to trial, and see where he might find fault with me. Then, and only then, will he take that which is his, Cromwell."

"Once you resigned, Lady Anne Boleyn would have convinced Henry to arrest you, and charge you with treason."

"Treason … how so?" More demands.

"The new laws would suffice to condemn you."

"Laws you wrote."

"Amongst others. The king has to be kept safe, until we have a male heir. These new laws protect his life, and bar anyone from speaking against him, either directly, or publicly. You voiced the opinion that the Bishop of Rome's decisions must be above those made by the king."

"Henry is King of England, but there is a King of Heaven, and Clement, for all his failings, is his chosen one, on earth. Of course the king must accept his ruling, but he can always appeal."

"Until he is too old to sire healthy children?" Cromwell shakes his head. "No, you must stick to what *is*, rather than what you wish. Clement refuses the annulment, so we have pushed him aside. Henry is now head of the church in England, and soon, we will completely break with Rome."

"I know all this," More says. "So, why bring me here, to listen to it all over again. The King of any nation must obey the Pope. To refute the church means excommunication, and the loss of ones immortal soul."

"Not any more, Thomas," Cromwell says. "The law says Henry is the head of the church within England, and all taxes, levies and artefacts belong to him."

"Ah, now you will steal bones, and take down crosses, and smelt them down, for their gold." More sighs. The wealth of the church will enrich Henry's coffers, he thinks, and ruin his soul. "The king will never destroy the church. He will stop short, when he sees how heresy becomes his bedfellow."

"We are already closing down monasteries, and cleansing them of their venal old pederasts." Cromwell pours a glass of wine for himself. "Next we shall start on the abbeys, and those clerics who dare oppose the king. I say all of this to show you but one thing. The Roman church, and the Bishop of Rome's power, will not survive in England."

"Then consider me shown," Sir Thomas seems weary, and rubs his chest, where he has, of late suffered stabbing pains. "Now, may I go back to Utopia, where my daughter has a stew waiting for me?"

"How is dear Margaret?" Cromwell asks. "Does marriage to young Master Roper suit her?"

"She is still a dutiful girl, and loves me better than any father deserves. I pray you, Tom Cromwell, *do not* threaten my family in this underhanded way."

"Dear Christ in Heaven, does it come to this?" Cromwell cries, genuinely stung by More's words. "I held your children in my arms as babes, and send them fine presents on their birthdays, do I not? Have I not written to you, commending your daughter's wit, and intelligence. She has the best Latin of any scholar in England, and is as dear to me as my own departed girls."

"Forgive me, Tom," More says. He remembers Cromwell's daughters as bright little things, tumbling around his ankles, and calling him Uncle Thomas. "I look for trouble in every corner, and ever fear for my family. They are my one weakness, as you well know."

"Your family will be safe, no matter what happens," Tom Cromwell promises. "I will guard them from all harm. Though I confess, you are a different matter. The situation is going to become ever more dangerous for you, and I am not sure how best to keep you alive."

"My life is, as always, the king's," More replies, calmly.

"Remember how Wolsey's death affected Henry?"

"I do. He often swears how he was going to restore him to his place, and forgive him."

"Yes, *after* he was dead," says Cromwell. "Let us have Henry bethink to spare you, *before* your head is in the basket!"

"He cannot think to do such a thing," More says. "I have been careful not to offend him in any way. Of course, I would not sign for him to put Queen Katherine aside, but he embraced me, and commended my scruples."

"That was then," Cromwell tells him. "Since then, he has flexed his muscles, and found that his boundaries are now limitless."

"And who made it so?" More snaps. "The lawyers. If ever Jesus came to save the world again, he will do well to first consign all lawyers to the fiery pit."

"Guilty, as charged," Cromwell replies. "The Boleyn woman has him at her mercy, Thomas. You must see that. She teases him to distraction, then makes her demands. She wants you dead. Once you went into your shell, I thought she might relent, but no, she is like the Devil's own whore, and wants to watch you die. You spoke against her, and that is enough."

"What do you suggest?"

"Would you rather live than die?"

"Yes."

"Really?"

"Of course."

"What if I asked you to denounce your faith?"

"Why would you?" More shakes his head, as he begins to see where Cromwell is going. "Ah, I see. There is to be an oath then?"

"It seems so."

"What have you done to us all, Tom?" More cannot believe that Cromwell has instituted such a calamitous thing. The swearing of oaths can lead to nothing but heartache, and destruction.

"Not I," Cromwell says. "Whilst I was busy tending to your duties, a viper entered the garden."

"Not Norfolk, surely?" More asks. "The duke is, in private, an ardent lover of the true church. He will lose his soul if he takes an oath."

"Not Norfolk," Cromwell says. "It was the Bishop of Winchester, who mentioned it, almost in jest, and Lady Anne overheard him."

"Oh, Stephen, what have you done?" More laments the folly of his old friend Gardiner. "How did he put it to Henry?"

"Some silliness. The king was speaking of a legal matter, where some fellow had lied under oath. The judge had him hanged, and Stephen said that an oath is sacred, and might bind a man tightly, whether to a king, or a cowherd. Anne Boleyn, very cleverly, asked which oath takes precedence."

"Oh, clever woman," More says. "For once it is sworn, no force on Earth might un-swear it. See how she plays on the king's fear of treachery? Can his realm be left to swear oaths to any they wish? No, of course not."

"Just so. La Boleyn told Henry that any subject might swear to any lord, or any faith, before him. From there, it was easy to make the king start thinking about a great oath. An all encompassing oath that binds his subjects to him."

"Dear Christ."

"Precisely. You see the implications at once. I set about tempering the oath, which Henry thought to be a splendid idea, but there are those about him who saw it as a useful weapon."

"Must every man in England swear?"

"I think not," Cromwell explains. "Only those of noble rank, all those employed by the king, and *ministers of state*. I could not remove the last."

"When will it come into force?" More asks, ashen faced.

"I explained the legal complexities to Henry, and said it might take years to enshrine in law, but he will have none of that, and gives me but a scant eighteen months to bring in the legislation. Then the Boleyn woman said that we might start to compile a list of all those who must take it, and prick out those who might refuse."

"She prepares a death list, for when she is queen," the Lord Chancellor says.

"Exactly so, Thomas," Cromwell concludes. "It will be a long document, written not in ink, but blood, if she gets her way."

"She is not queen yet."

"They will be married before this coming Christmas," Cromwell tells his friend, "Or it is my head for the block too."

"Then I must read this oath," More replies, "and hope I can take it, without compromising my beliefs."

"Can you not separate your beliefs from your public persona, and swear for one, but not the other? Norfolk will, and so shall I."

"No."

"I thought not. Then we finally come to the reason for your visit," Cromwell says. "You must cease being Lord Chancellor of England."

"You will recall that I once tried to resign my office," More responds. "Why would I be able to now?"

"Then, it would have looked like you were slighting Henry, and Anne," Cromwell explains, "and that would have led to your death. Now, the king is grown used to you not being about the place, and will soon forget you, and appoint a new man."

"You, Tom?"

"Not I," Thomas Cromwell says. "I do not want the poisoned chalice. It will be someone who is more pliable. I have Audley in mind for the post. First, we must get your resignation accepted, without anyone noticing what we have done."

"You have a scheme, Tom?" Sir Thomas More smiles for the first time. "Tom Cromwell always has a scheme. Where I rely on faith, you choose to use your low animal cunning. So, speak out."

"I will tell the king that you are of failing health," Cromwell explains. "I see how you often clutch at your chest, and will play on it. The king is compassionate, and does not want your death on his mind. If he thinks you close to the end, he will let you lay down the mantle, with honour, and retire."

"And then?"

"Go to the continent."

"No. That would be cowardice."

"God's teeth, Thomas!" Cromwell is almost distraught. "If you will not flee, then become like some hibernating animal, and bury yourself inside the walls of your precious Utopia. Do not write letters, welcome visitors, or speak out against anything that might bring you to our attention."

"You say 'our' Tom."

"Of course I do," Cromwell replies. "Considering how the world is working, whose side would someone like me choose?"

"What of this oath?" More is still agitated. "Will it not follow me, unto death?"

"As a private person, you *may* not be asked," Thomas Cromwell says, "but if you are asked to take it, use sophistry and guile when answering. You must do your very best to accept its wording. If you cannot do that, and must refuse to take the oath, I will see that your wife and family are safe abroad, before the end."

"Will they push me?" More is tired, and wants nothing more than to be left alone.

"They might, if Boleyn supports the move."

"Will she?"

"Yes," Cromwell says, honestly. "I believe she will."

"Then God help me, Thomas, for I cannot swear falsely."

"Then you will die." Cromwell takes More's hands in his, and kisses him on the cheek. "For the sake of friendship, Thomas, *please* take the oath."

"If I cannot, for the sake of my family, how can I for an old friend, Tom?"

"I shall do all I can to save you, my friend, but if it comes to it, I will draw up the charges, and see they are pressed. Your death will make you into a martyr, and that is the last thing I want."

"Better a living friend, than a dead saint?" More suddenly seems cheerier, and smiles at the thought. "My greatest sorrow is that you cannot love Rome, Thomas Cromwell."

"And mine is that you cannot love yourself. I cannot save you from yourself, Thomas More." They embrace, and More pulls his thin cloak tightly about him.

"I feel a chill," he says, "but it is nothing to the wind that is going to sweep across England. I fear for my country." Thomas Cromwell, cannot help but catch onto the remark and asks:

"Do you know something, Thomas?"

"Something?"

"Yes, something that is to smite England?"

"Other than God's wrath?" Sir Thomas More says, regaining his stiff manner. "No, Master Cromwell, I do not."

8   Business As Usual

"I cannot be locked away like a nun, Will," Miriam Draper argues. "I must keep an eye on our business interests, else they will fail."

"Fail?" Will almost laughs. In the brief time of their marriage, Miriam has managed their finances well, and they are worth over three thousand pounds, with an annual income of sixteen hundred. "We are richer than half of the merchants in London, and men of middle years ask your advice. We shall not fail for wont of a few days. Stay in, until the present danger passes."

"No."

"What?" He is a kind, and tolerant husband, but the stark refusal to obey his wishes edges him towards anger. He makes as if to rise from their bed. "You forget your place, madam. You will do as I say."

Miriam realises her mistake at once, and sets about repairing the damage by throwing her arms around his neck. Her chemise is unfastened, and gapes, displaying her superb breasts. He cannot stop himself from slipping a hand up to her cheek, by way of softening his rebuke.

"Forgive me, my darling husband, but my tongue is still Jewish, and apt to run ahead of my English brain," she says, and he smiles at the jest. "I mean only to express my concern for our general well being. If you wish me to be safe, then would I not be better sent out of London altogether?"

"Sent away?" Will considers the suggestion and, foolishly fails to see the trap. "That might be for the best. Yes, if you were in the country, your safety would be more assured."

"Such a clever idea," Miriam says, as if Will was

the instigator, and kisses him. He responds, and presses her back onto the bed. She slips to one side, and jumps to her feet. "So is that, but we do not have the time. You must search London for your villainous preacher, and I must go to Cambridge, this very morning."

"Cambridge?" Will sighs. He has been duped again, and wonders if he will ever get the better of his beautiful wife. "Why would you want to go to Cambridge, my sweet ... are you not already clever enough?"

"Such a jest," Miriam says, and smiles at him. "I have been invited to visit with Rob Buffery, who wishes to purchase my imported wines for his new hostelry in Cambridge. I have two carts waiting to leave, and have a mind to escort them. I shall be gone, and safe from harm for three or four days."

"Sergeant Buffery has fulfilled his dream then?"

"He has. He is now the proprietor of his own establishment, and wishes to sell fine wines to the clever town scholars. He sought me out, at your own suggestion."

"That is so. Buffery is a stout fellow, and will keep you safe," Will says. "Though I wonder if the university is ready for delicate Italian wines."

"Master Cromwell lets me buy from his Flanders contact, and I shall let Sergeant Buffery have a range of quality ... from the sweet and smooth, to the rough and ready northern stuff that the French call wine."

"Are your carters decent men?" Will asks.

"They are, and besides, I will have Gregory with me."

"Master Cromwell's son is but a child," her husband protests. "I did not even know he was back at Austin Friars."

"He is thirteen years old, and almost a man," Miriam replies, as she begins to dress for the day. "He has come to beg an increase in his allowance from his father, and is returning to school in Cambridge, quite empty handed. You know how Master Thomas thinks. Better a penny earned, than a shilling given."

"Poor Gregory. I will send him a purse of silver, for his father's sake," Will says. "A gentleman cannot go about town without a coin for his dinner."

"You will not," Miriam says, sharply. "Master Cromwell will not think it well done, and he might even think to be offended by such an action. I have engaged Gregory as my bodyguard, until we reach Cambridge, and will pay him the going rate, when he has done his duty."

"You are as hard as Cromwell," Will Draper says, and laughs. "What will he earn?"

"Five shillings." Miriam piles her hair up, and tucks it under a white linen bonnet. "It will keep him honest."

"Then he will be no use to Cromwell."

"Hush, Will," Miriam says. "We owe all we have to Master Thomas, and we must never forget it."

"Nor will I, but I must be allowed the occasional opinion, my dear," Will tells her. "Give my regards to Rob Buffery, and bid him keep you safe for me. As for young Gregory, let me at least give him the loan of a pistol, some shot, and a horn of black powder"

"Of course, my love," Miriam says. "Though I doubt he will have any need of it. The road from London to Cambridge must be the safest in England."

"True enough. Between them, Thomas More, and Master Cromwell have hanged enough rogues to deter most of the rest from threatening the king's road. Tell

Gregory that he may also have the use of one of my swords … though not the one I gained in Ireland, where I was … "

"Please, Will, I beg you not to tell me the Irish story again," Miriam says, with a smirk. "For I fear the excitement will set my heart a fluttering too much, and I must be about my duties."

"What kind of a woman have I married?" Will Draper returns, throwing his hands up in mock horror. "You have our vows all about face, my girl. You promise to *dishonour*, and *disobey*!"

"For that I am sorry," Miriam says, "but I shall never *dis-love* you, sir. Not even if all the stars in heaven fall down upon our heads. My love for you is stronger than …"

"Enough, I understand," Will says, and pulls her into his arms for a final kiss. "For my part, I will settle for richer, rather than poorer, better rather than worse, and health over sickness."

"Until commerce do us part?" Miriam concludes, and kisses him, long and passionately. After a moment, there is the sound of stones hitting their bedroom's shuttered window. The young couple break apart, then Will Draper crosses the room, and throws the slatted shutters open.

"Gawd, but I never thought you would wake, Captain," the small boy calls up. "Though I too would dally, if I was with Mistress Miriam."

"I'll dally long enough to box your ears, Sam Foxton," Will calls down. "What is it, boy?"

"I have a message from the Spanisher gent, as what lives by Austin Friars. He says as how he is waiting, with Master Gregory, an' the mistresses carts, by the St. John's Gate in Clerkenwell, an' that you should hurry the mistress along to him."

"Chapuys is going too?" Will asks of his wife, who looks back at him blankly. "What is this about?"

"I have no idea," Miriam replies. "Though I cannot refuse his company, can I?"

"It is Cromwell's doing," Will says, frowning. "It is always Cromwell's doing. Why can the man not simply tell us his wishes, instead of playing fast and loose?"

"Tell the boy to wait for me," Miriam decides. "He can lead me there quicker than I can ever find my way. Is it the best way from the city, Will?"

"For laden carts … yes. Once through the priory gate, the road runs free into the Fenlands." Will buckles on his favourite sword. "Come, I will accompany you to St. John's Gate, and pay my sincere compliments to Ambassador Chapuys. Perhaps he might enlighten me, as to why he is leaving London. It seems odd that he should, considering the dangers that seem to be growing about us."

"Oh, do not think poor Eustace is involved," Miriam says, scornfully. "He is a good friend to us, Will."

"And a loyal servant of Emperor Charles," Will Draper replies. "When the race starts, which horse will our friend, Señor Chapuys put his money on, my love?"

*

It is not yet the seventh hour, when Miriam and Will come upon their little caravan, stationed by the splendid, new St John's Gate. Built only twenty years before, the gate is imposing, and made from Kentish Rag stone. Once through the gate, there is a large quadrangle that is the priory of St. John.

Usually, access is denied to all, save clerics, but Eustace Chapuys has prevailed on the Prior to allow them to pass through the inner courtyard, and out the other side, onto the Clerkenwell road. This saves them a couple of hours, traversing muddy London streets, and the Prior is rewarded with a generous 'donation' to the religious house.

"Let us see Cromwell gain such a favour from English clerics," Chapuys says. "We Catholic's stick together. Thomas, who is a wicked heretic would have to find another way, and get his heretical boots wet."

"My humble thanks, sir," Will says. "Now, may I commend my precious jewel to your safe keeping? I presume, my master has asked the same service of you?"

"He has not," Eustace Chapuys replies. "It is just that I must travel the same road today, on an urgent mission, and Thomas mentioned Mistress Miriam's own journey. See, here is young Master Gregory, who must be the man in charge."

"Master Will," Gregory Cromwell says, bowing to the captain. "It has been a while."

"Gregory, how you have grown," Will Draper tells him. "Miriam has a good sword, and one of my pistols for you, just in case of trouble."

"My thanks, sir," Gregory says, drawing himself up to his full height. He is taller than his father, and of an altogether more athletic build. "I shall cherish them, as if my own. Good hunting today."

"Your father has told you?"

"I hear things," Gregory replies, smiling at him. "Father thinks me a small child still, and not worth confiding in."

"Not so," Will says. "He loves you, and wishes only that you have those advantages that we did not. A Cambridge education will do you no harm. It will see you well when those clever fellows like Norfolk and Suffolk seek to dun you."

"Perhaps, but for now, I am the commander of two carts loaded with wine, and guardian of Ambassador Chapuys, and your wonderful wife."

"Wonderful?" Will Draper cannot help but smile. "Does any man have a hard word for my dearest Miriam?"

"Can one ever be too clever, too nice, or too beautiful?" the little Savoyard diplomat says. "We will take care of your precious jewel, Will. You must take care of yourself, and do not let Tom Cromwell's enemies triumph."

"I shall not," Will replies. "Though, before I take my leave, I must ask … what is your business away from London?"

"Queen Katherine."

"The Dowager Princess of Wales, sir?" Will is confused as to where Katherine of Aragon fits in to the day's events. "How is she involved?"

"She is not," Chapuys says, firmly. "Henry, in his wisdom, has moved her out of London, at the Boleyn whore's request. I am going to visit her, near Cambridge, and ensure she is not implicated in whatever mad plot is afoot."

"A plot conceived by your emperor, sir."

"No, I think not," the little man responds. "I think his name is being taken in vain. Thomas and I are in agreement about this, and suspect that the infamous Anton Fugger is our man."

"You know him?" Will asks. It is right that one

should know your enemy, as best you can, he thinks.

"A money grubbing scoundrel, who will misuse the church, and my dear emperor, to gain a fat profit," Chapuys says. "I met him in Mannheim, some years ago, and formed a rather poor opinion of the detestable little man."

"So, you go to watch over your dear Katherine." Will nods his understanding. The ambassador will insinuate himself into her presence, and make sure she is not embroiled in anything dangerous. "God's speed to you all." He kisses Miriam once more, and the small party go through the open St John's Gate, and disappear from sight.

Will Draper turns from the gate, and sets off, back towards Austin Friars, where he is to meet with those agents of Cromwell's who are under his direct orders. It is time to cast the net wide, and see what can be hauled in.

*

"Your husband loves you very much," Gregory says, as he rides along side Miriam. Chapuys, and the two carts are a few yards behind. "I wish to make a good marriage, one day."

"One day," Miriam replies. The boy is becoming a man, and she does not wish to belittle his desires. "Though you should enjoy your freedom for a few years yet."

"Oh, you mean by drinking too much, gambling, and whoring?" Gregory asks, with the sublime innocence of youth. "I have no taste for any of those three vices. Though I do enjoy hawking, and running my hounds. Father thinks me to be a wastrel, and of little valid intellect."

"I doubt he was any different as a young fellow," the girl replies. She is still only twenty years old herself, and has no vices, other than a need to do her work well, and succeed at all she turns her hand to. "Why, I once heard he was a soldier, just like my Will."

"Yes, he has killed in the heat of battle," Gregory says. He is unsure of his feelings towards his father, and constantly hovers between reverence, and disdain. "Though he has a lawyer's heart. It is going to be a warm day, mistress. I hope your wine does not spoil in the barrels."

"I believe it prospers in warm weather," Miriam replies, but she has no real idea. Her task is to deliver her cargo to Rob Buffery, and encourage trade with him. The old soldier has used his bounty share wisely, and owns a fine tavern on the edge of Cambridge, that boasts stabling for a dozen horses, a large, enclosed courtyard, and eight rooms for guests to occupy, in some goodly degree of comfort.

The retired sergeant has, true to his promise, found himself a buxom, young wife, and runs a very fine hostelry, with two large rooms downstairs; one for drinkers, and another to be used as a dining room. His wife provides roast meats and fowl for hungry guests, whilst he keeps an eye on the four girls who work for him.

He has two tavern maids, and two more who act as bed warmers, and general whores. All in all, the man has a decent establishment, that lacks only a wider choice of drink. Most local inns serve ale, beer or mead, but Rob Buffery will break the mould and offer his patrons a choice of six different wines, by the cup, or by the flask.

"Sergeant Buffery sounds to be a man who wants to get on in life," Gregory says. "What does he call his tavern?"

"He is the proud Keeper of the Angel," Miriam replies. At that moment, Eustace Chapuys spurs his mount into a trot, and joins them. He is constantly on the lookout for other travellers, convinced that they will turn into wild, murderous outlaws, and descend on them, but he is constantly disappointed.

"There are some men ahead," he says. Gregory touches the heavy gun hanging on his saddle, to reassure himself, but in truth, he doubts he will be able to aim its great weight without it wavering in his hand.

"They are going our way," the boy observes. "I doubt they mean any harm. Perhaps they are travelling to some shrine, or other."

"Perhaps," the little Savoyard diplomat says, but he is uneasy. "The people here about are very pious, and there are many churches with holy relics to visit."

"How long will our journey take?" Gregory asks.

"Master Cromwell tells me that it is about fifty miles," Miriam tells the boy. "The weather is dry, and that makes the going much easier. If we keep on the road, until it begins to grow dark, we will have covered about twenty six, or twenty seven miles. So, with a dawn start on the morrow, we will reach our destination by late afternoon."

"Allowing for fine, dry weather," Gregory says, "and the carts holding up. When I came down from Cambridge, I did it in easy stages, so as not to tire my horse, and I stopped to see the sights. A little way on is a church which claims to have the shin bone of Saint Cuthburga, who was the benevolent Queen of Northumbria, over six hundred years ago."

"Did she hop down here from the north then?" Miriam says. She has little time for churches, and even less for the business of relics, which raises money from poor, ignorant folk.

"What ever do you mean to imply, Mistress Miriam?" Gregory is astounded by what she says.

"Why do they only have one shin?" Miriam persists. "Why not both shins? Or the whole of her?"

Gregory cannot understand that she is jesting, because he is being given a grounding in religion by his tutors that precludes the questioning of his faith. He is not yet of the mind to separate the bible from the attendant dogma, and believes, simply because that is what you must do.

"The blessed Saint Cuthburga was the first abbess of Wimborne, in Dorset," Gregory Cromwell pronounces. "She was the daughter, wife, and mother of great kings. She and her sister, St. Quenburga, founded a monastery at Wimborne in the year seven hundred and five, and she sent missionary nuns to Germany, where they worked with Saint Boniface."

"Good for her," Miriam mutters. She doubts she will be able to stand two days listening to the history of English saints. Gregory, like most young men, is oblivious to anything, other than that which he is currently thinking, and continues to bore his lovely companion without realising it.

"The saint was always hard on herself, but very kind to others," he says. "She died around seven twenty five, and her bones were sent to various churches from Dorset, right up to Northumbria."

"And did they give you board and food?" Miriam asks, sharply. "Or did you pay for it?"

"A donation was required, of course."

"And another penny to see the shin bone?"

"Why, yes," Gregory replies, surprised that Miriam should know such a fact. "I paid them double, because I was the only one who wanted to look. Money spent on God, is money well spent."

"God and the church are not the same thing, Gregory," Miriam tells him. "Does not your father tell you that? The church in England is corrupt, and in need of much change."

"The harsh wind of a new order," Gregory says. "That is what father calls it. He thinks Henry will become the English Pope, and that all men will read the bible, in English."

"Is that what you think?" Chapuys asks.

"I try not to have too many thoughts," the youth replies, solemnly. "It affects my sporting prowess, and makes my head ache. Father can think quite enough for both of us. After all, does he not think for the king, these days?"

"Master Tom is a loyal subject, and seeks only to offer his advice," Chapuys puts in. "The king's thinking, *these days*, is done by *la putain* Boleyn, young man!"

"Is the king to marry her then?" young Gregory asks.

"I fear so," Cromwell replies. "Now, let us get on about our business!"

*

"Well, what is it?" Will is becoming increasingly disturbed, as report after report comes to him. Cromwell's agents are working without rest to uncover a lead to the whereabouts of Father George Constantine and his men, but can find nothing.

"We have questioned the guards of every city gate, to no avail, sir," the agent says. "Each boatman has been spoken to, and they all say the same. The preacher and his men did not cross the river. They might have rode over the bridge, but so large a band would have been noticed."

"Then they came in one by one."

"Perhaps," the man says. "Or they never intended coming to the city at all. Might they have ridden out into the shires?"

"If so, we are confounded," Will Draper tells the man. "For we do not have enough men to cover all points of the compass."

A horse clatters into the courtyard, and Mush leaps from its back. He is covered in the dust of the road, and calls for something to drink.

"They are found!" He announces. "They used a ferry, far down river, and crossed over to the northern bank. The ferryman marked them down as a troop of the king's soldiers, for they were all armed to the teeth, and well mounted."

"Then we have them?" Will asks, and Mush shakes his head.

"No, they have a half a day's start on us," he confirms, "but the ferry man says they were heading north east, as if making for Suffolk, or Norfolk."

"Or any of another three counties," Will curses. "We must ride at once."

"Where to?" Mush is ready, despite a hard morning in the saddle. "Do we split our forces?"

"No, we ride for Norfolk," Will decides. "It is the most likely source of trouble. Fast gallopers must go to Ipswich, Buckingham, Cambridge, and Oxford. Have them rouse the local militia, and conduct searches of their counties."

"Miriam is on her way to Cambridge," Mush says.

"I doubt she will be in any danger," Will replies, trying to reassure himself, rather than any one else. "What would our treacherous preacher want with her?"

"Yes, you are right," Mush says, to convince himself rather than his brother-in-law. "Besides, young Gregory is with her, as well as Eustace Chapuys. If these rogues are the emperor's men, they will not offer the ambassador any harm. Rather, they would obey him."

"Let us hope they are not his men." Will says it, but does not believe it. "No, Eustace is a man of honour. He has sworn to look after my wife, and that is enough for me."

9   An Angel Falls

The great Palace of Whitehall never slumbers, and there is activity throughout the day and night. The quietest time is the early evening, when the diplomats have been seen, and everyone is preparing to dress for their evening repast. Some will dine with friends, and others in local taverns, where they must pay their own way. Most will eat sparingly, at the expense of their patrons, who demand their loyalty in return.

This evening Thomas Cromwell is honoured above all others in England. The Privy Councillor is invited to sup with His Majesty, and Lady Anne Boleyn. It is a meal he would rather miss, but duty demands his presence. With two of his toughest young men to keep an eye on him, he slips out of the Tower of London, and makes his way, unnoticed or, at least, ignored, through the busy city streets.

He arrives at Whitehall, just as the fifth hour is struck, and enters by a discreet side gate. It gives access to a small courtyard, surrounded by high windows, and there is a stone sundial at its centre. In one wall is a solid gate, which is guarded, and leads to one of the king's private walks. Thomas Cromwell is known to the guard, who salutes smartly, and allows him passage.

"Not your lads, Master Cromwell," the man says. "More than my life's worth to let them in, unannounced."

"Well said, Sergeant Cunliffe," Cromwell says, and hands over a shilling. "My young men will keep you company, whilst I dine, and speak with the king." He stoops, and goes through the low gate. Beyond is a long, rectangular space, with a central flower bed, in full bloom. The May weather has been better than of late, and everything is coming early ... like Cromwell.

The king is strolling along the furthermost path, accompanied by his young son, Henry Fitzroy. Behind them comes Norfolk, and Suffolk, the king's most senior councillor, and his best friend. The two men tolerate one another, knowing that the king loves them both in equal portion. It is Suffolk who sees Cromwell first, and coughs, politely, so that Henry might notice his Privy Councillor's unannounced visit.

The king looks up, and his broad forehead furrows into a deep frown. Usually, he is pleased to see the man, whom he thinks is a creature of his own making, so that they can exchange ideas, and come to decisions. Now though, he is concerned at the unplanned visitation, and unsure how to react.

Thomas Cromwell removes his cap, bows, and stands quite still, waiting to be either beckoned forward, or dismissed. After a moment, young Fitzroy returns Cromwell's bow, and gestures for him to come and join them.

"Forgive me, Your Highness," the young prince says, "but it is a while since I last saw Master Cromwell, and I still recall how he managed the saving of my life so well."

"Of course," Henry replies. "We cannot ever repay such a debt. Good day, Thomas, I thought it was for dinner that you are asked. You are here early. Have I forgotten a state meeting?"

"Your Majesty forgets nothing," Cromwell says, flattering his king. "For which I am eternally grateful. It makes my duties easier to perform. I am glad to see you in better health, young Harry."

"Yes, the coughing is improved today," Fitzroy replies. He is consumptive, and his present state of improved health will not last long. "But, enough of me, I assume you wish to speak with the king?"

"I do, sir." Thomas Cromwell glances over at Norfolk and Suffolk, who both, obtusely, stand their ground, until Henry waves them firmly away.

"Give us a moment, gentlemen," he says, then starts to stroll along the path again. "Walk with me, Thomas. You look troubled. Does that mean I should be, also?"

"If I am troubled, it is only because I am the bearer of some very sad news, sire. It is about Sir Thomas More …"

"Dear Christ, is he dead?" Henry's face drains of its usual ruddy colour, and he feels genuine regret at the thought.

"No, not yet, sire." Tom Cromwell puts on his most pained expression, even wringing a tear from the corner of one eye. "I am here, because I know the esteem you still hold him in, and because he is an old friend of mine. His health is declining each day, and I wonder if he will live much longer."

"What ails him?" Henry is glad the man has not died on him, which would make him look like a faithless dog, and also make him feel badly about himself.

"His heart," Cromwell says, truthfully. "I spoke with his doctors, and they fear greatly for his life. The heartbeat is most irregular, and his strength drains away, day by day."

"I cannot visit him," Henry says, and regrets his cowardly words. "Lady Anne would be furious if I show him any sort of favour. You know how she is where Tom More is concerned."

"I understand, sire, but that is not why I am here."

"No? Then speak plainly, Thomas, for we are alone, and I would hear what you think."

"Sire…"

"Come, call me Henry, in private," the king says. He is shocked at the news about More, and does not wish to seem like he is uncaring. The blacksmith's boy will feel honoured by his show of friendship, and think better of him when More eventually dies.

"Henry, we must both look to the Lord Chancellorship," Cromwell says. "If Sir Thomas dies, in office, there are those - the Spanish, the French, and many others - who will whisper lies behind their hands. They will remind people about Cardinal Wolsey's fall from grace, and say we are treating More in the same way."

"I was going to forgive Wolsey," Henry says, trotting out an old, familiar story. "I loved the man, as I love you, and as I love Sir Thomas!"

"Just so," says Thomas Cromwell. "It is time to let Tom More go, Henry. He is in very poor health, and cannot continue in office. You can do him a final kindness. Let him resign, due to his ill health, and retire into private life."

"Will that stop the gossip?" Henry asks.

"Most of it," Thomas Cromwell tells the king, honestly. "Sir Thomas will retire, and undertake to cease any involvement in court politics. Those who might speak evil of you will see him surrender his office, of his own free will. Then, a month or two from now, they will realise that you have no intention of taking action against him, and let it be. More will fade from men's minds, before Christmas. When he dies, he will not be thought of as a martyr."

"Yes, I see the wisdom of that."

"Then, prey, let it be done, Henry," Thomas Cromwell says. "I will summon him here, today, and he will resign. Take the seal from him, and let him thank you for the great honours you have bestowed on him. He will not want titles, or lands. Just let him keep the usual pension, which will keep him, until the end."

"Then it will be so," Henry decides. Then he stops, and utters a soft curse under his breath. "What will Lady Anne say?"

"She will applaud you, sire," Cromwell says, though he does not really believe it. "Lady Anne wishes More destroyed, and so it shall come to pass. He is a fallen angel … cast down from heaven."

"Yes, you are all my angels," the king agrees. "Below me in the English firmament. How goes the investigation of the monasteries, Cromwell?"

Ah, the Privy Councillor thinks, we are done with first names again. He smiles, and brings a small ledger from under his cape.

"Your Majesties agents are making good progress, sire," he reports. "Last month, thirty four establishments were shut down, and their land and revenues diverted to the Crown coffers. Over twenty thousand pounds of income, and seventeen thousand acres of good farm land, sire, and we are barely started."

"When this is done, I will have enough to go to war with the French again," Henry says, with a satisfied smile on his face. "The time may yet come when an English king sits on the French throne once more."

"Why fight them, when they can be bought?" Cromwell asks. "A hundred thousand dead, and you will be the ruler of a ruined France. Much better to use commerce, sire, rather than risk open warfare."

"A king must be great," Henry says, softly. He is in his middle years, and his health is beginning to fail, but he still wants to lead a charge, or storm a town wall, to show his bravery.

"You are great, sire," Cromwell replies. "What other king rules, without the Roman church at his elbow? What other king in Europe is even solvent? In your younger days, you led the charge which broke the French."

"True ... it was magnificent."

"In your middle years, you led the charge against Pope Clement, and broke his hold on your realm."

"By God, yes, I did."

"And in your later years, you will reign over the richest country in the world. Your navy will rule the seas, and your merchants will rule the entire continent. The French, and the Spanish will have to beg for your favour, if they want our wool, and they will, by God ... they will!"

"Without a war though?"

"Imagine, being the king who made England the greatest nation on earth, without losing a single soldier, or having to fire off a single one of his cannon," Cromwell continues. "Besides, Your Majesty will be too busy reforming his church, and planning for his wedding. Soon, the legislation will be in place, and parliament will ask you to produce an heir. To comply, you will be compelled, by parliament, to divorce Katherine, and re-marry."

"The word '*compel*' concerns me, Thomas."

"A mere legality. It is the duty of parliament to protect the realm, which '*compels*' them to '*compel*' the king to act. As no monarch would willingly fail to provide an heir, the word has no force, other than a moral one. It is your duty to sire a child, and you will not flinch from it. In truth, Your Majesty, you thus only '*compel*' yourself."

"I see what you mean. Then I shall re-marry, and have a son … for duty's sake. Lady Anne will be pleased. I thought a Christmas wedding might be rather nice."

"Perfect, sire," Cromwell says. "You are to visit Calais just before Christmas, for talks with your cousin King François. He wants us to lower import duties on French wine."

"Oh, and will we?"

"Why ever not? In return, we will extract a promise from the French that they will allow us to import mulberry bushes from the south of their country."

"Mulberry bushes?" The king is taken by surprises. "We lose revenue on wine, and gain a few bushes?"

"Mulberry bushes, sire. They are eaten by silkworms. The exchange will strengthen our silk trade. Later, we will quietly introduce some other levy, to make up the lost revenue."

"By God, if Norfolk, Suffolk, Gardiner and the like, are my angels, you are my archangel, sir." Henry mellows, and is in an expansive mood. "Name your reward, Thomas, and you shall have it."

"A reward is given for a job well done, sire, and the job of helping you to run England will last for ever," Cromwell says. He has little time for empty titles, and is content with his rents, and earnings from his duties with the Privy Council, and the courts of law. He is worth sixty thousand a year, which is three times the worth of any duke, or baronet in the land.

"There must be something?"

"Very well, sire, if you insist," Thomas Cromwell says. "Grant me but one request. Allow me to tell Lady Anne about More, so that she might look favourably on me, once more."

"Granted," Henry says, relieved that he does not have to explain to his beloved. She can, he thinks, be like a weathervane, and veer from one mood to another, at short notice. "It is the least I can do for so loyal a servant."

Cromwell bows, and retreats, confident that the evening's repast will now be a pleasant one.

*

"Sir Thomas, you wish to see me?" King Henry says, in a not unkindly manner. He notes the grey pallor of the man's skin, and his unsteady gait, and agrees with Thomas Cromwell's physical assessment of his estranged old councillor. They are in the same garden as Henry's earlier meeting with Tom Cromwell, and the light is now fading into a pink suffused evening.

"Your Highness," Sir Thomas More says, bowing with a little difficulty. "I come to you as a supplicant. It is plain that my health is failing me fast, and I cannot continue in even those lighter duties you ask of me. It is not my wish to bring the office of Lord Chancellor into disrepute, by dint of my health, and I beg you to let me lay down this heavy burden. Take my chain, sire, and bestow it on a worthier pair of shoulders, for mine are grown too weak."

"I thank you for your past service, Sir Thomas, and willingly grant you leave to resign your high office. You will retire to the country?"

"To Utopia, sire," More replies.

"I think not," Henry tells him, with one last twist of the blade, suggested by Anne Boleyn. "The country air will suit you better, I think. Cromwell will find you a place, down in Dorset, or Hampshire."

"As you command, sire," More says.

High above, Anne Boleyn is standing at a window, and observing the scene. She is there at Cromwell's prompting, and turns to him now, for clarification.

"What am I seeing, Master Cromwell?"

"The end of Sir Thomas More," he replies, simply. "See how he hands over his chain of office, madam? The king will accept it from him, and your enemy is finished."

"But he still lives."

"Pray leave him now, madam," Cromwell tells her. "Press further, and it might rebound on us. The man is without his high office, without his king, and without any hope. Left alive, he will suffer the agonies of failure. His fall is so complete, that even the hardest of hearts might pity him."

"You have done well, Thomas," she says, nodding her approval. "Only last evening, I advised Henry to send More far away from London. Let us hope he listens."

"Without Utopia, Sir Thomas will not last a month," Cromwell says, appalled at her cruelty.

"No, he won't, will he?" she tells him, and smiles benignly. "I am most pleased, and will reward you. What can I get the king to give you?"

"I want nothing for this days work, My Lady," Cromwell replies. "It is done, because it has to be done. By your leave, I must retire, and see that Sir Thomas is escorted home safely."

"Master Hot and Cold," Anne says. "That is what I shall call you. You are nine parts cold business, and one part hot passion. It will be the complete undoing of you, sir."

"Humanity often is the undoing of a man, Lady Anne," he says, as he leaves. "Have a care for your own."

Anne watches him leave, and sighs with satisfaction. More is gone, Henry is under her thumb, and even Master Cromwell seeks to do her bidding, despite his initial reluctance. She feels safer now More has finally fallen, and can turn her malevolent attention to Queen Katherine.

The new laws will ensure that Henry can divorce her, but she will still be there, in the background, like some spectre at the feast, and the king will never be at ease. Her father, and brother council her not to be hasty, but she will have her way. Once Henry marries her, she will be free to act against the old queen, once and for all.

It crosses her mind to involve Cromwell, but wonders if he is up to drawing up charges against the Dowager Princess of Wales, and the bastard child, Mary. Katherine lives in a dark, mysterious and foreign world, and it is easy to see how talk of witchcraft can start. Once Henry thinks Katherine is working against him, he will demand an investigation, and charges can be brought. She will be powerless to refute well constructed charges, which will point to her desire for revenge.

Any competent lawyer will do, but Anne wants it to be Cromwell. For only he has the king's ear, and can push for the correct sentence. Katherine and her daughter must burn, and their names be expunged from the realm's history. Then, and only then, will Anne Boleyn and her family be truly safe.

*

"That was not too painful, was it, my friend?" Cromwell asks on the return boat journey to More's house in Chelsea.

"He bids me leave Utopia." More is crestfallen. The house is the centre of his existence, and a magnet for the greatest minds of the age. In its time, Utopia has sheltered the genius, Erasmus, and entertained philosophers, royalty, and intellectuals, from across Europe.

"Leave it with me," Cromwell replies. "I will dissuade him from such a foolish act. We do not want to draw attention to you, do we?"

"No, Tom, you have all that you want."

"You should have come with me, Thomas," says Cromwell.

"Why, when I was on the right path all along?" More tells his old friend. "Yes, the church is corrupt, but we could have healed it, from within. Now we are ruled by a misguided king, who thinks he is one step below God. Heaven help you all."

"A new age is coming."

"No it is not," More argues. "It is the same old world, but with different masters, demanding different oaths. Men will still burn for heresy, and printing the bible in English will not make England a much more tolerable place to live."

"No more preaching," Cromwell says. "See, here we are, and your Margaret is waiting for you. Look, my dear girl, your father is home, safe and sound, once again."

"Is that the cat courting the mouse?" Margaret says, and turns her back on Cromwell.

"Am I such a monster?" Cromwell asks More, who only shrugs, and starts up towards the cold looking house.

"Do you want for anything, Mistress Margaret?" Cromwell calls to the retreating woman. He cannot bare the idea that she hates him too.

"We want for everything, Master Cromwell," she flares. "We want for my father's position, his good name, and his dignity. You have all three now ... see how they benefit you, sir!"

"I meant the comforts of life," Cromwell replies. "Your father's pension will not stretch to running so large a house, I fear."

"Sir, we will manage," Margaret says. "Pray do not give us a second thought. You have a church to destroy, and a vainglorious king to pander to. Will not they be waiting for you at their dinner table?"

Cromwell is hurt by his rebuff, but can see no other way he could have gone. More is, he thinks, too stiff necked, and set in his ways. A minister of state needs to know how to bend in the wind, and fight only those battles that one can win.

By the time he has dined, and reaches the Tower of London, he is once again convinced that he is in the right, and that England must tread the path he has chosen for it. It is very late, and a cold supper is laid out for him, but he has little appetite after having to indulge at Henry's lavish table. He goes to the warden's library, and takes down a book, but cannot settle to read. At length, he calls for one of his young men, and bids him take pen to paper.

"Make a list, Tobias," he says. "We must attend to the needs of Utopia. See that fire wood his delivered each week, together with enough basic food stuffs, and ale to feed them all. Have a couple of bolts of good worsted cloth delivered, for the ladies to make dresses, and throw in sewing threads, needles, and ribbons. No, forget the ribbons ... they will not be appreciated."

"Yes, master."

"Then see that my name is not on the transaction," Cromwell says. "If anyone seeks their benefactor, it must not come back home to me. Make it seem as though some Holy Order is helping them live." Cromwell knows that, even if Sir Thomas were able to accept his charity, his daughter would not. "Now, how goes the search for George Constantine?"

"Captain Draper is casting the net much wider, sir," Tobias reports. "The rascal is thought to be heading for Norfolk."

"Or a dozen places in between," says Cromwell. "Let him but reach his great personage, and things will go badly for England."

"More wine, Master Thomas?" Tobias holds up the jug of sweet, white Rhenish, from the vineyards of Hesse. Cromwell shrugs, and holds a hand over the top of his cup. His consumption, of late, is increasing, and he makes a mental note to curb his drinking from now on.

"I must keep a clear head," he says. "Have we anything more from our agents, as to the nature of this great threat to us?"

"Nothing, master," Tobias replies. "Our people in Augsburg tell us that Fugger is going about his business, as usual. The emperor's court in Flanders is quiet, and there is no news from Calais, other than the usual trading reports, and merchant's returns."

"No troop movements at all?" Cromwell asks, for he is surprised that no Holy Roman Empire forces are massing around the Channel ports. If the plot is under way, there must be several thousand skilled mercenaries, poised to land anywhere between Dover and Kingston upon Hull.

"The French military are posturing along the Savoy border," Tobias tells his master. "They gallop a few thousand men about the countryside, making idle threats against Annecy, but with ten thousand Swiss mercenaries protecting them, the Savoyards have nothing to worry over. The emperor will not allow Savoy to be overrun."

"Nothing in the northern ports at all?"

"No, Flanders is perfectly quiet, sir." Tobias turns to leave, then pauses in the door. "There is one thing … but no, it is only a minor irritation."

"What is it, Tobias?" Thomas Cromwell is wise enough to know that even the most seemingly trivial of things can be important.

"A report from the king's shipyards, concerning the purchase of timber from the continent. We use our own oak, of course, but with the increased ship building, we must buy timbers from the empire, to keep apace."

"Are they refusing to deal with us?" Thomas Cromwell asks.

"No, not at all. They will supply as much cut board as we require, and at a fair price."

"Then, I do not see what the problem is," Cromwell says. He is tired now, and ready for his bed.

So his mind does not grasp the significance.

"They insist on payment in Ducats, French Solaires, or Brabant gold."

"More fool them," Cromwell says. It is only in the deepest part of the night that he awakens, bathed in a cold sweat. The purchase of cut boards for Henry's new warships is on his mind, and he begins to realise the significance of it all, at last.

"Ah, and so I finally begin to see," Cromwell sighs into the inky darkness. " I have been a blind fool, looking for soldiers, where there are none to be found. Payment in Ducats... ha! *There* is the enemy!"

10   Old Bones

It is almost night when Miriam and her retinue arrive at the church of Saint Cuthburga. The six hundred year old place of worship is a little way outside of Hertford, and almost the mid point of their journey. Gregory trots ahead, to prepare the way for his precious charge, and her wagons.

"I am glad we managed the crossing of the river before dark," Chapuys says. He makes it sound as if a great obstacle has been overcome, but the crossing of the River Lea, in truth, was easy, thanks to the dry weather.

"The water scarcely came up to the axles of our carts," Gregory replies, but he is also relieved to be at this, their lodging for the night. "They are still up, for I could see a light within. The old priest will see we are fed and boarded, for a few pennies."

The church is lit by candles, and there are a couple of horses tied up to a nearby tree. Miriam is wondering who these other travellers are, when the church door opens, and a thin, weasel faced little man appears. He is dressed in layman's clothing, and does not seem to have the spirit of Christianity in him.

"Be off with you!" the man cries, rudely. "The church is closed." Chapuys trots his horse right up to the man, who steps back in fright.

"I am Eustace Chapuys, ambassador to the court of King Henry," the Savoyard demands. "Name yourself, rascal!"

"Rascal? Not I, sir," the man replies. "I am Herbert Worthy, a commissioner of the king. What is your business here, sir?"

"We seek shelter for the night," Miriam says.

"Not here!" the man says, again, but less rudely.

"Step aside, scoundrel," Gregory says, and draws the heavy gun from its holster. "Or I will …"

"Master Cromwell!" Chapuys cries, and the situation changes at once. The man steps back, and looks as if he has been slapped in the face.

"Cromwell, you say?"

"I am Gregory Cromwell, sir … and my father is Master Thomas Cromwell, Privy Councillor, and confident of the king."

"My apologies, Master Gregory," Worthy says, bowing. "The last time I saw you, it was as a small child, scarcely able to totter about. I am one of your father's oldest agents, sir. Please, dismount, and come inside. We have food cooking. My men will tend to your carts, and the horses."

"Your men?" Gregory says, and four armed men step out of the darkness.

"Thank God you were named, sir," the little man says, smiling. "Else you might have been shot from your horse."

Miriam supervises the settling down of her small convoy of carts, and sees the horses fed, before she ventures into the old church. Herbert Worthy, Gregory, and Chapuys are sitting around a makeshift table, laden with a cauldron of rabbit stew, some root vegetables, and two loaves of hard bread.

"Ah, Mistress Draper," Worthy says, rising to his feet. "Come and join us. The wife of the famous Captain Will must be our guest of honour."

"Where is the priest?" she asks. The church has been stripped bare of all its adornment, and the walls painted over with a drab whitewash. The magnificent depictions of Christ and Saint Cuthburga can still be seen striking through. Another coat will obliterate the scenes for all time.

"Gone," Worthy replies, casually. "He has been given the choice … Henry, or Rome, and the fool chose badly. His living is taken, and will be reassigned to another, more amenable priest. The revenues, for what they are worth, go to the crown coffers."

"This is monstrous," Chapuys says. "How can a man of God choose his king above the Kingdom of Heaven?"

"We do not ask that, sir," worthy explains. "We are not against God, but the Bishop of Rome. We love God in Heaven, and will always worship him in our English way. Though there are those who still fight against the changes, we will have an honestly printed English bible … and in my life time. What say you, Master Gregory? Your father is right, is he not?"

"I cannot go against my father," Gregory says, "though I wonder what will remain, after all is done. Where is the saint's relic?"

"Relic?" Worthy frowns. "You mean that scrap of animal bone in a box? Gone. Our new way will not tolerate the misuse of the people. Besides, what kind of idiot would pay a penny to look at a bone salvaged from the cooking pot?"

"It was part of Saint Cuthburga," Gregory says, then sees the look of derision on Worthy's face. "That is what they claimed."

"Master Gregory, let me tell you something about the holy relics that fill our churches," the little man says. "If we take all the pieces of the true cross, and put them together, we will have enough wood to build another warship for King Henry. It is a fraud, designed to take money from poor folk, who know no better. The new church will also ban the despicable sale of indulgences."

"Then how can sinful men ever hope to escape from their years in purgatory?" Gregory asks. He knows his father has sinned often, and does not wish him to stay in purgatory for ten thousand years. Better by far to pay for an indulgence, and free his soul all the sooner.

"Read your bible, Master Gregory," Worthy says. "There is no mention of the place. The Roman church invent Purgatory and other such places, to scare unwitting people into giving them their hard earned money. There are but two places for us to go. Heaven, or Hell. Let each man behave as to how he wishes to end up, is what I say."

"Then only the truly good will ever see Heaven?" Miriam asks. The convolutions of the Christian faith confuse her, and she likes her own Jewish beliefs, despite having to conceal them from a dangerous, Jew hating world.

"Who knows?" Worthy spoons more stew into her bowl. "The good book says that God rejoices in finding one repentant sinner. Perhaps that is the way?"

"Ha!" Chapuys can stay silent no longer. "You believe a man can spend his life in sin, but gain a place in Heaven, simply by apologising to God?"

"Perhaps that is all He asks of us, sir."

"Then, when I am in heaven, I will search you, and your like out … but in vain," the Savoyard diplomat concludes. "For no man that offends me, can redeem himself with a casual word. To forgive, I must needs see some genuine act of contrition."

"Then I am very pleased indeed that you are not God, sir," Worthy says, and grins at Eustace Chapuys' discomfort. "You are a long way from London … for an ambassador."

"I go to visit Queen Katherine, who is currently lodged near Cambridge." Chapuys has papers to explain his mission, but is disinclined to show them to so insolent a man.

"The Dowager Princess of Wales, you mean?" Herbert Worthy strokes his beard in contemplation of this news. "A popular lady, these days, sir."

"What do you mean?" Chapuys feels a grip of apprehension in the pit of his stomach.

"Only a couple of hours ago, a party of men were here, asking after her whereabouts."

"A party of men?"

"I took them for some of the king's men," Worthy replies. "The leader told me they were a protection detail, though he looked more like a priest than a soldier."

"Constantine," Miriam says. "He is making for Katherine, but why?"

"To spirit her away," Chapuys tells her. "It is as Cromwell and I suspected. Whatever is coming, they want Queen Katherine out of harms way. My guess is they intend removing her by force, and taking her abroad. It is utter madness."

"I don't know if it is," Worthy says. "A dozen, heavily armed men will be enough to take the old queen's guard unawares. Some fast horses, and they can be across Norfolk, and aboard a waiting cog, in no time."

"If the plot fails, and Katherine is taken, it will mean her head … and the head of her dear daughter." Chapuys stands, and starts for the door. " I must ride through the night, and try to stop this lunacy."

"I too," Gregory Cromwell says, jumping to his feet. "We must stop the priest, Constantine, and save Queen Katherine from a horrible fate."

"The horses are fed," Miriam says, standing.

"You mean to give chase to them now, good people?" Herbert Worthy sighs, and wishes they had never happened upon him. "Very well, take my four men. They are armed, and the villains do like a good fight. I will send word to London, and raise a hue and cry for their leader."

"What?" Gregory asks. "Did he not leave with them?"

"He did not, sir," worthy replies grimly. "He sent his men on towards Cambridge, but he set off on the road to Norfolk. He has another errand, perhaps?"

*

Will Draper's troop, over thirty strong, and armed to the teeth, make good time. They can afford to ride hard, as fresh mounts await them every ten or twelve miles. Despite starting off several hours behind his wife, they clatter into the cobbled churchyard of Saint Cuthburga scarcely an hour behind.

Herbert Worthy appears with a lantern, and in the moonlight, explains to Will what has happened. He is keen to emphasise that he has sent his men with Miriam, Gregory, and Chapuys.

"My lads are all Cromwell men, Captain Draper," he says, "and will defend your good lady to the death."

"You should have stayed her from so foolish a course," Will replies.

"There was no stopping them, sir," Worthy concludes. "Though, if you ride on, you will overtake them, before they reach their destination. God's speed, Captain Draper."

Will selects six of his best men, and places them under the command of Mush, with orders to take the Norfolk road, and track down Constantine.

"I will ride on to Cambridge, and try to halt this mad caper," he says. "Once I am done, I will leave Richard to guard Katherine, and send word for Tom Wyatt to make haste to Norwich, with as many men as he can muster. If Norfolk is the heart of the plot, we might be able to bring our enemies to battle before they are ready."

"Take care, Will," Mush says. "For these enemies are still invisible to us, and how can you cut down a phantom?"

*

Despite the fullness of the moon, Miriam Draper, and her companions, can only advance at a steady walking pace. Their only consolation is that Constantine's men can only do the same. It is a cause of frustration to Chapuys, who fears for his queen, but he dare not go any faster. It is still a couple of hours before dawn when they hear the sound of other horses approaching. Gregory reaches for his pistol.

"It cannot be Constantine's men, Gregory," Miriam advises the nervous youth. "They are coming from the wrong direction." Suddenly, two dozen mounted men are milling around them, and a familiar voice shouts out for them to reign in their mounts.

"Will, is that you, my love?" Miriam is relieved to see her husband, and Gregory gives a childish whoop of joy.

"Now we are an army," he cries.

"Ambassador Chapuys," Will Draper says, "we are here to escort you to the Dowager Princess of Wales. Miriam and Gregory, you must turn aside now, and return to your original task. Master Worthy has orders to deliver your carts to you at the Angel Inn at Cambridge. My regards to Sergeant Buffery."

"I shall ride with you, Will," Gregory says, firmly.

"And who will look after Miriam?" Will Draper replies.

"Master Worthy's men," Miriam tells him. "Do not stop Gregory from earning his spurs, husband. Though make sure he is not too brave, or Master Cromwell will be angry with you."

*

Thomas Cromwell finally abandons his quest for sleep just before dawn breaks, and calls for his servants to help him dress, and prepare for a move back to Austin Friars. His deliberations during the night lead him to the conclusion that it is not he who is under threat, thus freeing him to take matters in hand.

By early morning, he is standing in the great kitchen, with the breakfast table's chairs and benches filling with his young men. Rafe Sadler is there, along with Barnaby Fowler, and a half dozen of the trainee lawyers and financiers he sponsors. Each one will gladly give his life for Cromwell, and they await his instructions.

"Soon, gentlemen, we will be at war," he says. "Though not one that is to be fought with cannon, and swords. The enemy is more powerful than any king, or emperor, and it will take all of our wits to beat them."

"You begin to frighten us, master," Rafe says, speaking for them all. "Are we then up against something beyond human ken? Is Mush right, when he talks about invisible spirits?"

"To a degree," Thomas Cromwell tells them. "Though there is nothing of the supernatural about them. Rather, they are out of sight, than invisible, and they will strike from afar. Tell me, Rafe, how do we keep the French from our shores?"

"A good navy, and strong coastal defences," Rafe replies, his brow furrowing. "They do not yet have enough wealth to match our arms."

"Precisely. England is strong, because she is wealthy. You need gold to buy ships, and pay for soldiers, do you not?"

"You do."

"Then how would you defeat us, Rafe?" Rafe considers the question, then smiles as he understands the answer that Cromwell seeks.

"Why, by making us poor," he says. "Without wealth, we cannot defend ourselves, and will fall prey to any who wish us harm. It is an easy answer, sir, but an impossible one to achieve. We have the wool trade, Cornish tin, and Welsh goldmines. Then we have the coastal trading cogs, who control import and export in the Channel. Not to mention our rich pastures, fishing grounds, and fine craftsmen's skills. Our people are the finest stone masons, bridge builders, cannon makers, and ship builders in the world."

"True. This little island of ours is a cornucopia of wealth," Cromwell says. "It would take an audacious plan to dry that wealth up, and reduce us to poverty. Some might think that only a great war of attrition would suffice, with our armies smashed, and our land laid waste, but who could do that alone? It would take the entire might of the Holy Roman Empire, and France combined. As they are at war with one another, I cannot see that as a likely proposition."

"We know what cannot be, sir," Barnaby Fowler says, "but what of that which *can* be?"

"I have a strong suspicion, but that is not enough," Cromwell tells the assembled young men. "We are lawyers, and lawyers deal in proof. You must go out, and find me the facts I need to confirm that which I suspect."

"We await your instructions," Rafe replies. "Though I doubt we will be much use, in the event of any trouble."

"I need minds, not swords," Cromwell tells his favoured assistant. "We must fight this battle with our intellects. I need copies of all foreign bills of lading, for the last month, and sight of any government contracts, where they concern dealings with foreign merchants."

"We will need several days," Barnaby tells his master. "Most of those documents will be spread from here to Dover."

"I also want to know the extent of lending, between us, and the Fugger banking house in Augsburg. I do not mean crown loans, but private transactions. That will do to start with."

"What of our men in the field?" Rafe Sadler says. "Tom Wyatt is rounding up troops, even as we speak."

"Have him stay close by," Cromwell says. "We may still have recourse to violent solutions. Let Will Draper complete his mission against these mysterious interlopers, and let us keep on looking for George Constantine. If he is taken, we might find out the entire plot, and be able to counter it."

Cromwell's young men disperse, about their allotted tasks, but Rafe Sadler hangs back. He is concerned, and wishes to know what Cromwell suspects.

"I cannot conceive what harm you envisage," he says. "One treacherous preacher, and a dozen men cannot bring down England."

"The men, I fear, are an escape party, sent to remove Katherine to safety," Cromwell explains. "I pray they are stopped, before the queen is foolish enough to join their scheme. As for Constantine, he is little more than a messenger... sent to awaken a 'great personage', and rouse them to some terrible action. That is the second part of this plot. The third part is more insidious. I believe that some event is planned, that will ruin our economy."

"But what?" Rafe cannot conceive of anything, short of war and plague that would lay England low.

"I don't know," Cromwell admits, "but there are odd things happening. Why would a Flanders timber merchant ask for payment in Ducats, rather than our English coin?"

"I don't understand," Rafe says. "English gold is preferred over all other coinage. The exchange rate will cost him dear. How does that benefit him?"

"It does not," Cromwell replies, "and that is the true mystery in all of this."

"Do our enemies seek to stop us buying broad timber?" Rafe conjectures. "Even if they manage to stop imports, our own forests are sufficient to keep the ship yards building war ships. Perhaps they mean to burn down every wood in England, and starve us of precious oak`/"

"Forget about wood," Cromwell replies. "We must see what else they seek to sell only for French or Brabant Ducats. The answer is staring me in the face, Rafe, but I cannot grasp it to me."

"You are tired, master," Rafe tells him. "Perhaps if you rested?"

"Whilst England is destroyed about us?" Tom Cromwell shakes his head. "I shall not be able to rest, until I have answers, my boy. Answers!"

11   The Manor of the More

The Manor of the More is, by any standards, a magnificent house, which is thought by many to be the equal of King Henry's opulent Hampton Court Palace. It has a modern, and elegant red brick façade, and comprises of a long, central building, with two shorter wings, which house stables, staff, and kitchens. The soaring towers, to right and left, conceal the very latest design of chimneys, that cleverly service the multitude of fireplaces below.

There are sixty four bed chambers on the upper floors, a magnificent long gallery to walk down, and sweeping staircases, built in the French style. The dark stained, oak panelled, walls are hung with one of the finest collections of oil paintings in England, and the great library is said to contain over two hundred books, from beautifully illuminated bibles, to the most risqué modern Italian love poetry.

Once owned by Cardinal Wolsey, the great house has played host to King Henry, and the French ambassador, during the celebrations of the last peace treaty between the two realms. It is now owned by the king, and is staffed by almost two hundred servants, and another dozen ladies in waiting. The grounds are bounded, on three aspects, with high stone walls, and cleverly concealed ha-ha ditches to the fore. The estate is closed to outsiders, and guarded by a half dozen armed men, sworn to the king's service.

These days, the sumptuous Manor on the Moor is home to Katherine of Aragon, and it is where the ex queen must, for now, live out her quiet retirement. The solid, red brick house is a comfortable place of exile, and it boasts a long gallery, that is fifteen feet wide, and over two hundred and fifty feet in length. The deposed queen spends her days strolling up and down, gazing out over the rolling parkland that is her only allowable view.

It is from this gallery that she first sees the distant group of horsemen, and wonders who it might be who dares visit her. Henry allows her visits, but makes it plain that to request an audience with Katherine means swift disfavour back in court. The figures are less than a half mile away, when a second force appears, and closes on them. She turns, and claps for a lady in waiting to attend.

"Your Majesty?" the girl asks, bowing.

"We have guests arriving, Donna Esmeralda," she says, excitedly. "Pray ask the cook to set the great banqueting hall table for … let me think … forty, or so."

"Madam, the guards will not admit them," the startled Spanish girl says.

"I very much doubt the guards can do much to stop them," Queen Katherine replies, testily. "Now, be off, and see to it!" So large a band can mean one of only two things. They are coming either to rescue her, or kill her. She hopes for the former, and wonders if they will be able to get her safely away. Then she pauses, and thinks of her daughter. To leave England without Mary will be an intolerable thing, and she dreads the possibility.

"They have stopped," Donna Esmeralda says, softly.

Katherine stares into the distance, and sees that the girl is right.

*

"Hold fast, gentlemen," Will Draper says, as they come within a dozen yards of the twelve armed men. "I will know your business here."

"I am Sir William Cross," one of the men shouts back, and we have urgent business at the house."

"Then state it, sir, for we are under orders to protect Queen Katherine from unwelcome visitors." Will uses Katherine's old title, to gauge the other band's reaction. Sir William touches a hand to the saddle bag by his right knee.

"I have orders to remove the queen from the Manor of the More, and convey her to a safer place. These gentlemen are all true Englishmen, sir." Cross is not lying. He does have orders, but not from Henry, and his companions are all men of good birth, devoted to saving England from what they perceive to be a disaster.

"That I know," Richard Cromwell mutters to Will, as he draws alongside him. "I see at least three devout Roman Catholic gentlemen amongst them, who are currently barred from court because of their obstinacy. Cedric Barton is a born Papist, and John Freeman has no love for the king. They are a nest of vipers, and no mistake."

"Sir William, the queen is safe enough where she is, and the outlook will not improve with some sea air," Will shouts over. "Lay aside your arms, and come with us."

"And if I refuse?"

"Dead or alive, sir, it makes no shift to me!" Will draws his saddle pistol, and his men follow his lead.

"Put away your weapons, good Englishmen," one of Cross's men calls. "We seek only to rescue the rightful queen, and take her from Henry's wicked clutches. Would you have the Boleyn whore decide her dreadful fate?"

"Enough," Will Draper snaps. "Surrender, or fight!" One of the men draws his sword, and the air is filled with the crack of pistols being discharged. As the smoke clears, there are three or four men unhorsed, and the rest spur their mounts forward, eager to hack at one another. Will charges, and is horrified to find young Gregory by his side, waving his borrowed sword around his head like a demented butcher.

The boy rushes straight at Sir William Cross, but Will rides into his flank, and pushes the boy's horse wide, and out of reach of a vicious slash, that would have cleaved him in two. Will rides on, and drives the point of his own blade into his enemies side. Sir William screams, and slides out of the saddle.

Gregory continues his wild rush, waving his sword about with no ill effect, until he is through the enemy. Richard is being far more economical with his thrusts, and has unhorsed another two men. Then, suddenly, it is over. Four men cry for quarter, and eight more are either dead, or wounded on the ground.

"Did you see?" Gregory says, as he rides back to them, his face flushed with excitement. "I charged right through them. Did you see, Will?"

"I saw," Will tells him. "Your father will be proud of you, lad. Now, let us bind these fellows fast, and take them to the house."

*

"Your Highness," Will bows low. He has chosen his form of address carefully, so as to avoid the difficulty over titles. Highness implies, but does not admit that Katherine is still a queen. She is satisfied, and beckons him forward.

"Why, my dear Captain Draper, I never see you without some attendant bloodshed. On the last occasion, you slew my physician, and my two Moroccan bodyguards. Pray explain yourself."

"The men we fought, were sent to steal you away, madam."

"Then I owe you no gratitude, sir!" She turns to leave, but Will is not finished.

"Had they taken you, the whole countryside would have been raised against them, and you would be taken within the day. I think it was intended to be that way. Once you left here, your life would be forfeit. Think, My Lady, how convenient to certain people, if you were to be tried, and executed. Anne Boleyn would clap with joy, and though your nephew, the emperor, would shed a few tears, his councillors would rejoice at the outcome."

"Not so!" Katherine snaps.

"Madam, they see that you tie Charles' hands, and would have you gone. Your untimely death would rebound on Henry, and make him into a monster, all across the Christian world."

"I wish no harm to my husband," she says. "Why would those men sacrifice themselves for a lost cause?"

"Because they were lied to, by a man called George Constantine," Will says. It is the only thing that fits the facts, and he begins to see some of his enemy's plan. "There are plots hidden within plots, and your ultimate death, along with your daughter's, was but a part of the overall scheme."

"You speak in riddles, sir," Katherine says.

"Though I do not doubt your sincerity. That is twice you have saved me now. Have a care, sir, lest the Boleyn whore finds out, for she will not forgive you. Here, take this, as a token of my grateful thanks."

Will Draper bows, and takes his leave. It is not until he is back with his men that he opens his palm, to gaze at the beautiful ruby ring therein.

"God's teeth!" Richard Cromwell exclaims. "How will you divide that amongst Cromwell's young men?"

"I shall not. Rather, I will pay Austin Friars a bounty for it, and place it on Miriam's finger."

"A nice Jewish girl, wearing a queen's ring," Richard says, with a broad grin. "What is the world coming to?"

*

"You must explain yourself, sir," Katherine says, sharply. "How do you come to be in the company of my enemies?" Eustace Chapuys sighs, and realises that he is in for a difficult interview with his mistress.

"It is the only way I can gain access to you, My Lady," he replies. "Your husband refuses me a private audience, time after time. Now, he banishes you here, to this palace, so far from London."

"It is Cromwell's doing," the queen says. "He is my enemy, and wants me put aside. Well sir, it shall happen only over my dead body!"

"God forbid such a dark day ever comes," Chapuys tells her, earnestly. "Thomas Cromwell cannot change the king's mind, so does what he can to make you safe. Court is too dangerous a place for you, these days. He seeks to keep you in comfort, and works towards a time when you might see your daughter again."

"He is a perfect saint," Katherine sneers. "Yet he sends men to foil my rescuers."

"Leave here, and you sign your own death warrant, madam," Chapuys replies. "It is eighty miles to the nearest port, and there are a thousand men waiting to halt your flight."

"The good Captain Draper tells me as much, Chapuys." Katherine sees the truth of what they say, but she is disappointed not to have had the chance of taking flight.

"Forgive me, Your Majesty, but I must ask a question of you, that requires a truthful answer. The fate of England might hang on your reply."

"England has stopped loving me, Chapuys," she says, "so why should I care?"

"Madam, you are under a misapprehension." Chapuys waves an all encompassing arm, to signify the general populace. "The people would line the streets, if you ever returned to London, and each night, those still of the true faith pray for your soul, a hundred thousand times over."

"Yes, I believe you." Katherine composes herself. "Ask your question, Ambassador Chapuys, and I shall answer it with all honesty."

"Did you expect this attempt at rescue?" There is a long pause, and the little Savoyard begins to think she will refuse an answer, but then she speaks.

"Yes, I did," she says.

"How so?" Chapuys asks. "You are so closely guarded, and your letters, both in and out, will be opened. How did you receive word of such a plot?"

"Oranges."

"Oranges?" Chapuys asks.

"There are messages concealed within gifts of oranges," the queen confesses. "They are delivered, from time to time, and have letters concealed within them."

"And these letters informed you of this attempt?"

"The last one did." Queen Katherine is struggling to give a fuller explanation, as she has no wish to incriminate anyone. "Before that, the notes were private communications, sent by my nephew."

"The Emperor Charles writes to you?" Chapuys is surprised, as his master has told him absolutely nothing of this.

"On family matters only," she replies. "There is nothing treasonous in them. He tells me of deaths and births… of marriages and engagements. The last note , however, was not from the emperor. It said only that I should prepare myself for a visit from some loyal Catholic gentlemen."

"And who is this mysterious benefactor, who sends you oranges, My Lady?" The queen shrugs, and shakes her head at her ambassador.

"I do not know," she tells him.

"Then how do you know they are not poisoned?" Chapuys does not believe her, and presses the point. "Why trust this fruit above any other sent to you, Your Majesty?"

"Because I know its provenance, sir," Katherine replies. "The oranges come in a wicker basket, and always have an embroidered napkin with them. The warders recognise the coat of arms, and so allow their delivery to me."

"Whose coat of arms, madam?"

"Why, Tom Howard's, of course." Katherine

smiles, sure of the love of the noble Roman Catholic lord. "The guards would never refuse a gift sent from the Duke of Norfolk."

"*Norfook?*" Chapuys high pitched pronunciation would sound comical, under any other circumstances. "His Lordship is the most pre-eminent peer of the realm. You suggest he is betraying the king?"

"I am not," Katherine retorts, sharply. "I am merely stating a fact. The napkin comes from the Duke of Norfolk's household. It may be a gentleman in his service, or a lady in waiting of my dearest friend, Elizabeth."

"I regret that she is no longer a part of Thomas Howard's life," Eustace Chapuys tells the queen. "He has cast her out, and installed a ... low *putain* in her place."

"It is very much the fashion, these days," Katherine says. "Poor Elizabeth. She is a devoted friend, and has stood by me loyally. I hear that she dislikes her niece, *la grande putain, Anne Boleyn*, and refuses to even curtsey to the woman."

Chapuys blushes. Not so long ago, he was forced to bow to Anne Boleyn, and is compelled to chat with her, whenever they now meet. In his heart, he feels as if he has betrayed his queen with this craven action.

"Sometimes, there is no other option, than to bow the head, or unwillingly bend the knee," he says, "but the heart knows the truth, madam. I think Lady *Norfook* should mind her manners for now, and keep her private thoughts private. She will live a much longer, and happier life."

"That is not Elizabeth's way," Katherine of Aragon replies.

"No, madam?" Chapuys shakes his head. "Then

may God protect her from her own foolishness."

*

The principal servants of the house are lined up in front of Will Draper, and have an air of collective guilt about them. It is their sworn duty to keep Queen Katherine secluded, and they have failed in their allotted task, miserably. They look fixedly down at their feet, and wait for the righteous scourge to be levelled at them.

The Head Steward, the Senior Cook, Keeper of the Chambers, and senior Lady in Waiting expect a harsh punishment, and can only hope to mitigate their fate with the truth. Will Draper has no intention of hurting them, but has his men to hand to frighten them, should they prove recalcitrant.

"Who amongst you knew that the Dowager Princess of Wales was receiving illicit letters?" Will uses his best 'military' voice, and the four servants quake in terror. The steward is the first to regain the power of speech, and he denies all knowledge of the event.

"Nor would these good women know, sir," he confirms. "We are all chosen, especially, for our devotion to His Majesty."

"Who brought the oranges?"

"Oranges?" the Keeper of the Chambers, a portly, red faced woman of indeterminate age, asks. "I don't understand, sir."

"The letters were placed inside gifts of oranges," Will Draper persists. "Such a rare delicacy. Surely you saw them?"

"Why yes, sir," the woman replies, "but oranges

is oranges, ain't they? I know naught of any secret letters."

"Nor I," the cook puts in. "They just comes in, at the back door. A serving fellow, on a horse. 'Here,' says he, and then he gallops off. I must have seen him three or four times, these last months, sir."

"Did you not think to examine the basket?"

"I did, sir," the woman replies. "An' it were a basket, plain an' simple. I sent the fruit up to the princesses chambers, but did not touch it, for fear of bruising. I ain't never seen such fresh oranges before, sir. They must usually get a battering on the way from Spain, but not these. Fresh as the day they was picked they are!"

"I am sure," Will replies, frowning. All four sound to be telling the truth, and the trail is cold again. True enough, there is the evidence of the napkin, bearing the coat of arms of the Duke of Norfolk, but other than that, nothing comes to his mind. "Very well, you may go. I will send a report to Master Cromwell, asking him to be lenient towards you all. If anything else comes to mind, I will be outside with my men."

He steps out into the gardens, where Richard Cromwell is playing dice with another of his men. The big man stands, and looks at him enquiringly.

"Well?"

"Nothing."

"By the buggering horns of Satan," Richard curses, and the men laugh. "If we cannot find out the truth, Norfolk will escape us."

"What if it is not Tom Howard?" Will says. "The duke spends his time swiving Bess Holland these days. What benefit will he have in kidnapping Katherine, and putting England into a rare turmoil?"

"None, I suppose," Richard says. He tends to think in slow, straight lines, and cannot abide a mystery. "See, here is the steward, who has held back from leaving with the rest. What does the rogue want now?"

The Head Steward approaches, diffidently, wringing his hands. Will sees that he is in mortal fear for himself, and smiles.

"Come, good sir, I will not eat you," he tells the man. "Do you have something to get off your chest?"

"I do not have a shred of guilt in this matter, Captain Draper," he replies, becoming a little bolder. "Though I have had a thought that might be of some help."

"Pray speak up, sir," Will says, and places one hand on the pouch of silver coins hanging at his waist. "I can be a generous benefactor … if what you say pleases me."

"Thank you, master. It is the oranges, you see."

"You noticed something odd about them?"

"No, I never saw them," the man says, "but I am minded as to what the cook says. They were as fresh as any she had ever seen."

"Yes, that is odd, I suppose," Will says.

"It is, if they came from Spain, sir."

"Where else?" Will can only wonder what the man is getting at. "Oranges grow in warmer climes. I have yet to see an orange tree in England."

"There are some," the man says. "Puny things, that lack the heat of the sun. But I recall something I was told about Framlingham Castle."

"In Suffolk?" Will Draper has only a vague recollection of the place.

"It is an imposing sight, I hear," the man tells them, warming to his story. "There is a Great Chamber, a strong gatehouse, a moat, and twenty odd fine bedrooms. It also has a chapel … dedicated to the Papist church … and an extensive pleasure garden, with ornamental ponds, terraced walkways, fountains, and a herb garden."

"Come to the point, sir," Richard Cromwell growls. "What is so special about this place?"

"It has a high walled garden, which is kept warm all year around, with exterior fire places that burn day and night," the man concludes. "Within, the duke's gardeners grow exotic fruit trees. Pears, damsons, apples, and oranges."

"That might account for the oranges' fresh state," Will says. "Who owns the place?"

"Though it is in Suffolk, the Duke of Norfolk holds the key to it. He does not live there, of course. He lives in Kenninghall, with his new … lady."

"Then who?"

"The Duchess of Norfolk is in residence, sir," the man says. "She is banished there, in the hope that it will stop her slanders against Lady Anne Boleyn, and Master Cromwell."

"The queens best, and most loyal friend," Chapuys says. He has been sitting close by, and has heard everything. "Can you not see, Will, that you have found the identity of the 'great personage' you seek?"

"A woman," Will Draper says. It is possible, he reasons, for some women, like his beloved Miriam can function in a man's domain. "Yet she is still a great power in England. She is descended from kings, and must have many influential ears to whisper her secrets into."

"Of course it is her." Chapuys is relieved to find that it is an English hand, and not a German, or

Spanish, that is involved in the treason. "*Norfook* has thrown her over, and Lady Elizabeth Howard swears vengeance on him, to any who will listen to her. Why, she has even asked me to arrange a visit to Queen Katherine."

"You did not find that odd?" Richard asks.

"She is a friend of Her Majesty's, and a devout Roman Catholic person," Chapuys says, in his defence. "Besides, what could a mere woman do? I, like you, was looking for a masculine piece in this puzzle."

"A puzzle that is beginning to unravel," Will replies. "We must take horse for Suffolk, at once."

"But we have not slept!" Chapuys complains. "Can we not set out tomorrow, refreshed, and able?"

"You may stay here," Will tells the ambassador, "but we must get to My Lady Norfolk, before she can act. Once we have her, we can find out what her part is in this matter."

"Chapuys does not shirk his duty," the little man snaps. "I will come with you, and see this out to its wicked end."

"Good man," Will says, "though I have a mind to split my forces, and send some back to London."

"For what possible reason?" The ambassador asks. "Send one man back to Thomas Cromwell at Austin Friars, and warn him that he must look to *Norfook's* lady. Then, if she escapes us, he will seize her as she tries to enter the city."

"Wise advice, sir. Pray, take your leave of your queen now, and join us at the horses."

My queen, Chapuys thinks. Yes, I am one of a dwindling band who still keep up the fiction. Soon I will have to stand alone, and fight for a lady whose titles have gone, and whose life is ever at risk.

11   The Good Samaritan

Elizabeth Howard pauses, with her quill poised above the letter she has been writing since daylight. In it she asserts, for the three hundredth time, that she has been a most dutiful wife to the Duke of Norfolk. She mentions how she has served her husband well, at court … daily for almost sixteen years …and accompanied him to Ireland when he was posted there. She re-reads the part where she details the bearing of his children, and states, clearly, that Tom Howard was always a devoted, and loving, husband.

She dips into the thick ink, and writes that anyone might think them to be bonded together, by mutual love, and respect, until the unhappy day that he took a mistress. *'A woman without breeding, and of previous immoral character'*, she pens. Then, after a moment's thought, she adds a final paragraph to her letter, which is directed to Pope Clement in Rome.

'No man can put aside his lawful wife, and expect to remain within the grace of God, Your Eminence, so I beseech you, write to Thomas Howard, 3ʳᵈ Duke of Norfolk, and command him to return to me. By the time you receive this, great things will have happened, and England will be upon its knees, and begging for your forgiveness.'

As she signs the sad plea for help, her steward knocks, and comes into the room. She ignores him whilst she dusts the letter with sand, and blows on it, to aid in its drying.

"What is it, Dallard?" she asks, finally glancing

up at the tall, young man. He holds out a gentleman's riding glove for her inspection, and smiles when she does not ask where it is from.

"Someone was in the house, during the night, My Lady" he says. Elizabeth remains silent, for she is quite aware of the fact. A gentleman, purporting to be an old friend of her husband arrived, after the servants were settled in the stable block, and begged a bed for the night. "It seems he had free access, and was able to search the house, at his leisure, madam."

Elizabeth, starved of both company, and affection, has accepted the man, Stephen Vaughan, at face value, and spent the evening drinking large amounts of wine with him. He is witty, charming, and knows her husband and his business well. Some time around midnight, he had helped her to her bed chamber, and into bed. She is unsure exactly who first kissed whom.

The love play, she recalls, was quite exquisite, and bore none of the bestial traits common to her clumsy, malodorous old husband. Stephen had told her the sweetest lies, and coaxed her into acts that she thought only the French were prone to employ. After the third time, she was too drunk, and too exhausted to continue, and fell into a deep sleep. She woke up, as if from a beautiful dream, to find him gone.

"How do you know this?" she asks. Her lack of funds is almost complete, and she cannot afford to keep servants for the house. One steward, and a couple of village girls, is all she can keep, and they sleep on straw, in the stables. Her midnight tryst should have remained a sweet secret.

"Effie answered a call of nature, My Lady, and saw the rogue leaving." The man was beginning to feel rather satisfied with himself. The girl was a regular bed companion, and shook him awake at once. "I saddled one of the carriage horses, and gave chase. He was not expecting any kind of pursuit, and I came upon him on the top Ipswich road."

"Dear God, what has come about?" Lady Elizabeth is now completely mortified. If Stephen Vaughan is taken, the whole story will come out. He will tell the whole of England of how he pleasured her, and her privileged life will be ruined beyond redemption. Norfolk will have her charged with adultery, and divorce her at once. The king, if he is so inclined, might even demand a harsher punishment. So much to lose, she thinks, mournfully, for one or two hours of glorious passion.

"Fear not, madam," the steward tells her, smugly. "I struck the rascal down, with my cudgel. I bring the glove as proof of my action. In his saddle bag, I found many important looking papers, taken from your library."

"Sweet Jesus … the man was a spy then?"

"It is a wonder he did not come upon Your Ladyship, in a state of … undress. For who knows what might have happened to you. Thank God your honour is still intact."

"Just so," Elizabeth says. The steward grins, and gives her a look that says he knows what has happened. "How can I ever repay such a noble deed, Master Dallard?"

"Perhaps I might come to your chambers, a little later … and we can discuss my reward."

"You are too saucy, sir!" she snaps. "How dare you suggest such an improper action?"

"How dare I, madam?" Dallard replies. "It is you

who have dared, and almost lost everything. I can see from your face that you have given of yourself to the fellow. The papers I recovered are inflammatory, and border on treason against the king. No doubt, your 'friend' was sent to spy on your husband, and settled on you instead. Was his time well spent, madam?"

"You are too clever for your own good, Master Dallard," Lady Norfolk snaps.

"Come, madam, and stop this nonsense at once," the steward sneers. "You have betrayed your husband, and your king. The papers tell me the one thing, and your blushes the other. Do not fret, for do not the nobility swive as well as we mere servants?"

"I will not speak of it."

"Then I will, madam," the steward leers. "You have been had, and to get out of your predicament, you must be had again."

"What of the man?"

"Dead. I could feel no heart beat, and there was a great deal of blood." Dallard, in truth, is not sure, for the night was dark, and the man had tumbled from his horse, and into a field of stubble. The blow, however, struck from behind, had been prodigious. "It will look as if thieves have waylaid, and robbed an unfortunate traveller, Lady Elizabeth."

"Then you have done me a good deed," she says, forcing a smile to her lips. Once it is open, she realises, Pandora's box cannot be closed again. Adultery is adultery, whether it be one gentle lover, or a hundred fierce ones. "Have you a mind to lay with me then, sir? I am a full ten years your senior."

"And still as desirable as a peach," Dallard replies, touching her hair with his fingertips. "A woman with your looks, and fulsome body, will be a welcome change from the low sluts you employ."

"Come to me tonight then, and I will reward you well," the duchess says. The steward bows, slightly, and smiles a crooked smile. Then he reaches down with his hand, and slips it into her chemise. She closes her eyes, and wets her lips with the tip of her tongue.

"No, My Lady, the reward will be yours," he says, and squeezes, harder.

"You promise much, sir," she tells him, but his insolence excites her, and makes her wish for nightfall again. "Have you the papers?"

"Safe, My Lady," Dallard says. "I will return them to your keeping, page by page … as reward follows upon sweet reward!"

"Then I am to be your creature?" Lady Elizabeth can feel her heart beating in her breast, and wonders if he will be as gentle as the previous night's lover. As if in answer, he pulls her to her feet, and lets his hands roam where they will, pinching, and squeezing, until she moans at the casual misuse of her soft body.

"You smell better than my usual fare, My Lady," Dallard tells her, and crushes his lips down onto her exposed breasts.

*

Richard Cromwell is a big man, in every way, and it is because of his great height that he sees over a hedgerow, and wonders at the sight of a man, curled into a ball, and covered with blood. He draws his sword, and calls a halt. Will gallops up to him.

"What is it?"

"A dead body, in the field," Richard says. "I almost missed it. There is some mischief afoot, and we must be on our guard."

"What, here?" Will gestures to the hedgerow, and Richard nods. "You two men," he says, "bring the poor dead wretch to me. We must see if we can identify him."

"I doubt his purse will be there," Richard mutters. The two men dismount, and push their way through the hedge. A minute passes, and then, one of them shouts to Will.

"Captain Draper, the fellow is still alive, and I know him. It is Master Vaughan!"

"Stephen?" Will cannot hide his surprise. "I knew he was helping in our search, but what brings him here?"

"Perhaps he suspects Tom Howard's wife?" Richard says.

"Or the duke himself," Will Draper conjectures. "Handle him with care, lads, for he is one of ours, and dear to Master Cromwell's heart."

A half hour later, Stephen Vaughan is bandaged, and being loaded onto a makeshift litter. Two men will take him to Ipswich, where a doctor might be found to tend his injury. He is delirious from a head wound, and unable to tell his saviours what has befallen him.

"We will play the Good Samaritan, and see him safely to a doctor, sir," Jake Stoodley, one of Cromwell's rougher young men says. "But 'tis a pity he spoke only a few words."

"He spoke?" Will asks. "What did he say."

"Nothing that made sense, sir," Jake replies. "As I picked him up in my arms, he says *'it is the angel'*, and passes out."

"The Angel!" Wills senses reel. Miriam is, even now, travelling to the Angel Inn, in Cambridge. "By

God, Richard … are we going the wrong way? Is Miriam in some kind of trouble?"

"Calm yourself, Master Will," Gregory Cromwell says. "It is nought but a strange sort of a coincidence. Mistress Miriam is safe. She has four good men with her, and your Sergeant Buffery sounds like a sound fellow, who will not allow your lady to come to any harm."

"Yes, you are right, Gregory," Will says. "Why would Stephen seek to warn us though? Which angel does he mean?"

"Perhaps he meant the Angel of Death?" Gregory says with a sudden clutch of horror. He is young, and still fears the darker corners of Roman Catholicism. "Might he have seen him, hovering over him, as he lay, close to death?"

"Well, he has flown off now," Will tells the boy. "Let us hope he has other souls to gather, before we have to meet with him."

"Bugger angels. Our answer lies ahead," Richard says. "Let us get on to Framlingham Castle, and catch Norfolk's bitch at her filthy treason, before it is too late."

*

The Angel Inn is on the southern approaches of Cambridge, and is popular with travellers of all kinds, from pilgrims to scholars. The new owner is proud of the place, and the alterations he, and his new wife, have made to it. He is standing at one of the new windows, with its polished horn panes, looking up the road, when Miriam's party trundles into sight.

Rob Buffery's usual friendly smile turns into a

frown as they come into the yard. He steps behind the wooden bar, and retrieves his old army sabre. Then he stands it just inside the door, handy, should he have need of it. Mistress Miriam Draper is here, but has brought a disturbing puzzle with her. The carts come to a halt, and the old soldier fixes the smile back on his face, before stepping out to greet them.

"Mistress Draper, I presume?" Rob Buffery is a big, well muscled man, who still keeps a keen sense of military discipline, to go along with his natural amiability. "Welcome to the Angel Inn. My wife has food ready, and there is a comfortable room waiting for you. Though I was not expecting you to bring so many men along - six is it?"

"It is, Master Buffery. I have been in an adventure, and apart from my two carters, I have acquired four further bodyguards. They will be happy to bed down in your stable, if it be warm, and there is enough food and ale for them."

"I shall see to it, at once," Buffery says, ushering her inside the well lit inn. "What do you think of my Angel then, mistress?"

"Divine," Miriam Draper replies, smiling at her own small jest. "How many can you feed and board at once?"

"Enough," the old soldier replies. "Most of my trade is done with travellers coming from Oxford, or London. Once they get a taste for your foreign wines, they will want more."

"Have your men unload my carts, and we will settle accounts," Miriam tells him. "My husband vouches for your honesty, and I am minded to make you a good price, providing you are ready to listen to my offer."

"I am always open to offers," Rob Buffery replies. "What have you in mind, Mistress Draper?"

"Cheese, smoke cured hams, salted beef, wines, Italian sausages, salt, pepper and nutmeg," she says. "I can supply all your needs. Make me your single supplier, and your inn will prosper."

"I have never heard a woman ... lady ... talk so," Rob Buffery replies, scratching his thick beard. "You must have dealings with half the world. Can you truly do all of this?"

"I have swift cogs bringing me wines, and foodstuffs from afar, and I can import from as far away as Venice, or even the Ottoman states," Miriam concludes.

"Then we have a bargain made," the retired soldier tells her, holding out a big hand. He refrains from spitting into his palm, in deference to her fair sex. "Though I am quite puzzled by your choice of carter."

"What do you mean?" Miriam asks. "Both men are good workers, and keep themselves in orderly fashion. They are just common fellows I sometimes find work for."

"The one with the eye patch, perhaps, mistress," says Rob Buffery, "but not the younger man. He is no more a carter, than I am Queen of the May!"

"You know him?"

"No, not know him," Buffery confides, "but I have seen him before now."

"You frighten me, sir," Miriam Draper says. She and her husband live in a world of intrigue, and secrecy, and things are seldom what they seem. "Pray, tell me what you know."

"Your husband gave me a promissory note for my share of a horse deal, and bade me present it to Master

Thomas Cromwell, at Austin Friars, in London. I found the place easily enough, as the man is well known, it seems. I went in, and asked to see Master Cromwell."

"I trust he honoured the note?" Miriam says.

"He did, mistress, and even offered me a position, working for him. I declined the offer, as my heart was set on running an inn, and he paid me six pounds in gold coins, and five shillings in silver, without further ado. Waiting in the hall, to see him, were three other men … young men … who all looked as though they might be able to handle themselves. It seems Master Cromwell was hiring likely fellows, to swell his entourage."

"And one of these men was the carter, Alfred?"

"Yes, Mistress Miriam. He was better dressed, and clean shaven back then, but I knew him at once. He walks like a military sort, and I wager his hands are too soft for his current profession."

"Curse the man," Miriam mutters. "The fellow is set to watch me."

"I can see he vanishes, if you wish," Rob Buffery tells her. "A swiftly cut throat, and a deep hole in a field will not be a problem."

"No, he is not here to do me any sort of harm," the girl explains. "but rather to keep a caring eye on me. Master Cromwell is far too diligent when it comes to my safety."

"Then he is set to spy on you, and watch that you come to no harm?" Rob Buffery is not completely convinced. "Why should that be … and is he the only one?"

"Yes, here. I suspect there are a few more in my employ, who also take a wage from Master Cromwell."

"Funny that." The big ex soldier worries at his

fulsome beard, and frowns deeply. "He did not seem the sort."

"The sort?" Miriam asks.

"Yes. The sort of old bugger to covet a younger woman in such a manner." Rob Buffery reaches the wrong conclusion, and believes Thomas Cromwell to be the worst kind of panderer. "Does Captain Will know of this?"

"You misunderstand the situation, I think," Miriam replies, hastily. "Master Tom holds my husband in the highest regard, and treats me like a favourite child. His two daughters died young, you see, and I am by way of being a comfort to him."

"Then you are a very lucky girl," the old soldier says, smiling. "He has you watched for the noblest of reasons, and helps you where he can. Thank God, and accept it, mistress."

"Miriam," she says. "I am just Miriam."

"A Hebrew name, is it not?" There is no malice in Rob's voice. The name simply reminds him of sermons, half remembered from his childhood. "Was she not an old time prophetess?"

"Yes, she was. The bible says she foresaw the closing of the Red Sea over Pharaoh and his multitude and sang about it to Moses and Aaron.

'*Sing to the Lord, for he has triumphed gloriously;*

Horse and rider he has thrown into the sea.'" she sings the words in a lilting chant, and Rob Buffery is spellbound by her gentle voice.

"You sing well, and the choice of name was a good one," he tells her.

"My father liked the sound of it," she says, telling the usual tale concocted to keep her safe from persecution. "I am originally from Coventry."

"Things are much laxer in Calais," Buffery says. "There, people are judged on their worth, not their religion. I am sure that Coventry is a very nice town. You must call me Rob, Miriam from Coventry."

The girl smiles at the small jest, but cannot help wonder how deeply Cromwell has infiltrated his people into her everyday business. Are they all there to keep her safe, or do they use her business to act as spies, and agents for their real master? One day, she will sit down with her benefactor, and demand the truth.

*

The Spaniard has never been to Bruges before, and he is surprised by its beauty. The city is a prosperous one, and is well furnished with grand houses. Gomes is directed to one of the grandest, by a wide canal, and arrives at the appointed hour.

"Ah, Gomes, there you are!" Anton Fugger says, as he is shown into the main hall. "We feared you might have been taken, in Calais." The Spaniard bows to his master, and nods at the other four men, who, he assumes are fellow bankers to Fugger.

"The town is a melting pot of every nation in Europe, sir," he says. "If you are careful, one may move about freely. My agents in Calais ensured I was safe."

"Excellent. Now, what news?"

"The men we sent to Queen Katherine were taken, as we thought they would be. Cromwell's men ran them to earth."

"Before they freed the lady?"

"Yes."

"Damn," Fugger says. "It might have been better had they removed her, before being stopped."

"The emperor will be pleased," Gomes says, coldly. "He has no desire to have his aunt's head displayed above traitor's gate. She might yet be allowed to retire honourably, or even enter a nunnery."

"Yes, yes." Fugger is a practical man, and knows that Charles would be better off being free of his moral obligation to his aunt. "I'm sure the emperor will rejoice at the news."

"The lady is still much loved in Aragon, sir," Gomes replies, stiffly. "I myself am an Aragonese."

"I see, and what of George Constantine?" The banker has several irons in the fire. "Is our tame preacher still at large?"

"My agents tell me that he is still free, and was last seen seeking shelter at a friend's house in Suffolk. He should be with the Duchess about now," Gomes replies.

"And what of our Keeper of the Angels? Fugger asks. "My friends are keen to know of his progress."

"Assuming that Thomas Cromwell's men are still looking for Constantine in the wrong county, he will contact Lady Howard soon. In the next few days, she will have the Keeper of the Angels visit her. He is a relative, and this will not cause any suspicion. With the exchange done, Constantine will slip back across the channel, and be brought to us, here."

"Hear that, my friends?" Anton Fugger can scarcely contain his excitement. "Within a few days, we will hold the fate of a nation in our hands. You must prepare for the next stage."

"Some of us have already begun," one of the men, a heavy set German says, glaring at a thin faced

Frenchman sitting across from him. "I hear that wood from the Ardennes forest can only be bought for Ducats, or French gold coins."

"What else would you have me do?" the Frenchman snaps back. "Must I stand by, and lose thousands?"

"We all swore," Fugger tells them. "Did I not promise to make good any losses?"

"You did, Anton," the same stone faced German agrees. "And I have kept to my part. I have two shiploads of trade goods on the way to Dover, and must accept English coin." The Frenchman looks about for support from the other members of the banking cartel, but finds only stony looks.

"You speak as if our plan has already come to fruition," he says, defensively. "Let me see these precious Angels, and I will fall in with all that you say, Fugger!"

"Until then?"

"I am the richest man in France, and I wish to remain so," he says. "Your guarantees are nothing to me. I believe in actions. Pay me now, against any future loss, or I must withdraw my support."

"You have me over a barrel, my friend," Anton Fugger says, coldly. "I cannot have you pulling out now. You would break faith with us, and our plot will fail. Stay, if only for another week."

"Will you pay me?" the Frenchman asks. "I cannot live on promises."

"Then go," Anton Fugger says. "For even if I pay, you will still choose your own, selfish path. Escort my friend off the premises, Señor Gomes."

Gomes bows to his master, and takes the Frenchman by the elbow, roughly. He is affronted by this rude treatment, and tries to pull loose, but the Spaniard is far too strong for him.

"Come, sir," Allesandro Gomes says. "Your continued presence is an offence to these fine gentlemen, who seek only to bring down our natural enemy."

The Frenchman is taken into the courtyard, and made to stand under guard, until his carriage is ready. His hopes of forcing the immensely rich Anton Fugger into buying his co-operation are scattered to the winds, but he can still use his knowledge to profit in other ways.

The coach clatters into view, and Gomes opens the door for the French banker. He gestures for him to climb in.

"There, sir. Go, but remember this ..." As the Frenchman turns to hear Gomes' final words, the Spaniard slips a thin dagger up, under his ribs. The man shudders, and stares in horror at his murderer. Gomes leans against the mortally wounded Frenchman, and pushes him into the coach. He closes the door, and steps back.

"Drive out, deep into the forest, and make it look like robbers have done this," he instructs the coachman. "On your return, there will be a purse of silver waiting for you." the man nods to the Spanish assassin, touches his hat, and whips the horses into a swift trot.

Gomes watches the coach vanish from sight. He stoops, and wipes the bloody blade on a tuft of grass, then returns to his master who is waiting in the great hall.

"Is it done?" Anton Fugger asks.

"It is." The Spaniard touches the hilt of his dagger to indicate the method of the Frenchman's despatch. "He is on his way, sir."

"Excellent." The banker smiles, and addresses those who remain. "Now, gentlemen, are we all in this together … to the very end?"

"We are, Anton" Horst Grunewald, the German, says, raising his wine glass in the air. "Let us drink to the downfall of the heretic, Henry, and the complete destruction of England!"

Anton Fugger, the richest man in Christendom, is content at the way things are going. The Frenchman, Jacques Verrier, was always a weak link, and likely to betray them all for money. He is better dead, than allowed to upset things at this late stage. All that remains is for Constantine to return, safely, and England is doomed, but the financier is loath to leave anything to chance.

"Gomes, what if Constantine fails us?" he asks. "What if he is taken, or loses his nerve?"

"Rest easy, sir," Gomes tells the worried banker. "I have a band of men close to the duchesses castle. They are heavily armed, and know their trade well. These men have instructions to protect the house, and see that Constantine returns to us, exactly as we planned."

"Good. There must be no loose threads in this tapestry, Gomes," Fugger says. "Once we have the Angels, our treacherous preacher must vanish."

"The ship's captain has orders to cut his throat, and then drop him overboard, once he is in deep water," Gomes replies.

"Most apt. The coward fears the flames, but will perish in water," Fugger says, and they all laugh politely at his small jest.

"There is also the matter of the Duchess of

Norfolk, sir," Gomes says. "She thinks she is helping Queen Katherine, whilst embarrassing her estranged husband. Once she understands what we are about, she might cause an upset at court."

"Kill her." The banker pronounces the death sentence, as if speaking of a small change in interest rates. "Have your men kill them all, duchess, servants … the lot."

"I have already given the order," Gomes says, relieved that he has not overstepped his authority. "My men will see to it, and burn down her house. It will look like the work of marauding French pirates. They often raid along that part of the English coast."

"Well done, Gomes. I will see you are well rewarded."

"Thank you, sir, but I must confess that I would do all in my power to hurt the heretical English, even without your gold."

"Ah!" Anton Fugger laughs, coldly, and drops a heavy purse onto the table. "Revenge does not put bread and meat on the plate, my friend. Take the gold I offer. You have earned it."

"Thank you, Señor Fugger," the Spaniard replies, hefting the leather pouch. "Brabant Ducati, I hope … and *not* English coin?"

The others burst into laughter then. They are all in on the secret, and have been quietly buying up Spanish silver for some months. Even so, the price has begun to rise, and they must go carefully, lest they alert the English, and expose what they are up to.

12   Framlingham

Elizabeth Howard is still, at the age of thirty five, an attractive lady, and she cannot understand why her callous husband has thrown her over for a younger woman, of much lower birth. It is his lack of good taste which appals her most.

"He is mad," Matthew Dallard replies. He has the duchess straddled over a padded bench, and is taking her from behind. She is gasping, and urging him to even greater endeavours. He slaps her exposed behind, and speaks to her like a common paid whore. "There is more on an old bird, than a spring chicken. I will ride you, madam, 'til the cock does crow!"

"Such a crowing cock," Elizabeth moans, and turns to face him. She runs her fingers across the hair on his chest "Come, look at me. Let me see your eyes as you swive with me, sir."

The steward, safe in the knowledge that she must surrender to his basest wishes, smiles, and takes hold of the mass of hair that cascades down over her bare shoulders. He pulls her by it, and makes her slip to the floor, and on to her knees.

"Come, woman," he sneers, raising her chin with his free hand. "Tend to me, in the French way, like a penny slut!"

Elizabeth, Duchess of Norfolk is aghast at the crudity of the man, but feels tempted to fall in with his wishes. It is an art that she is untrained in, but is willing to learn if it increases her own pleasure. The steward understands that she is only playing the innocent, and draws her lips onto him.

"A pretty picture." The steward spins around, and Elizabeth screams, as the man framed in the bedroom door saunters in. "My humble apologies, Your Ladyship, I did knock, but you were otherwise engaged.

"Who are you, fellow?" Dallard says, clutching at his hose.

"Captain Will Draper, sir. The man who is minded to have you hanged from one of those nice orange trees in the garden."

The steward blanches with fear, and starts to step away from his erstwhile lover. She, for her part, draws a chemise about her nakedness, and stands to face the newcomer.

"I am the Duchess of Norfolk, sir," she says, as if greeting him in her sitting room. "What is your business with me?"

"Madam, I have fifteen men outside. Pray, instruct this rude fellow to have them fed, and given shelter for the night. Then you must make yourself decent, and attend me downstairs."

"Must?"

"Must madam. Your castle is now under my orders," Will says. "You are already guilty of two crimes, and I must question you about a third."

"What two crimes?" Elizabeth asks.

"Adultery…"

"Is it a crime to seek love, when your husband will not do his duty?"

"… and attempted murder."

"What?"

"Stephen Vaughan, a friend… struck down not two miles from here," Will says, coldly. "Now, get dressed, or I will drag you downstairs, as naked as you are, Madam!"

"That was not any of my doing," the duchess

cries, pointing a finger at Dallard. "That foul rogue struck the blow, before coming back here, to force himself cruelly on me."

"I witnessed the *forcing*, madam," Will Draper tells her, bluntly. "Now, for the last time of asking, get dressed."

He leaves a man on guard, and goes back downstairs, where Richard Cromwell is detailing men to keep an eye on the two servant girls, and take up strategic points around the grounds.

"We don't want any surprises, lads," he is saying. "Keep out of sight, and keep an eye open for this accursed preacher. You all have an idea what the rogue looks like. Take him alive, whatever happens, or Will Draper will have your heads on poles!"

"With an apple in the mouth," Will adds, with a smile. They are good lads, and will follow orders to the letter. "Richard, there is a naked steward upstairs. It seems he was being favoured by the duchess. She claims he was the swine who tried to kill Stephen, so bind him fast, and lock him in the cellars."

"Why not just hang him?" Richard replies, sternly. "The treacherous dog deserves nothing better from us."

"I need him, to bear witness against the duchess," Will explains. "I care not who she lets swive her, but *she* does. To keep her base lewdness a secret, she might confess all … whatever 'all' may turn out to be."

"Then she was…"

"On bended knee," Will confirms.

"And Norfolk has tired of such a woman?" Cromwell's nephew says, and laughs.

*

Lady Elizabeth takes her time dressing, doing her own hair, and adorning it with her newest, pearl embroidered hat, and an array of ivory beads, and rubies. Just as Will is about to send men to drag her down, she makes her appearance. In the candle light, she looks like a twenty year old, and a fine looking one at that.

Neither Will nor Richard can understand why her husband has chosen to put her aside, and take up with Bess Holland at Kenninghall House. She sits, and awaits their questions, with her hands, demurely in her lap. The action presses her bodice down, slightly, and displays the twin orbs of her full breasts, to very good effect.

"Madam, you are in serious trouble," Will starts.

"What you witnessed, sir, was a lady being forced against her will, into performing an abominable *French* act."

"The man is your steward, and he tried to kill one of my friends earlier. Was it because Stephen Vaughan has discovered your involvement in a crime against the king?"

"If swiving is a crime, sir … then you must lock up every man at court, including the king. He puts the queen aside for a whore, whose sister and mother he has already covered. Do not tell me I have done him any wrong."

"Your illicit animal couplings are a matter for the Duke of Norfolk to sort out, My Lady," Richard says. "You are charged with harbouring George Constantine, an enemy of the realm."

"Have you found him under my roof?"

"Not yet."

"Nor will you," Elizabeth replies. She turns to Will, and bestows a beautiful smile on him. "What else am I charged with, young man?"

"You conspire to free the Dowager Princess of Wales from her confinement."

"Then she is under arrest?" the duchess asks, in mock surprise.

"Not actually," Richard Cromwell says. He is not the man his uncle is, and is more used to getting confessions with his big fists, or at the point of a blade. "The king thinks it meet that she does not wander the countryside."

"Then she is not restrained, which means she cannot be freed," Elizabeth tells him, as if explaining to a small child. "How have I angered the king?"

"You send oranges, madam," Richard snaps.

"Oranges?" She takes a deep breath, and watches the younger Cromwell's eyes slide to her bosom. "Are you a lover of fruit, Master Richard?"

"You placed messages inside them," Will says, trying to bring some order to the questioning. "Do not deny it, My Lady, for I have the evidence."

"Were not the oranges consumed then?"

"Then there is the treasonable congress with George Constantine," Will says.

"Whom I have never met, nor written to," Lady Elizabeth replies, demurely.

"He comes here to further the treason," Richard Cromwell says.

"What treason?" the duchess asks of him. "I hear only talk of oranges, and mysterious preachers. My only crime, if crime it be, is to have a dirty rogue's pintle *forced* upon me. Now, is there anything else, gentlemen?"

"You do not know Constantine?" Will asks.

"No."

"You have never heard of him?"

"Never."

"Then how does it happen that you know him to be a preacher, madam?"

"I tire, young man," the duchess says. "Might I retire to my bed?"

"Alone?" Richard asks, nastily. The Duchess of Norfolk runs a finger, delicately down her cheek, her neck, and into the ample cleft of her breasts.

"Pray, do not put your puerile thoughts onto me, sir. Better you go and swive one of the servants, in my pigsty. It might satisfy your baser feelings."

"You rut like a whore, and play the traitor without a second thought, madam," Richard Cromwell cries across the room. "Let us see what happens when Tom Howard hears of your adultery!"

"Let us," Elizabeth replies, calmly. "For my action is no man's business, save his, and he will not want his dirty laundry washed in public places. Do your absolute worst, sir, but until then, I am for my bed … alone."

She stands, and with the most regal of bearings, heads for her chambers. Will raises a hand, to stop Richard dragging her back, and watches her climb the long marble staircase. Half way up, she pauses, and looks back at them. There is the hint of a smile about her mouth, and he cannot help but smile back. One last thing remains to be tried.

"Madam… we know about the Angels," he says.

"Do you, sir?" she returns, giving him a most quizzical sort of a look. "Then, if that be so, why are you here … save to peep through my keyhole." She continues mounting the steps, allowing her slender body to sway with each movement.

Were I a free man, Will tells himself, with stark honesty, I would be joining her. How can any man throw such a pearl aside?

*

Thomas Wyatt is tired of his allotted task. He and his men have been criss-crossing the county for three days, in the hope of stumbling on Constantine, or his band of rogues. The search has been quite fruitless, and he is finally reduced to sitting atop a low hill, and watching the Ipswich road. It is the only byway of any note within twenty miles, and travellers can be seen from miles away, stopped, and questioned.

After a night sleeping on a bed of straw, under a clear May sky, the poet is refreshed, and atop his horse, like some silent sentinel of the road. He watches the small party of men ride towards him, recognises at least one of them, and grins. He turns in his saddle, and addresses the dozen men clustered behind him, in clear stentorian tones.

> "*Lo, here comes our Prometheus bold,*
> *With stolen fire from above,*
> *To save those souls within Cromwell's fold,*
> *And snare them with his father's love.*"

There is a scattering of applause, a few hearty 'hurrahs', and from the back, a very rude noise, which makes them all break into raucous laughter. The smaller group of riders are close now, and the poet can make out Mush Draper, Rafe Sadler, and Barnaby Fowler trotting along, with their master. Tom Cromwell is riding a sturdy hunter, and looks out of place on the huge beast. He is getting too old and fat for these adventures, and only the need for speed has enticed him back into the saddle.

"Well met, Master Wyatt," Thomas Cromwell says, easing his mount to a stop. "Have you come upon any fellow travellers this morning?"

"No, sir, we have not. Our search for the elusive preacher goes badly," Wyatt replies. "Have you come to help in our task?"

"Not to find Constantine any more," Cromwell says. "I fear that he was yet another trail, set to mislead us. We are in pursuit of a greater quarry."

"Then you know what is happening, sir?" Wyatt asks.

"I do, Tom," Cromwell says. "Thanks to my young men, and their diligent paperwork. I was too obsessed with plots, and could not see the blindingly obvious. Come, we must ride on to Framlingham Castle, and end this thing, once and for all time."

"You speak in riddles," Wyatt replies. "Is not Framlingham one of Norfolk's castles? Then we have our enemy, for …

though Norfolk be held in so much awe,
He is n'er a match for Cromwell,
Who'll wrap him up in England's law,
And send him to the flames of Hell."

"A poor effort, Thomas, even on the spur of the moment," says Cromwell. " Nor do I like being rhymed with Hell. Besides, you leap to the wrong conclusion. It is not Tom Howard we seek, sir, but his cast off wife … and her rather clever cousin."

"The nobility have so many poor cousins, that I

am lost as to whom you mean … but I have never known you be wrong … so, to the road men. Let us follow Master Cromwell to the bitter end."

"Oh, not bitter, I hope," Rafe Sadler says. "For life is just becoming sweet, my friend."

"What's this, Rafe Sadler smiling?" Tom Wyatt looks his friend in the eye, and nods. "Ah, you are in love. I see it in the stupid look on your face. Who is she, and is she good looking?"

"Do not try to bait me, you rascal," Rafe replies, "for my new love is proof against your taunts."

"Then she is plain?" Wyatt asks, suppressing a chuckle. "If she is, it is unlikely that I know her."

"Enough," Mush says, riding between them. "She is a clever woman, and though of a certain age, most comely."

"A name, I must have a name, so that I can write a poem for her, Rafe." Wyatt spurs his mount, and the small, well armed force set off on the Ipswich road. "How certain an age?"

"Ignore him, Rafe," Cromwell says. "We live in the same house, and I have been too blind to see. I hope you will consult with me, before you marry, so that I might attend to your household needs." Rafe Sadler cannot meet Cromwell's gaze. "What ever is it, my boy?"

"She does not know yet."

"Know what?"

"That I love her … or that she *must* love me in return."

"Ah," Cromwell says, and lapses into silence. He remembers so well how much he once loved, and craved nothing, but its return.

"We will be there in a couple of hours, master,"

Mush says, to try and change the subject of their conversation. "What if we are too late, and our quarry has beaten us?"

"Catching the Keeper will not help us. It is his Angels that we must take," Cromwell says.

"The ports are guarded." Rafe has seen to this in person, giving orders that every boat is searched, and every traveller's papers are checked. "Their only hope is to find some deserted beach, and have a small sailing ship waiting."

"Then we must stop it now, before we have to search the whole of England." Cromwell digs his knees into the big hunter's flanks, and it steps up its pace. The Privy Councillor clings on for dear life, and prays for a safe delivery to Framlingham. Tom Wyatt and Rafe gallop alongside the older man, ready to try and stop him from falling, if he should stumble.

"Then you are in love with her dowry?" the poet persists.

"Thomas, I beseech you to shut up," Rafe Sadler replies. "For I fear she will repulse me, and break my heart."

"You must have the right words," Wyatt decides. As an ardent seducer of women, he knows the power of a well turned phrase, or a casually dropped compliment. "I shall write something for you to study, so that you might whisper it into her lovely ear."

"That is so thoughtful of you," Rafe replies, smirking to himself. His dislike of poetry is almost as great as his love for Ellen Barré.

"It is the very least I can do for a friend," the poet says, oblivious to the sarcasm in his friend's reply. "Now, some facts, if you please. I must know her hair and eye colour. Is her nose pretty, or is it far too big, like yours?"

*

"Did you sleep well?" Will asks, yawning.

"Well enough," Richard replies, sheepishly. In truth, he took the duchesses advice literally, and has been with one of the two serving girls for most of the night. She has fulfilled his immediate carnal needs, and then demanded two silver shillings in return.

"I can get as much for sixpence in London," he complains.

"Then you can bugger off to London then," the girl replies, saucily. "You're in Suffolk, Master Cromwell, and you must pay Suffolk prices for your pleasure."

Now, he is dressed, and buckling on his sword. After taking his pleasure, he has ensured that the guards are still awake, and sought out the kitchen, where an old crone from the village is making bread.

"Bacon, eggs and sausages," he says to her, and drops a couple of pennies onto the kitchen table.

"Some fresh baked bread, cut ale, and a few slices of hard cheese," she replies. "Lest you want to pay more, and I must send to the village for it. My Lady Nose in the Air owes everyone of us, and cannot pay. I'm paid for by His Lordship, and am told to do nothing, but keep her alive. The duke is as mean as a Jew money lender, and will not spend gold, where silver will suffice."

"Then she lives on watered ale, and a peasant's food?"

"Of course. The duke is done with her, sir." The old woman shrugs. "Soon, she will have to part with what jewels she has left."

"The Duchess of Norfolk is the first lady of the land," Richard says, suddenly feeling sorrow at her plight. "I want this kitchen overflowing with food, within the hour. Cured hams, wild fowl, chickens, fresh vegetables, and a decent barrel of wine. The bill is to be sent to Master Thomas Cromwell in London."

"Some will not like it."

Richard frowns, and drops a hand to his sword hilt. "I will visit any who refuse," he says. "Tell them that I am an ogre, and will smash to pieces their shops, and break off their arms and legs. Tell them that we are the only law here about, and shall deliver justice our own way. Now, be off, woman, and do as I command!"

"Trouble?" Will asks, coming into the room.

"No, I'm just organising breakfast for us all," Richard replies. "How has our lovely duchess fared?"

"She has slept the sleep of the innocent, and looks even fresher and lovelier than last night."

"Dear Christ, the woman is almost as much of a force as Uncle Thomas." Richard considers their options, which seem few. "Can she not see which path she must take?"

"We can prove nothing against her," Will tells his friend. "She claims the steward was forcing her, and will be believed. The fellow is still under lock and key?"

"He is. Perhaps he will speak out, once he knows his fate."

"Why should he confess anything?" Will says. "I caught him, with the duchess on her knees before him. Norfolk will have him strung up. What has he to gain?"

"We can promise him a quick death."

"A cheering thought," Will replies. "Confess all,

and I will cut your throat, rather than burn you at the stake, or dismember you, whilst you still draw breath. He will keep silent. Rather be killed for violating a member of the nobility, than admit being involved in high treason."

"Can we not hang her ladyship up by her pretty ankles," Richard asks, only half in jest. "Until she tells us what we must know?"

"Good Christ, Richard, she is the Duchess of Norfolk," Will replies. "The king would boil us alive for such an unauthorised act."

"Then we are no further on," Richard says. "Do we mount up, and continue our search for the preacher?"

"I think not." Will considers his one remaining option, which is to stay put, and sees that it is a case of damned if you do, and damned if you do not. Perhaps, he thinks, there is no more to do, other than hope for a stroke of luck, or a small miracle. He is saved from making a decision by a cry from one of the lookouts.

There is a party of men approaching, the man shouts down to them, led by none other than Thomas Cromwell. Richard sees the relieved look in his comrade's eyes, and roars his delight at this turn of events.

"Ah!" he cries. "Here is the chess master now, Will … and the game is suddenly changed for the better!"

"Let us hope Master Tom can checkmate the enemy king, and win the day for us," Will Draper says, with relief in his voice.

"His presence means we are absolved of responsibility," Richard replies, cannily. "The game will be his... I assure you, and our part in it will not require any dangerous decision making, my friend."

*

Cromwell's approach to Framlingham is also being watched by another. Father George Constantine is holding the head of his horse, whilst concealed in a copse of woodland. Since early childhood, he has been afraid of everything, and he is no better now. The plot is coming apart, and he knows he cannot get to the duchess, and collect Fugger's precious Angels.

When taken by Sir Thomas More, eight months before, it was the fear of losing his own life that made him confess, and so consign two innocent men to the stake. Then, under threat of the stake, he allowed himself to name another man, Stephen Vaughan, whom he had never even met. Once started, it is hard for a coward to stop his mouth, he thinks.

There is only one thing to do now, and it is that which comes naturally to one of his weak nature. He must mount his horse, and gallop away, for dear life. By the time Elizabeth Howard is broken, and the plot revealed, he can be on a fishing boat, and seeking refuge in France, or Flanders.

Once he decides to abandon his mission, and let his confederates be taken, he feels better. There is nothing more precious than a human life, and George Constantine will do anything in his power to preserve his own. Let the duchess be damned, and may her precious Keeper of the Angels make his own way out of trouble.

13   Understandings

"What is it, Charles?" Henry calls from the heavily laden breakfast table. "Come and eat something, before we get off after our sport."

Charles Brandon, Duke of Suffolk, and the king's childhood friend, is undecided as to what to do. A messenger has come, with an urgent despatch for Henry, and he has him at the door. Under any other circumstances, he would take the sealed letter, and toss it to one side, unwilling to bother the king before a stag hunt.

"A moment, Hal," he calls, with a good humoured smile on his face. "Lay into the eggs, and I will soon catch you up."

"Ho!" Henry is in a good mood, and senses a sporting proposition. "I wager ten pounds that I can eat more than you!"

God help us, Brandon thinks, must he be ever thus? Always there must be a game, or a wager, to keep his royal attention, and a string of bawdy humorous stories to lift his spirits. Nothing should get in the way of a fun packed day, on pain of Henry's displeasure. He cannot turn the message aside, however, because the bearer is in Cromwell livery, and to do so will insult a man who owns his very soul. Now the king must win another foolish wager.

"You're on," he says, heartily. He takes the sealed letter, and dismisses the messenger with a curt nod of his head. "Boiled, coddled, or raw?"

"Raw?" Henry is amused by the prospect of this, and wonders why anyone might do such a thing.

"Marvellous for too much wine, sire," Charles Brandon explains. "Though can one *ever* drink *too* much wine?"

"Well said, old fellow. See, here are some soft boiled eggs in mustard sauce ... let us begin."

The Duke of Suffolk, second most powerful noble in England sits, and spoons an entire egg into his mouth. Henry whoops in delight, and follows suit. They repeat the performance another five times, until Charles judges the time right to concede defeat. He raises the sixth egg to his mouth, pauses, then shakes his head.

"A draw, Hal," he says. "Unless you can manage one more?"

"You doubt me?" Henry says, and pops a sixth egg into his mouth. He hardly chews, then swallows it down. "Ten pounds, you rascal. Pay up, or must you go borrowing off Master Cromwell?"

"He is a most amenable fellow," Charles says. "Please, never cut his head off, sire, else we will all be stuck for a few shillings in our purses. Cromwell is a wonderful conjurer, and can turn anything he touches into money. I almost forgot ... he sends a message."

"I am going hunting, Charles," Henry says. "Will it not wait until we have our stag at bay?"

"Of course," Charles Brandon replies, tossing it onto the table. "Though I have never known the man waste your time with nonsense."

"You think it important then?" Henry is hooked. His Privy Councillor does not waste time on fripperies, and any message from him is usually well worth reading.

"Cromwell does," Brandon says, covering himself from blame. "Perhaps it explains why he has left London."

"What, my blacksmith has left me?" Henry likes to know where his principal ministers are at all times, and worries when one is up to something without his knowledge. "Why did he not tell me?"

"Mayhap he has," Brandon says, nudging the sealed message. "All you need to know might be within."

"If I open it," Henry says, darkly. "It might ruin the hunt."

"Or bring something of the very greatest importance to your immediate attention, Hal," Suffolk says, climbing down from the fence at last. "Cromwell rode off with his best young men about him, and he has a hundred more, armed with guns, scouring the eastern counties. Open it, sire, I beg you .. if only for duty's sake."

"Yes, duty," Henry says, ripping open the wax seal, and opening the sheet of parchment. "The king must always do his royal duty. God's teeth!"

"What is it, Hal?" Brandon is unnerved by Henry's reaction to the contents.

"Where is Norfolk?" the king demands.

"He has lodgings in the city."

"Why is he not in court accommodation?" Henry does not understand why his most important lord is sleeping in a common house, outside of the court precincts.

"He has his tart with him," Brandon explains, "and does not wish to cause any offence. Her father is an under steward on one of Lady Anne's estates. To present her would be most inappropriate, and might well cause both ladies great distress."

"You mean Anne hates the girl?"

"No, sire, she enjoys the fact that Bess has displaced the duchess, whom she dislikes, but cannot accept her uncle's whore as an equal. So Norfolk swives her in a tavern. I fear he cannot leave the poor girl alone."

"Is she so comely?" Henry's curiosity is suddenly aroused.

"She is, sire, and a most accomplished lover."

"You rogue, Charles," Henry says, and chuckles.

"Not I, Hal, but that poetical tomcat, Tom Wyatt," Brandon replies, without thinking. "Why, he even wrote a saucy verse about humping her, before Norfolk ever got into the saddle."

"Master Wyatt again," Henry says, thoughtfully. "Still, that is for another time. Have Norfolk brought to me, at once. Master Cromwell is considering arresting his wife, and talks of treason against the state. He bids me keep the duke with me, so that he might not be unsupervised for the while."

"Then he does not suspect Tom Howard, and seeks to have him kept aside," Brandon says. "What can Elizabeth Howard be up to? A mere woman can hardly …"

"Let us not dwell on the matter," Henry says, reading the remainder of the message. "After Norfolk is secured, you must take some trusted men, and go to the Tower. Master Cromwell says we are to detain certain people, if they be there. Here, see their names?"

The Duke of Suffolk takes the proffered letter, and reads where the king indicates. His eyes widen in surprise as he recognises several names.

"These people are all your loyal servants, sire," he says. "Why, one of them is even married to a cousin of mine, and as for Sir Ragnar Delabord, why he is closely related to …"

"Elizabeth Howard," Henry says, his suspicions now fully aroused. "To business, Charles, and let us take heed of what Master Cromwell tells us. At least the stag will be happy for, it seems, he will live to fight another day."

"What men shall I use, sire?" Suffolk asks. "The duke's troops currently garrison the city gates. I doubt they would answer to me."

"Use my own guards," Henry replies. "For if they are disloyal… who can I trust?"

*

Tom Howard is still dressing when they come for him. He is commanded to come along by a thick set sergeant at arms, who has a half dozen armed men at his back. The duke is speechless with shock, and leaves his young mistress, Bess Holland, sprawled naked in bed. To the delight of the crowd already milling about Whitehall, the duke is marched to the king, flanked by stone faced soldiers of the court guard.

"What ho, Your lordship," a nameless voice calls out from the tumult. "Have you lost your new whore already?"

"Better lose the whore, than your head," a woman cries, and there is a burst of laughter.

"By God, sergeant, send your men into this mob, and crack their heads open for me," Norfolk demands, but he is ignored. "You filthy scum. I shall have you all flogged for your insolence!"

"Let's wait to see what Bluff Hal wants you for first," another wag calls. For such an unusual action to take pace, they are sure that Norfolk has fallen from grace, and that his head will soon adorn a spike on the city walls.

Norfolk is marched into Whitehall Palace, and

escorted right up to Henry's inner chamber. The doors swing open, and he is ushered inside. The king is stooped over a table, studying some documents. He looks up as the doors open, and smiles, broadly at his visitor.

"Ah, there you are, Thomas," he says, his face a picture of happy innocence. "I have the new land reformation documents, freshly delivered from Tom Cromwell, and wish to discuss the finer points with you. Is not Mistress Bess with you?"

"Your Highness, forgive me," Norfolk says, bowing low. "I was not asked to bring her."

"I see. Perhaps that is for the best," the king replies, "though Charles tells me she is a beautiful, and most *spirited* young thing."

"She suits me well, sire."

"And a few others too, I hear." The king smiles at Norfolk's obvious discomfort. "You will dine with me tonight, My Lord Norfolk… and bring Mistress Bess along with you. Lady Anne is down at Hampton Court, and will be none the wiser for it."

"Sire, my Bess is not yet fit to be presented at court," Norfolk says. He knows the king well, and realises that he is being invited to lend out his mistress for the night.

"Oh, I am sure she is well acquainted with the company of gentlemen, Thomas," Henry replies, tartly. "I shall put it to the test, and let you have my considered opinion. If the girl pleases me, I might make her into a lady in waiting. Then you can dally in court with her as you wish, and spend the rest of your time with your *lawful* wife, sir."

"We no longer live together, sire." Norfolk is affronted, but suspects there is more to this than is first obvious. "She remains in the country."

"Perhaps that is why you do not know what she gets up to at her leisure, Norfolk." Henry remains calm, and the effect is quite chilling. "I expect you to come to a more cordial understanding with the duchess. I cannot have my nobles running off with shilling whores at the drop of a hat."

"Bess is no whore, sire!" Norfolk flares, before he can control his temper.

"No, sir?" Henry asks. "Then I suggest you speak with Thomas Wyatt, should he ever appear in court again, for he seems to have taught your sweet love most of her tricks."

"Thomas Wyatt is infamous for his disgraceful debauches," Norfolk replies, coldly. "There are few ladies in court who he has *not* tried."

"Take care, Tom Howard," Henry growls, as he perceives the insult, "for once aroused, I am a dangerous man to bait."

"What?" Norfolk realises his error, and tries to retract his thoughtless words. "I mean no inference about my niece, sire. The girl is as different from her sister as can be. She will make you a fine queen. Our two bloodlines will produce a dynasty that will last a thousand years. When I am long gone, men shall still call you the 'father of kings'."

"You believe so?" Henry says, tugging at a stray red hair in his side whiskers. "Anne will give me sons then?"

"Why not?" Tom Howard affects an intimates voice. "You certainly know how to sire a boy. The evidence walks amongst us, does he not?"

"Young Harry is my joy," the king replies. "I pray he soon has a little brother to bounce on his knee."

"Amen," the duke says, relieved that he seems out of immediate danger. "Now, how can I help you in your task, Henry?"

"Thomas Cromwell's plans are far too clever for me, Uncle Norfolk," Henry tells the older man, and uses the pet name to calm him further. "He seems to want us to give *my* land away to .... well, to my subjects."

"What, give land to the lower orders?" Norfolk is dismayed.

"Yes, he claims that it will easily increase my wealth, almost four fold," Henry continues. "A small landowner works harder for himself, and that means we get more in tax. Does that seem right?"

"Give me an army, and point me in the right direction, sire, and I'm your man," the Duke of Norfolk confesses. "But this finance is a mystery to me. Old Archbishop Wolsey was your man for that."

"Ah, Wolsey," the king sighs. "Did I ever tell you that I was about to pardon him, and forgive his transgressions?"

"Yes, Hal. The world knows you loved the man well... but sometimes, duty comes before friendship."

"That applies equally to a man's duty to a wife, before his friendly mistress," Henry says.

"Consider me reprimanded," Tom Howard replies. "From now on, I shall have to keep two stables running."

Good, the king thinks, providing the duchess survives Master Cromwell's careful attentions.

*

"Thanks be to God," Will Draper says, as

Cromwell strides in, covered in dust. "Here, sir, drink some wine, and rest yourself."

"There is not the time," Cromwell replies. "Tell me what you know … not what you might think, Will."

"There was an attempt to release Katherine," Will starts. "We foiled it, and took prisoners. They were all Catholic gentlemen, sworn to make the plot work."

"Fools," Cromwell mutters. "They could never succeed."

"We learned that the priest, George Constantine, had left the troop earlier, and rode away. Thanks to some oranges, we were able to establish the involvement of the duchess."

"Oranges?" Cromwell asks, then holds up a hand. "No, the details can wait until later. So, you came to Framlingham Castle?"

"We did, sir, hoping to overtake the preacher. Instead we found Stephen Vaughan, cruelly beaten, and almost dead. He spoke but a few words, about angels."

"Angels?" Cromwell's face lights up. The threads are coming together, and he is close to knowing the whole, tawdry thing. "Does he still live?"

"He is in Ipswich, and still alive, as far as we know," Richard puts in. "We guessed he was spying on Norfolk."

"No guesses, nephew," Cromwell replies. "It often leads to wrong conclusions. The Duke of Norfolk may be guilty of many things, but not high treason. I take it that you have Constantine in your power?"

"No, sir." Will is uneasy, and hates letting his benefactor down. "I fear he is long gone."

"Then you have the duchess?"

"We do," Richard says, loudly. "Will caught her playing with her steward. She claims rape."

"Then, because she is a great lady, we must accept what she says," Cromwell explains. "Is the man taken?"

"Locked in the cellar," Will tells him. "He is the same man who tried to kill Stephen."

"Then we do not need to trouble the law courts," Thomas Cromwell decides. "The man is guilty of enough to warrant the action, and him airing his love life in public will do him no good. As a Privy Councillor, I am empowered to act as judge in such cases. Guilty, as charged. Richard, take him out to the main gate, and hang him from it."

"Yes, uncle." Richard hovers, unsure if he is to stay, or go.

"*Now*, boy," Cromwell says. "Make it quick, and do not let him dangle overly long. I never like to see the birds pecking at a dead man's eyes. It is not dignified." Richard bows, and retires to carry out the arbitrary sentence. "Now, what of the lady?"

"I can get nothing from her, master," Will confesses. "She knows I cannot beat her, or throw her into a deep dungeon, without risking the king's wrath. So, she smiles prettily at us, and denies everything, save that her steward was about to rape her, when we turned up, and saved the day."

"A clever woman," Cromwell says. "She will hold her tongue, and hope to come to an understanding. The rape, we must believe … you witnessed it, in part."

"She was on her knees, and seemed very willing," Will protests.

"She gives in, hoping the fiend will spare her poor life," Cromwell says what her lawyer will say, and shrugs. "Both Henry, and Tom Howard, will believe every word of such a tale. They are gullible, and wish only to think the best. I am more pragmatic, and seek only the truth of certain things that threaten the state."

"She will say nothing about her involvement with Constantine, and stares blankly if we question her about her oranges." Will sounds, and feels foolish. Twice he mentions oranges, and Cromwell smiles, and shakes his head.

"Forget these oranges, my boy," he says. "It is for *Angels* that I come so far from home. Fetch the woman to me, and I will bring forth the truth, and her part in it all."

*

Richard Cromwell cannot coax the steward, Dallard, to stand like a man. The wretched fellow is quite undone at the prospect of hanging, and clings to the big man's legs, imploring him for mercy.

"Get up, and face it like a man," Richard growls, and catches him by the ruff of his shirt. "Your pleas cannot move me. Master Cromwell is arbiter here, and considers you guilty of attempted murder, attempted rape, and attempted treason. So many attempts, and so many failures doom you, Dallard."

The man manages to stagger up, but still clings to Richard, as if he were a raft on a stormy sea. Then a glint of an idea comes into his head, and he tries a final gamble. A single throw of the dice, that may yet save his poor life for him.

"Spare me hanging, good sir, and I will prove the duchess's treason," he says. "I am but a casual victim of her wicked plotting." Richard pauses, and considers for a moment. The man claims he can show Elizabeth Howard to be guilty, and that might well save some time.

"Convince me of what you say, and I shall spare you from being hanged," he offers.

"She has received letters from a foreigner. I cannot read the language, but the signature is that of someone called Anton Fugger," Dallard says. "Then there are drafts of letters, in French, or Latin, to that bastard Pope Clement, and one note to Katherine, warning her to be ready for flight."

"You lie." Men will say anything to avoid their own deaths, and Richard Cromwell must see the proof, rather than listen to tawdry tales, made up to gain a few moments of life.

"No, your fellow stole them from her chamber," Dallard confesses, "and I took them from him. I did not mean to hurt him overmuch. It was but a single tap to the head. You must believe me."

"Then you actually have these letters?" Richard Cromwell cannot believe his luck, and prays the man is not a liar.

"I do."

"Where?"

"Your promise, master?"

"If you have the things, I swear on my immortal soul that you shall not hang, and further than that … you shall have a full purse for your trouble." At this, the younger Cromwell takes a purse from his belt, and holds it up for examination.

"Bless you, sir," Dallard shudders at his close escape. "The letters are hidden under a bale of straw in the first stall to your left, as you come into the stable."

"All of them?"

"Yes … all of them."

Richard Cromwell nods his approval, and keeps

his word. He pushes the purse filled with silver into Dallard's eager hands. Then, with fearful ease, he grabs the man by the chin, and twists. There is a sharp cracking noise, and Dallard collapses to the floor.

"My word, sir," Richard says. "You have a purse, and you did not hang." He calls for a couple of men, and instructs them to take the body away. As they manhandle the corpse from the house, Elizabeth, Duchess of Norfolk is coming down the long sweep of the stairs. She raises a hand to her mouth, and stifles a gasp at the sight of her erstwhile ravisher's lifeless body.

"Is it so easy then?" she says, touching her own throat.

"Life is like a candle's flicker, caught in a draft," Richard sneers. "I can snuff out a great lady's flame as well as any."

"Did you enjoy my pigsty, Master Cromwell?"

"The lass was more wholesome than anything you have to offer," the big man replies. "The only difference betwixt you is the price, and at two shillings, she is worth a shilling more than you, madam. Now, I suggest you hurry along. My uncle awaits you, and he is in an unforgiving mood."

She is shown into the lavishly furnished library, where Thomas Cromwell sits by the hearth, with an open book balanced on his knees. It is a warm enough day, and so, there is no fire in the soot blackened grate. He stands, and bows, as if acknowledging her at court.

"My Lady, I trust you have not been ill treated, other than by the rogue, Dallard?"

"I cannot complain, sir," she replies. "Though Master Dallard is not so disposed."

"Ah, you have seen?" Thomas Cromwell purses

his lips. "A necessary death, if I am to prevent yours."

"Mine, my dear Master Cromwell?" Elizabeth smiles, and sits down in the next most comfortable chair. "Your fellow, Draper arrived before the rape was done. Other than that, I am what you see before you now. A wronged wife … a poor victim. Wait until Henry sees my tears, and offers me a consoling shoulder to cry upon. He might even wish to console me throughout the night. The king is still susceptible to a powdered bosom, and a pretty face."

"Which is exactly why you will not have the chance to meet with His Majesty," Tom Cromwell says. "He is far too soft hearted. No, a quick trial, here, and a swift end, I think."

"You bluff well, sir," the duchess says. "I am no steward, to be strangled, and thrown aside. I am born a Stafford … the beloved daughter of the Duke of Buckingham … descended from three kings."

"Buckingham died a traitor's death, madam," Cromwell replies, quietly. "Then again, one of those precious kings you claim descent from suffered the death of a sodomite. Impaled on a red hot poker, if I recall my history. You must tell me all you know about Constantine, madam."

"I do not know the man."

"Anton Fugger?"

"No, I am at a loss," the duchess says. "He sounds like some foreign rogue."

"Sir Ragnar Delabord?" Cromwell notes the flicker of concern that shows, then vanishes from her eyes. Ah, he thinks, she is wondering how much I know, and how much she can safely tell to save her neck. There is a knock, and Will Draper comes in, begging forgiveness for the intrusion.

"Richard has found these, sir," he says, and hands a sheaf of papers to Cromwell. The Privy Councillor needs only a quick perusal to understand the content. He nods, and turns an icy cold eye on his prey.

"One should never put anything dangerous in writing, madam," he says. "Failing that, you must not append your signature to such treasonable rubbish as this."

"I have never seen …"

"Enough!" The single word echoes from the wood lined walls, and abruptly silences Elizabeth Howard. "This is almost too much proof, madam. Now, I will ask my questions again … for one last time. Answer me straight, and I will see if I can keep your head on your shoulders. Do you know George Constantine?"

"No, I knew only the name."

"In what context?"

"He was to come to me, here, and collect something. He never came."

"Anton Fugger?"

"I met him in Bruges, last year," the duchess admits. "He sent me gifts, and entertained me, whilst Tom dallied with his latest little whore. I thought nothing of it at the time."

"Until he asked what you thought of Queen Katherine's sad plight," Cromwell says, drawing out the tale from her.

"Yes. He guessed I was a sympathiser to her cause, and suggested a way of me helping her."

"A rescue?"

"Yes."

"You knew it could not work."

"I thought it might," Elizabeth tells him. "Then,

he drew me into his net. Before I realised it, he knew everything about me, and how best to use the knowledge for his own ungodly ends."

"He found out about Ragnar Delabord, and saw his opportunity to damage England," Cromwell says. "Imagine, his pet duchess ... cousin to the Keeper of the Angels."

"Yes. I did not understand the significance, until Anton sent a man called Gomes to me. This Spaniard had me write a letter of introduction to Ragnar. Then, I do not know how, he brought my cousin over to Fugger's camp."

"So, there it is," Cromwell says. Will Draper is standing to one side, and does not understand what is going on. He knows that Elizabeth Howard is in the process of confessing, but has no idea what she is confessing to.

"I am still in the dark, sir," he says, and Thomas Cromwell explains, occasionally glancing at the duchess, as if seeking confirmation of this fact or that.

"We were looking for an invading army," Cromwell tells him. "A hundred thousand of the emperor's troops landing at Dover is hard to hide. Anton Fugger is no general ... he is a financier of kings, and a banker to Europe. How does a banker beat you? Why, by calling in a debt, or refusing a loan. Fugger saw his chance to ruin England financially, by using Sir Ragnar Delabord."

"Forgive me, but the name means nothing to me."

"I am not surprised. It is often the shadowy figures who are the most important," Cromwell explains. "Sir Ragnar is a devout Roman Catholic, as is his cousin, Lady Elizabeth. He has been convinced that England must be brought low, so that Henry returns to the Roman church. As Keeper of the Angels, he is in a unique position to cause this country the greatest harm."

"What are these Angels you speak of?"

"Forget any religious involvement, Will, and look to your own purse."

"What, you mean the coins?" The currency of England comes in denominations from a farthing, to a gold pound, and includes silver pennies, groats, sixpences, shillings, crowns, and the gold angel - a coin worth seven shillings and sixpence.

"Yes, the coin," Cromwell confirms. "The Angel is, after the penny, the most widely used coin in England, and is often the preferred currency demanded by foreign merchants. It is used to pay a craftsman's weekly wages, and is the price of a bale of raw wool. There are about eight hundred thousand of them in circulation, and they are the bedrock of our economy."

"And Sir Ragnar?"

"He is one of several gentlemen working in the Tower Mint, entrusted to be Keepers of the King's Moulds. Delabord's task is to attend to the striking moulds for Angels, and ensure they are always fit to use."

"How do you know this, sir?" Will asks.

"My young men found disturbing irregularities. Certain foreign merchants, and one French banking house, had started demanding payment in Ducats."

"But why?"

"Because Delabord was going to steal a set of the Angel moulds, and bring them to the duchess. She was to pass them to Constantine, who was to return to the continent with them. Once Fugger had a genuine set, he was going to start minting Angels, but with a much reduced gold content."

"How does this bring England low?" Will is not of a financial mind, and does not yet understand.

"Tens of thousands of fake Angel coins, flooding the market place," Cromwell says. "Then, he lets the cat out of the bag, and every merchant in England will know that the coins are, potentially worth less than the mint value. Trade will stop, almost over night, and business will only carry on where full weight golden Ducats are available."

"Then I might have found some fake coins in my purse?" Will shrugs.

"Imagine that on a grand scale, Will," Cromwell tells him. "What if the king cannot guarantee the worth of his coins. He is a bankrupt, and no one will deal with him. Only Spanish, or Venetian money will be held good. Instead of an Angel being worth a Ducat, men will demand two for one, because Fugger's coins have much less gold in them."

"But most of the coins will be good." Will thinks his argument a good one, but Cromwell shakes his head.

"Who will stand surety? How can you check every coin, every time it is spent? No, Will, our economy will be ruined. The king will be forced to mortgage his realm, just to keep it solvent, and the repayments will be crippling. Catholic bankers in Italy will demand high interest, and a return to Rome."

"Henry will not."

"He will have no choice," Cromwell says. "I have left orders for Delabord to be taken at the Tower, but if he is already on his way here, we must catch him, and regain the moulds. The Keeper of the Angels will go to the Tower, but under lock and key."

"What of Anton Fugger, and this Spaniard?"

"Without the moulds, there is no plot," Cromwell concludes. "Fugger cannot claim our money is debased, without showing it to be so. He will have to think of another scheme."

"Can we not simply change the mould?" Will asks with the simplicity of a soldiering man, whose lack of financial knowledge is all encompassing.

"And admit that every Angel in circulation might be a fake?" Cromwell shakes his head. "The moulds must never leave these shores."

"Then we must take Delabord," Will says. "He might still come to us here, but we must search the countryside too."

"Well, My Lady Norfolk?" the Privy Councillor asks. "Can you help us, or will you stay tight lipped?"

"I cannot," Elizabeth says. She is only now beginning to realise the scope of the Augsburg banker's plot. "Ragnar is due here at any time. If he suspects a trap, he might simply head for the coast, and slip across the channel."

"God help us if that is the case," Cromwell curses. "For if he eludes us, England may never recover."

"I have told you what I know, sir," the duchess says. "Do we have an understanding?"

"For whatever good it will do you, madam," Will says. "You sought to ruin your country, because of your husband's desire for a new woman. You should rot in Hell."

"And what of his guilt?" Elizabeth asks. "His foul adultery is more important to him, than his loyalty to the king. How will *he* avoid Hell, Master Cromwell?"

"Perhaps that is a fitting punishment for the both of you," Thomas Cromwell says, with a smile on his face. "That you should spend all eternity, together in the same hell?"

14   Conflict of Angels

The dull crack of a musket being discharged makes Will Draper order Thomas Cromwell, and the Duchess of Norfolk, to stay put. Then he spins on his heel, and strides out of the library.

"It comes from the gate," Richard says. "I have men on guard there." They run to the main gate, where one of the men is busy reloading his gun, whilst the other is aiming at a small copse of trees in the near distance.

"Riders, sir," the man reports.

"At least twenty, from the dust," the first man says. "I thought it best to rouse everyone to the danger with a shot."

"You did very well, Adam," Will Draper says to the young man. "Richard, get men onto the battlements, until we see what is afoot. How many are we?"

"Two dozen," Richard says. "Enough to ride out, and put these fellows to flight."

"No, have our lads keep down, out of sight. Let them think we are weak in numbers, until we wish otherwise."

"Fair enough, Will. Look, here comes one of their number now … to parley, I suppose." The lone rider comes on at a trot, and draws up, a dozen strides short of the dry moat. He sees the narrow bridge, and wonders if those within have enough men to stop a strong charge. He cannot see Rafe Sadler, Mush, and Tom Wyatt, crouching out of sight with most of their men.

"At your service, sir," the man says, bowing in the saddle. "My captain bids me demand entry to the castle."

"No."

"We have business with the duchess,"

"State it then." The man is well versed in what to say, as Jan Gruyer, his Dutch leader, expects this reply. He pretends to consider his words, whilst assessing the defences. The young mercenary can count only four or five armed men, and only two of them with muskets.

"Captain Jan Gruyer has a message for the duchess … from her devoted husband, the Duke of Norfolk, and it is of a delicate nature," the man says. "It is for her ears only. As a gentleman, you will understand this."

"I am no gentleman, sir," Will says. "I am a soldier. As for any message from Norfolk … you surprise me, for he is closeted away in Whitehall Palace with the king. Now, state your real business, or be off, before my fellow puts a musket ball into you."

"Very well. Captain Gruyer demands your immediate surrender, and free access to the duchess. He will not negotiate, and these terms are his final offer. Refuse, and I am instructed to say that no one will be spared."

"Then we are in for a fine scrap," Richard calls. "Let us hope your captain has a few cannon with him, or he is in for a sorry time of it. Will he fly over the battlements?"

"You jest, sir, when I predict your death?"

"Bugger off," Richard tells the astonished mercenary, "or I predict I will kick your scrawny little arse!"

The rider turns, and gallops back to the line of trees, where Captain Jan Gruyer, a veteran soldier of fortune, and leader of the mercenary band awaits. By his side is Sir Ragnar Delabord, who has just stumbled onto them, as he rides to Framlingham.

"What do they say, Lieutenant Thorpe?" the Dutchman asks.

"Their leader bids us leave," Thorpe replies. "His name is Will Draper, and he knows his fighting craft, very well."

"You know him?"

"He was in Ireland, as I was," Thorpe explains to his commander. "I never served under him, but I saw him at headquarters once."

"And you say he is a competent man?" the Dutchman asks.

"He knew how to kill Irish rebels well enough, or so I heard." Thorpe tells his commander.

"What of his strength?" the mercenary leader asks of his second in command.

"I saw only five of them. Two have muskets, and one is a great lump of a man, who does not know his manners. The moat is dry, but twenty feet wide, and easily as deep. Once go in there, and we will have nowhere to go. The only way in is straight over the bridge, and through the gate. It is a fixed structure, and cannot be drawn up."

"They will close the gate as soon as they see us riding at them." Jan Gruyer considers his various options. Once they do that, he can put his own men close up, and pour musket fire through the crossbars of the wooden gate. That will drive the defenders back, and give them time to chop their way in with axes. He tells his lieutenant this, and the young man nods his approval.

"We may take a few losses, if they put their muskets high up above, and fire down on us." Thorpe strokes his beard. "By the time we are through, they might kill four or five of us. The men will not be happy at that prospect, sir."

"Why must we get inside?" Delabord says, gruffly. "I have what we need, and we can be on a boat in hours. Leave my cousin Elizabeth to her own devices, sir. She is a cunning girl, and will win through."

Jan Gruyer casts a sharp look at the Keeper of the Angels, and has to remind himself to be wary of what he says. His orders are to bring the coin moulds back to Fugger, and leave no witnesses to complicate matters. Once the duchess, and her protectors are all dead, he is to kill Delabord too.

"Anton Fugger's orders," the Dutchman replies, evasively. "He wants the lady safe abroad. Perhaps he has developed a passion for her?"

"More fool him," Ragnar Delabord says. "She can be a shrew, when the mood is on her." He knows her quite well, having been related to the Stafford family. As a youth, he used to visit the Buckingham estates to hunt, and often saw the spoiled little girl having a tantrum. In later life, she has changed little, and can still drive a man mad with her looks, and her sharp tongue. "If your men are not up to it, Captain Gruyer…"

"Silence!" The mercenary is losing what scant patience he has, fast. With the coin moulds in his possession, he would prefer to ride for the coast, and take ship, but orders are orders, and he has yet to be paid his quite substantial fee. "We will take the castle, and be damned to it. Lieutenant Thorpe, let us be frugal with the lives of my valuable soldiers. This place must have more than one point of entry. Seek it out."

"There is the gate in the east wall," Ragnar

Delabord suggests. "As I recall, it is not that stout, and leads into the walled gardens. Once amongst the fruit trees, your men can work their way to the main gate from the rear … and do your worst."

"You are a strategist, Sir Ragnar," Gruyer says, nodding with satisfaction. "There then is our plan, Lieutenant Thorpe. I will take the best part of my men to this gate, and force entry. You will mount up six men, and gallop to and fro, at the main gate. Discharge your muskets, and make as if you are going to storm the place. They will defend the gate, and we will come upon them from behind. Yes?"

"A good plan, sir," Thorpe replies. He has been with the captain for almost two years, and fought several skirmishes in Flanders, and two of the Germanic states, against protestant reformist troops. Gruyer fights well, and knows how to win. "Might I suggest you withdraw to the far side of the woods, and proceed to this rear gate on foot. The ground is dry and hard, and your horses will kick up too much dust."

"Very well. Give us a half hour start, and commence your diversion," Gruyer says, then as an afterthought he adds. "Sir Ragnar will come with me." He knows that Thorpe will do his duty well, but does not trust him to kill either the Keeper of the Angels, or his shrewish cousin, the Duchess of Norfolk.

"You wish me to fight?" Sir Ragnar has served in Henry's army, and once fought in France, but he is a stout forty two year old man now, and no longer skilled with a sword, or pistol.

"No, I wish you to walk," Gruyer replies, testily. "We will do the killing, but you must be there to calm the lady. Has she many servants?"

"A couple of girls, I think," Ragnar replies,

remembering their willingness to please. "Oh, and a sly faced steward. Other than that ... nothing."

"Very well, we go!"

*

George Constantine cannot believe his good fortune. His horse, urged on at a gallop, has collapsed under him, and sent him sprawling to the ground. The grass is sparse, and the soil is of a sandy   feel. He staggers to his feet, and climbs the low dune to see the waters of the English channel lapping on the desolate shore.

Out in the bay, a sleek little skiff tacks, and turns towards the beach, and the preacher mutters a selfishly offered prayer of thanks for his safe deliverance. The boat is exactly as Anton Fugger's agent, Gomes, promises. In a few hours, he will be across the water, and free to hide from those who would seek him out.

True, he does not have the promised parcel to deliver, but that is hardly his fault. He frowns at the thought of not receiving the balance of his fee, but recalls the hundred pound advance, safe in the keeping of an Antwerp banking house. It will keep him in some comfort for a couple of years.

The skiff is manned by three men. One is at the tiller, a second is lowering the sail, and the third, a rough looking fellow with a beard, and a scar across his forehead, hails him.

"A fine day, sir," the man calls. "Do you hark to the song of the meadowlark?"

"And to the cry of the wild geese," Constantine replies, using the carefully memorised phrase.

"Then you are well met, sir. Though I was told

there might be others?"

"All taken up by the king's men," the preacher says, hurrying to the shore. As he comes alongside the skiff, he sees two men lying in the scuppers, their faces grimaced in death. He stops, and gulps in terror.

"As are you, Master Constantine," the scar faced fellow tells him. "Move, and I shall cut you down where you stand."

Constantine can feel tears of frustration running down his cheeks, and he weeps for himself, and knows he is in the worst trouble of his life.

"You are the king's men?" he asks, wondering if they might accept a bribe to let him slip away.

"I am Jethro Brent," the man says, laying a big hand on the preacher's shoulder. "Agent for Master Thomas Cromwell. It is he who bid me watch the coast. It was a simple matter to take these two, and make one of them talk. I almost pissed myself laughing when I had to '*hark to the bloody lark*'. Now, sir, you are in my custody, and will spend this night in a prison cell."

"Then I am to live?"

"I have no orders to kill you," Jethro Brent says, coldly, as if such an order were an everyday occurrence. "My master, Thomas Cromwell wants you kept alive … for now."

"Cromwell?" The preacher's eyes roll up into his head, and he slips to the ground in a dead faint.

"Gawd help us," one of the crew says, "and why do they always faint so, Master Brent?"

"True enough," Jethro Brent replies, "for were it me he were after, I would as like soil myself instead!"

They laugh, and haul the insensate preacher aboard the small craft, where he is tossed down onto the two dead seamen, who had been foolish enough to to work for the wrong side.

*

"Mush, secure the main gate," Will Draper says. "Pick four men, and have them give shot at any who venture too close. Richard, collect the rest of our lads, and follow me to the east wall."

"Where the orchard is planted?" Richard asks.

"It provides the best cover, once inside the wall," Will explains, "and I cannot believe there is no gate to the outside. These men are trained soldiers, and will think to look. If they find it, they will force an entry, and come on us from behind."

"I see. Then we will give them a most hot welcome," Richard replies. He has twenty men at his disposal, and a dozen have muskets. "Are you sure of this, my friend?"

"Hell, no," says Will with a grin, "but battles are won, and lost, this way. Fail to guard our rear, and we are sure to get the worst of things. If they do not come from the rear, then we will rush back, and fight them to our front."

"Then let us get to it," the big man replies, drawing his sword. "God spare us, Will … and let us be about the Devil's work!"

*

The gate is old, and made of a few oak planks, clout-nailed roughly onto a willow frame. It is the height of a small man, and only wide enough to admit one at a time. The Dutch mercenary signals for his best sergeant to try the latch, and he is surprised to find that the rear entry way is left unlocked. Sergeant Scottus pushes the gate back, and slips inside the high walled garden. Gruyer lets two more men go next, then follows, when there is no immediate sound of fighting. He places a hand to his lips, ordering those that follow him to keep silent, and ushers them all within.

Once all fifteen are accounted for, he signals for them to move through the closely ranked fruit trees, towards the main building. There is a movement ahead, and a branch cracks under a boot. Gruyer realises his approach is expected, but has no time to shout out any orders.

One of his men, keener eyed than the rest, sees a man ahead, kneeling into a firing position, and raises his own musket. The shot cracks out, and all Hell breaks loose, as almost thirty muskets spit fire at one another. The man to Gruyer's left grasps his throat, and falls, spitting blood to the ground, and another to his right takes a lead ball in the knee, and tumbles over, screaming in pain.

The Dutchman knows there is but a moment to act, and runs forward, sword in hand. His men drop their now useless muskets, draw blades, and follow their captain. A great bear of a man suddenly comes out of the trees, yelling, and barrels into two of Gruyer's men, slicing one down, and driving his fist into another's face.

The Dutchman parries a murderous cut from one of the defenders, and stabs at him. The young man cries out in agony, and drops his sword. Jan Gruyer finishes him off with a second thrust, and turns about to face the next man. All about him, men are being hacked and smashed at, and a dozen broken bodies already strew the earth. Then the noise of battle ends, as soon as it began, and men stand, panting with bloodlust, and wondering what will happen next.

*

Will Draper sees how his muskets have devastated the enemy, cutting down a third of them, and he urges his men to the attack. Richard is already there, beating man after man down with his sword, and delivering a killer blow. To his left, Tom Wyatt is deftly parrying and thrusting, driving his opponent back, until he stumbles, and begs for quarter.

Then it is almost done. The invaders are all either dead, wounded or taken, save for their leader, who sees Will, and comes straight at him. Gruyer thinks that in killing him, he might yet turn the tide. His first cut whistles past the Englishman's ear.

Will dances back, parries a second thrust, and steadies himself to go on the offensive. He feints, and drives in for the kill. It is a trick he has used a dozen times, but he finds his opponent has guessed, and danced away. Gruyer is on Draper's blind side, and has only to thrust into his unguarded flank.

It is then that Richard Cromwell steps forward, and lands a crushing blow with his fist. The Dutchman staggers sideways, and drops his sword. Will regains his composure, and puts the point of his own weapon to the man's throat.

"Yield, sir," he says. "It is over, and you are my prisoner."

"I see I am at a disadvantage," Gruyer replies, spitting blood from a split lip. "Will you give quarter to my men and I?"

"Gladly, sir," Will tells him. "Honourable terms

for honourable men."

"Then we surrender to you, Captain Draper."

"You know me?"

"My officer does, and would that I had paid more attention to him. He thinks you to be a fine soldier."

"I regret the loss of so many of your men, sir," Will says. "Though you have killed two of my own."

"*C'est la guerre*, my friend," Gruyer says. "It is the best way to go … sword in hand."

One of Will's men has gone to make sure there are no more lurking outside, and comes back with Sir Ragnar Delabord at the point of his sword.

"Another one here, Captain Will," young Adam calls.

"I am the king's man," Delabord blusters. "I serve him within the Tower of London. You must not offer me violence!"

"Ah, the Keeper of Angels," Will says. "Come along with me sir, Master Cromwell will wish to speak with you."

*

"So much trouble, for such insignificant things," Thomas Cromwell says, as he examines the coin moulds. "If these had reached Anton Fugger's minters, England would have bene flooded with debased coinage."

"Then we have done a good day's work," Will says. "Delabord, Gruyer and his few surviving men are locked up, and the duchess is in your power."

"Now comes the awkward part," Cromwell says. "Will, I must ask you to escort Lady Elizabeth back to her husband in London. I shall give you a letter for the king."

"Will she lose her head?" Will does not like the idea that he might have, in some way, brought about her death.

"No, she will not. I will ask the king to force Norfolk back into her life. His slut can take a cottage, and wait for his attentions. I do not think a public trial will do any good."

"And the others?" Will has an affinity towards Gruyer and his mercenaries, and he wishes to put in a word for them.

"Exile, I think." Cromwell sighs. "Such a waste of fine fighting men, eh?"

"Then I will set off at once, sir."

"Excellent. Once the duchess is in London, you must take a few days off, and retrieve your wife from darkest Cambridgeshire. I think she will be missing you. Take Tom Wyatt with you, for I do not yet think him safe in London. He still has far too much love for a certain lady, whom we both know, my friend."

"His wits are addled," Will replies. "I shall have him put his sad longings into verse."

"God forbid!" Cromwell laughs then. "I would rather hear about 'moon' and 'June' conjoined with 'dove' and 'love'. It would not be as sickening."

"Yes, God save us from poets."

*

It is only when Will, Mush, Elizabeth Howard, and an escort of Cromwell's best men are on the London Road, that the Privy Councillor sends for his young nephew, Richard.

"Uncle?" Richard is not the cleverest of

Cromwell's young men, but he is amongst the most loyal. "What can I do for you?"

"I have a problem, nephew," Thomas Cromwell says. "Will has placed me in a quandary. He has given quarter to Gruyer and his men, and would have me give them all parole."

"Is that a bad thing, sir?"

"Not for me, but it is for England, my boy." Cromwell sighs, and thinks of how history will paint him to be such a villain for what he must do. "Delabord is a traitor, and the others know about the plot. I know it has failed, but they might spread enough rumour to still cause damage to us. You see what must happen?"

"Yet, the duchess can live?" Richard asks, sensing the innate injustice of it.

"She is a noble," Cromwell says, "and that excuses her much in this world. A better time will come, when all are equal."

"Utopia, Uncle Thomas?"

"Perhaps, but not in our lifetime."

"Or in theirs," Richard replies. There will be no written orders, or court records for posterity, he thinks, just some unmarked graves in a Suffolk meadow. "Will Draper will not be happy. He will hate us for it."

"It was his word given, not mine," Cromwell replies, sharply. "I am the king's man, and cannot allow sentiment to cloud my better judgement. Let it be as quick as possible, so that they might not suffer unduly."

"Yes, uncle." Richard pauses in the door. "What of George Constantine, now we have him … is he to die also?"

"No, he must live," Cromwell says. "I have a use for him."

"He betrayed his friends, and almost had Stephen

Vaughan burnt as a heretic, uncle," Richard argues. "Surely, the rogue must die, for is he not the most guilty of them all?"

"Constantine is consistent," Cromwell tells his nephew. "He can be relied on to betray anyone to save his own skin. Once I convince him to fear me more than any other, I will have the man's very soul in my hands."

"Let me kill him." The younger Cromwell cannot see beyond the next action, and has no idea what his uncle is planning. The older man loves his nephew dearly, but wishes he might posses even a modicum of forward thinking. He takes a deep breath, and explains.

"We have thwarted a plot against the king, have we not?"

"Yes, uncle."

"To do so, I am forced to put hundreds of men out into the city, and across three counties."

"Yes."

"Each man must be paid, given a horse, fed, and rewarded afterwards," Thomas Cromwell says. "Rafe … come here … have you a tally yet?" Rafe Sadler, who is ever in a corner, waiting on his master, produces a thin ledger, and consults it.

"I have yet to reckon a full account, sir," he says, apologetically, "but to date you have expended seven hundred and eighty three pounds, eleven shillings, and four pence. I expect the final amount to reach a thousand."

"And my profit?"

"We have twenty-two horses taken from Gruyer's men, their purses, and the worth of their weaponry." Rafe Sadler does a swift mental calculation. "Allowing for the depressed market in muskets and horseflesh, I think we might recoup around two hundred and forty pounds … give or take the odd Angel."

"When I tell the king, what will he give me, Rafe?"

"His gratitude."

"Then I am eight hundred sovereigns out of pocket," Thomas Cromwell says, shaking his head. "Do you see, boy?"

"You have lost a fortune," Richard says, awareness finally dawning.

"And must make it good," Cromwell concludes. "George Constantine will help us, and in return … he might just survive."

"And Jan Gruyer and his men?"

"They must hang," Cromwell says. "See to it, my boy… for your old uncle's sake."

15   A Time to Pay

"I am sorry to see you and Mistress Miriam leave us, Captain Draper," Rob Buffery says. "It has been a pleasure talking with another military man, these last few days. I sometimes miss the thrill of battle." The retired sergeant, now a well respected inn keeper, will miss the company, and has enjoyed hearing Will's carefully censored account of his recent adventures in Suffolk.

"I am sure Miriam and I will have need to call frequently, Rob," Will replies, as he tightens his horses girth. His stay has been a pleasant one, and he is just a little ashamed to have suspected the man because of the name of his inn. In hindsight, he is surprised that he did not think of Gold Angels in the first place.

"God keep you, and your's, Master Buffery" Miriam Draper says, climbing up onto one of the carts seats.

"And may he protect you ... and your's, mistress," the old soldier replies, giving her a pointed look. Miriam colours slightly, and drops her voice to a whisper.

"You can tell, sir?" she asks. Rob Buffery smiles up at her, and shakes his head.

"Not I. The wife knew right away though. Does Captain Draper know?"

"Not yet," Miriam replies. "In truth, I was not yet sure myself."

"Then he is in for a pleasant surprise," Rob replies. "May your first born be a fine son, mistress."

"May it be healthy, whatever comes," Miriam tells him. The pain of her earlier miscarriage is still with her, and she hopes that this new child will fare better.

"What are you two whispering about?" Will calls over. "Not trying to sell the poor man more wine and cheese, I hope, my love?"

"Leave her be," the old soldier calls back, winking at the girl. "Soon enough, you will be praising her for making a fine delivery!"

*

"Damn your eyes, Norfolk!" Henry slams the parchment down on the desk. "Have you no idea about this new tax structure?"

Norfolk dips his head, and has no answer. He is fresh from a screaming row with his newly restored wife, and is a thoroughly chastised man. He tries to divert blame.

"Thomas Cromwell is your legal man, sire," the duke says, slyly. "Should the Blacksmith's boy not be here, explaining it to you?"

"And if he were to drop dead with the pox whilst on his way?" the king replies, sharply. "Who then will guide me?"

"There are other lawyers."

"None as fine as Cromwell."

"Sire, you say that of Wolsey." The words are out before Norfolk has thought them through, and he almost chokes at his own stupidity.

"Yes, and who was it who advised me to have him arrested, my dear Norfolk?" Henry is working up into a fine rage. "Why, it was you, as I recall. Then, when I realised *your* error… and just as I was about to forgive him … he dies on me."

"I was but one of many, sire," the Duke of

Norfolk replies. "You will recall that it was that scoundrel, Harry Percy, who rushed off and arrested him, so abruptly. Percy was the prime mover, with ..."

"With whom?" the king demands. "Tell me no names sir, for I am of a mind to shorten the list of my enemies, and that will be most unfortunate!"

"With a grudge against the poor man ... I was about to say, Your Majesty." Norfolk clutches at one of the many talismans he has secreted about his person, and prays for some calm. Where is Cromwell, he thinks, and what the devil is the man doing, showing Henry such inflammatory stuff. "Might I read these new laws again, sire, and try to unravel them?"

"Why bother," Henry says, with an air of defeat. "The fellow is as clever as Cardinal Wolsey ever was. Did I ever tell you, Norfolk, of how I was just about to pardon the man?"

"You have mentioned it, sire," Norfolk says, and has a sudden idea. Not being a thinking sort of a fellow, he blurts it out without a moment's consideration. "As for Harry Percy, you should show your disapproval in a way that will hurt him most."

"Would you have me do to him, as I did to Buckingham?" the king asks, narrowing his eyes, and frowning.

"Buckingham was a wicked traitor, sire," Norfolk replies. "Harry Percy is just a malicious young fool. Hit him hard, in the purse. Levy a tax on him that will make him squeal."

"Such as?" Henry asks.

"Have Cromwell think one up," Norfolk says with all the malice he can muster. "When he finally turns up."

"Yes... where is he?" Henry asks, and the duke

simply shrugs his shoulders. Who knows the workings of a blacksmith's lad's mind?

*

"Are you feeling any better, sir?" Rafe Sadler asks his benefactor. "It was a rather rough crossing, for the start of June."

"I do so hate sea voyages," Tom Cromwell replies, dabbing at his lips with a linen cloth. "I have never had so empty a stomach. Are we safe in harbour now, Rafe?"

"Docked, and tied up fore and aft," Rafe informs him. Richard and Mush are already ashore, seeking out the best lodgings for us all."

"Have they enough money?"

"They have, sir … for everything." Rafe is pleased to find himself free of the debilitating sea sickness that often attends channel crossings, and has been busy making arrangements. "I have been into Calais, and found a stable that can provide enough good horses. The owner, an Englishman, can even loan us a sturdy cart … should it be needed."

"Can we depend on his silence?"

"Mush put the point of a dagger up one of his nostrils, just to confirm the need for secrecy. The man does not know who we are, and cares not, thanks to the generous price I paid."

"Not too much, I hope," Thomas Cromwell replies. "Pay a rogue too much, and he will grow curious."

"Trust me, sir," Rafe Sadler says. "You have taught me well, these last few years."

"I see that." Cromwell loves the young man like a

son, and is pleased with all he does. Still only twenty-five, Rafe is a successful lawyer, and is becoming a man with a noted political mind. "What are you worth now?"

"It is all yours, master, if you need it," Rafe Sadler replies, without a moment's hesitation. "Every penny I have is because of your patronage, and it is yours… if …"

"A pretty compliment, my boy, but I asked you 'how much'."

"I am earning about three thousand a year," he admits, "and have some savings… which amount to a goodly sum."

"Twenty-six thousand pounds," Cromwell says, and watches Rafe's surprised look. "You bank with Blackshaw in the city, who has dealings with the Lombard, Celli, in Paris. His nephew is married to Bartelli's youngest daughter in Milan, who is friendly with the Doge, Andreas Gritti. Andreas listens to all the gossip, and writes letters to his friends."

"Then I am undone, for I thought my affairs safe from prying eyes," Rafe says, a little discomfited.

"Every penny you have was honestly earned," Cromwell tells him. "In all these years, you have not stolen a single groat from me, or misused my good name in any way. This, my boy, I know."

"Then you know I love you, as a father, and what is mine, is yours."

"I do not want your money, Rafe." Cromwell sighs heavily. He has to tell his protégé something that will change the dynamics between them, for ever more. Rafe nods, and smiles like a mischievous little child.

"That is good news, sir, for I am just about to buy a plot of land in Hackney. It is in the heart of the village, yet still only a three mile ride into the city."

"Why?"

"To build a house on, master," Rafe says, and his face lights up with ambition and pride. "It will be almost as grand as Austin Friars, and I shall build it with bricks ... not timber and wattle."

"Why, I ask again." Cromwell must have the reason from Rafe's own lips.

"I wish to marry."

"Ah, then it is serious?"

"The lady has consented to marry me," Rafe says, but he expects opposition. The young woman, a servant at Austin Friars, has been married once before, and has children. "Mistress Barré is of good repute, and will make a fine wife, sir."

"She will, Rafe, but not yet." Cromwell sees he must explain matters to the love smitten young man, and indicate the course his life must take. "Ellen's husband may not be dead. Though it is believed that he lies in his grave in Ireland, there is no proof. We must make diligent enquiries, before you can marry."

"I have it from a man in Braintree that Matthew Barré is long dead. Why else is nothing heard of him?"

"We must make proper, legal enquiries," Thomas Cromwell insists. "Once we know for sure, I can petition the king, and ask for his dispensation for you to wed your love. A year, or eighteen months, will suffice."

"Sir, we wish to be together."

"Of course. You will carry on living at Austin Friars, and Ellen can remain as a servant. Discretion now will help when I ask Henry for the favour."

"Can he do this for us?" Rafe asks, warily.

"He can, as head of the English church,"

Cromwell explains. "As such, the King of England is all powerful."

"Let us hope he takes wise council."

"Indeed. That brings me to a more urgent matter," Cromwell says, and must compose himself for what he must impart.

"What is it, master?" Rafe is worried, for Cromwell never hesitates.

"You must leave my service."

"Never!"

"You must, Rafe. The king has noticed you, and wants you to enter into his service."

"Why me?"

"You are one of the sharpest minds in England, Rafe," Cromwell says. "Henry wants you, and that is that. Stay with us, of course, until your brick house is finished … then move, and take your lovely Ellen with you. Once you can marry, take her to wife, and live long, and happily."

"But master," Rafe has tears in his eyes. "Might I not still work for you?"

"Not openly. Norfolk will whisper in Henry's ear, and your career will suffer. From now on, we must remain friends … and talk to one another, but only in a casual way."

"You are not happy with the arrangement, I can tell."

"It is Henry's wish. Join him, and we will help rule England for him," Cromwell concludes. "Now, who do we have for the task in hand?"

"Mush was first to volunteer, of course," Rafe replies. "Then Richard and Barnaby have dragged along poor Hans Holbein. Tom Wyatt wished to stay in London, but his verses, and proximity to Anne Boleyn has come under scrutiny again. Rather than end up in the Tower, he threw his lot in with us."

"What news of the Bishop of Winchester?"

"Stephen Gardiner landed in Calais yesterday, and is already on his way to Bruges."

"I sincerely hope he understands his part in all this." Thomas Cromwell, like all great thinkers, often considers things too deeply, and he is in danger of finding fault, where none lies. "I preferred the man as a friend, and wish, with all my heart, that Henry might not have elevated him so high."

"Henry calls his ministers his angels, or his falcons, as the mood takes him," Rafe says. "Sir Thomas's wings are clipped, and Gardiner can easily go the same way. He will not fail you, sir, for like George Constantine, he fears you greatly."

"I would rather rule men with love, than with fear," says Cromwell. "Though, if they cannot love me … I suppose they must fear me."

"Perhaps you should have stayed in London, master." Rafe knows there is an element of danger in their escapade, and does not want his benefactor put at risk.

"Bugger that!" Cromwell wipes his mouth, and struggles to his feet. The boat is swaying slightly, and he wants to get ashore, if only to still his heaving stomach. "I have fought battles, and killed men, before you were born, my boy. Let us get to it, and damn the danger!"

"At your service," Rafe Sadler says, but vows to keep the old man safe. A stout man in his forties should not be wearing a sword, and ready to fight for that which he most wants … the utter defeat of Anton Fugger.

*

"Good of you to see me, Your Eminence," Alessandro Gomes says, kissing the English bishop's ring. "I hope your visit to Bruges proves to be a great success."

Stephen Gardiner, Bishop of Winchester, smiles, and, raising two fingers, he blesses Alessandro Gomes. The Spaniard notes his behaviour, and thinks to himself that here is a true Catholic soul, and not a pawn of the protestant English king.

"I, and my dear friend, are here on a private matter," the bishop replies, softly. The tall, handsome gentleman by his side bows, and introduces himself.

"I am Thomas Wyatt, late of the king's diplomatic service, sir." Wyatt bows, and touches a finger to his lips. "Henry thinks me too clever a poet, and mis-likes my ardent ways."

"Ah, Master Wyatt, I know of you," Gomes says. "Is it true that you have slept with every one of your king's ladies in waiting?"

"Only the pretty ones, Captain Gomes," Wyatt replies, and winks at the astonished Spaniard. "You should visit Henry's court, sir. With your dark looks, I dare say several ladies will wish to make your *close* acquaintance."

"I regret, my duties keep me here, close to my master."

"Do you mean the Emperor Charles, or the banker … Anton Fugger?" Stephen Gardiner asks, slyly. "For I would have words with one of your lords."

"How so, Your Eminence?" Gomes is at once on guard. The bishop sees the wary look in his eye, and plays one of his better cards.

"I hear that Herr Fugger likes religious art," he says, smiling benignly. "I wonder if he might be interested in the effigy of an angel?"

"Angel, you say?" Gomes realises that he is soon going to be out of his depth, and casts about the large outer court for his master.

"Yes, I have come into the possession of a certain kind, which might interest a banker." The bishop folds his arms across his chest, and waits for Tom Wyatt to play the next card.

"I am a close friend of Sir Ragnar Delabord," the poet says, dropping his voice to a conspiratorial level. "He is detained in the Tower of London, because of an unexpected audit. As we are both good sons of the church, he begged a favour of me. I was to ride to Framlingham Castle, and deliver a certain package to George Constantine."

"Really?" Gomes says. He is wondering how to reply, when he sees Fugger, and waves him over. After a speedy introduction, Gomes tells his master what has been said so far.

"Then you actually have these Angels?" Fugger asks. "What proof have you?"

Tom Wyatt fishes a piece of gold out of his purse, and hands it to the wary banker. It is a golden Angel, but the obverse side is blank.

"Half struck, to show we have the moulds, sir," the poet says. "The bishop is with us, and wants nothing more than Henry's ridiculous English church to fail. With the protestants defeated, he expects the pope to be generous, and bestow Canterbury or Westminster upon him. For my own part, I wish to be disgustingly rich."

"Ah, greed," Anton Fugger says, flipping the half minted coin back to the poet. "That, I do truly understand. What do you want, sir?"

"George Constantine is in Calais, with the moulds. He wants his rightful share, and suggests we set up, and mint, Angels somewhere in the *Calaisis* hinterland. He surrounds himself with tough rogues, and says he will chisel the moulds into scrap, if we do not comply."

"That was not the arrangement."

"No, the arrangement was to kill him, along with the duchess, and anyone else who knows," Wyatt replies, smiling. "Your Captain Gruyer is inept, and failed to do anything, but get us involved, and himself hanged. Will we barter, Master Fugger, or stand here smiling, all day long?"

"How do we work this?" Fugger says. "There must be a careful plan, to suit us all."

"Constantine has the moulds hidden away. I have taken possession of a remote barn in the Calaisis, and equipped it with anvils, striking blocks, and a good furnace for the smelting. All we lack is the metal."

"Then we must deal, sir," Anton Fugger says. "For I have promised the emperor that England will be brought down low. He is not concerned with making a profit, but I am. I will take eight tenths of all the coins we mint. You and the bishop shall have a tenth part each."

"And Constantine?"

"Once you have the moulds, kill him, and save his portion for yourselves." Fugger thinks this is a good deal, but Wyatt shakes his head.

"No, sir, that will not do." He raises a finger, and beckons over one of his servants, who is wrapped tightly in a cloak. "See, here is my bargaining piece, Herr Fugger. Speak, sir." The servant opens his cloak, and reveals himself to the banker and Gomes as George Constantine. He is terrified of Thomas Cromwell, and speaks his part to perfection.

"I have the Angels, and will only produce them when I am safe in Calaisis. I do not want to mint them, or be involved in any other way. Master Wyatt has a proposal that will satisfy us all. If you decline it, I will go on to Paris, and try my luck with the French king, François."

"Please, take your hand away from your sword, Captain Gomes," Tom Wyatt whispers. "I have a dagger in my sleeve, and will cut your master's throat in a trice. Now, do we deal?"

"Very well," Fugger says. He has no wish to die, and is eager for his plan to come to fruition, one way or another. Revenge is a dish best served cold, and retribution can always come later.

"My men will mint all the gold and silver you wish into debased, counterfeit coinage, and keep them all," Wyatt says, and watches the look of surprise on their faces. "In return, we will pay you one third of their face value. That way, you get real money, and do not have the risk of distribution."

"What then?" Fugger is calculating how much silver he can get together, and works out that his share will almost double his personal fortune. "How will you get the coins into circulation?"

"That is the wonderful part," Wyatt says, smiling broadly, and playing the last card. "Once in England, I will have them placed into the vaults at the Tower Mint, by Sir Ragnar Delabord. Then, over the months, he will release them into general usage. The gold saved by using the debased coinage will be spirited out, and sold to you, for Italian Ducati, Herr Fugger."

"Why?" Fugger cannot believe such a scheme.

"Because you are the only man in Europe who can afford so much gold in one delivery. You will strike it into genuine Ducats, or send it to my private mint, to be mixed with silver, and made into even more Angels."

Fugger is astute enough to know that this ploy is not limitless. After three or four such deals, England will be flooded with fake coins, and almost destitute of real gold.

"England will collapse." Gomes cannot resist gloating. "They will starve, and have to crawl back to Rome, on their heretical knees."

"Just so," Bishop Gardiner says, with a sigh of pleasure. "The king will be ruined, and have to crawl to Pope Clement. Once we are reconciled with Rome, my country, and I, will prosper once more."

"Then we have a deal," Fugger says. "Give Gomes the details of your secluded barn, sir, and I will arrange the first shipment. Be sure that the preacher keeps his end of the bargain."

"Rest assured, Herr Fugger, Master Constantine is in fear of his life, and will not fail us." Fugger watches Gomes and Wyatt step to one side, and fall into plotting. He smiles, and makes small talk with the bishop, who is a fool to think the Pope will forgive Henry so easily.

There is enough silver to mix with the gold at a ratio of four parts to one. This means that he can turn his investment of around twenty cight thousand Ducats into a little over one hundred and fifteen thousand Angels. The banker will clear a profit of almost fifteen thousand Brabant Ducats, with each transaction.

"May God bless our venture, Herr Fugger," Bishop Gardiner mutters.

"Amen, Your Eminence ... amen," Fugger replies, grinning broadly. He is to be blessed in many ways. The deal will make him even richer, the Pope will return to power in England, Henry will be humiliated, and Thomas Cromwell will fall from power, and go to the gallows...or the block.

Yes, he thinks, revenge is a sweet dish... taken hot, or cold.

*

The *Calaisis* is a beautiful piece of France, that is under the direct rule of the English king. The farms, villages, and wayside taverns are owned by Englishmen - often retired soldiers - and most inhabitants speak both English and French. The local laws are English laws, and Henry's face is on its coinage.

Captain Alessandro Gomes rides at the head of his little convoy of heavily laden wagons, and keeps a wary eye out for stray rogues, or bands of bandits. The countryside still teems with outlaws, and men disinherited, out looking for trouble. Each wagon has a driver and an armed guard, and there are another thirty armed men on horseback riding in close order.

They are a half mile away from where Tom Wyatt is meant to be waiting with his illicit mint, when the road is seen to be blocked by a huge fallen tree trunk. A lone ox cart is sitting on the far side of the blockage. A thick set man in his forties is sitting on the fallen trunk, drinking from a flask of watered down red wine. He raises his flask in greeting, and hails the advancing convoy of wagons.

"Good day to you, sir," the man calls. "I fear we have a problem. Each side of the road has a deep ditch running along it. The ditch is filled with mud and water, and I cannot pass."

"English?" Gomes asks, and the man nods.

"That I am sir, as are my companions." Mush, Richard, Tom Wyatt, and Barnaby Fowler stand up from behind the fallen oak, with muskets held at the ready. Tom Cromwell is enjoying himself, and plays the part to the hilt. "Might we trouble you and your men to put aside their weapons, and help move the tree from the road?"

"Five against thirty, old man," Alessandro Gomes says. "We will cut you down, and you Wyatt, I will kill, personally."

"Your arithmetic is somewhat lacking, Captain Gomes," Cromwell says, pointing to the trees on the Spaniard's right. Brushwood, and uprooted bushes are thrown aside by men in armour, to reveal four canon and forty muskets, pointed straight at him. And to your rear, you will find a troop of horse from the Calais garrison. That, I fear makes it your thirty to my one hundred and fifty. Now, kindly turn about, and gallop away. These wagons are contraband, and are now the property of King Henry of England."

"My master will have you all killed for this!" Gomes is furious and can hardly restrain himself from drawing his sword, but his men are already wheeling about, and galloping back to the border.

"My regards to your master," the thick set man snarls. "Tell him Thomas Cromwell accepts this in part payment, and will submit the final account at a future time. Now go!"

*

"George Constantine is gone," Mush reports to Cromwell, once they are safely back in Calais. "He must have slipped away when we were taking the wagons. Shall I put out word for him to be taken again?"

"Do not bother," Cromwell says. "The man must wake each day with another black mark on his soul. Each betrayal takes him closer to his own personal Hell. If he disappears, then so be it, but if he should be fool enough to surface again, and comes within our reach … have him killed. Let that be his punishment … to always wonder when some stranger might step out of the dark, with a knife in his hand."

"Richard is supervising the gold and silver being loaded at the docks," Mush Draper continues. "It is hard to say for sure, but the gold alone comes to something like twenty five thousand… and the silver about the same." Thomas Cromwell realises that the young Jewish man has something else preying on his mind.

"What is it Mush?" he asks.

"With my share of Fugger's treasure, I will be very well off, sir. It comes to me often as I sleep. The very same dream. I want to travel far, and visit the land of my forefathers."

"Why tell me this?" Tom Cromwell asks him. "You are a free man, and can follow your heart, wherever it takes you."

"My heart is ever at Austin Friars, master, and my devotion is to you alone." Mush struggles to carry on. "But if I do not go … I will surely regret it for the rest of my life."

"Go, with my blessing," Thomas Cromwell replies, but he does not mean it. First Will and Miriam move away, then Rafe will have his house of brick, and wed a woman who still has a husband. His son never visits, unless he is out of funds, and now Mush, and his pretty little Gwen, will leave him all alone.

"Are you sure, master?"

"I am," Cromwell tells him. All things change, he thinks. It is the way of the world. His clever plan to cheat Anton Fugger has paid him out in kind. It has made Mush financially independent. So, he will lose yet another of the small band he loves.

*

Anton Fugger downs a fourth glass of wine, in the hope that it will help him sleep. Since being fooled, and robbed by the Englishman, Cromwell, he has trouble sleeping. Thirty nine thousand Ducats out of pocket, and half of the world laughing at him, is a heavy burden on his mind.

Gomes eventually came back with the disastrous news, and he has banished him back to Spain, where he can rot, for all the banker cares. To add insult to injury, the Spaniard delivers a message from Cromwell, threatening further revenge. It is an empty threat, of course, for he is behind thick stone walls, and has a personal bodyguard of a hundred.

A fifth glass does the trick, and Anton Fugger drifts off to sleep, next to his new wife. He has a disturbed night, and wakes up at dawn, with a start. He sits up, and sees something odd on the low table by his bed. He fumbles to light his tallow candle, and stares in abject horror.

Beside his head, sticking in the wooden table is a long, thin knife. At last, he realises that it is another message.

Beware, Thomas Cromwell is saying from across the sea, for I can reach you, wherever you might be.

Anton Fugger shudders, and cries out for them to bring him a light. From now and forth, he will never sleep without his chamber being lit by a dozen candles.

In darkness, there is fear.

~End~

Postscript

Once more I find myself having to apologise to the reader, for my real characters behaviour, and for the shameless way I tailor them to fit into my fictional stories.

By now, readers familiar with my earlier books will recognise Thomas Cromwell as a real person, dressed up in a set of morals and ideas that he might never have possessed. As for poor Richard Cromwell, I can only say that my characterisation is at odds with his later life. Though a big man, there is little evidence that he was so violent, though he did serve in the army at one point. Far from him being slow witted, he was, in fact, a competent civil servant in later life, and a loyal supporter of his uncle, to the very end.

Anton Fugger is real too. He was a very rich banker, and was the man who financed the occupation, and terrible, exploitation of the so called New World. For the sake of profit, he visited untold misery on native populations, and encouraged their forced conversion to Christianity. Like most unpleasant men, he led a rich, happy life, and died in his bed - not from a dagger, but of old age.

George Constantine was also a real man. Taken prisoner by Sir Thomas More, he betrayed friends, and saw them burn as heretics, to save his own life. He was forced to flee England, and lived abroad, until circumstances at home changed, and he was allowed to come back.

Constantine was born around 1500, and in 1523 gained entry into Cambridge University to study for a Bachelor of Canon Law degree. He later adopted the Protestant doctrine, and fled to Antwerp, where he met and assisted William Tyndale . Here he helped to translate the New Testament into English, and compiled books denouncing the Catholic Church.

Constantine later moved to Paris, where he studied Lutheran scriptures and began to smuggle banned books into England. He was arrested in 1531 by Sir Thomas More. After revealing the names of some of his Protestant colleagues he was allowed to escape in December of the same year, returning to live in Antwerp.

He returned to England in 1536, following More's death, and entered the service of Sir Henry Norris. Later, Constantine was made the vicar of Llawhaden in Pembrokeshire. He made some ill judged remarks in 1539, which led to his imprisonment by Thomas Cromwell in the Tower of London.

Seven years later Constantine was released from prison, and regained favour with the new English church. He became the registrar of St David's in Wales, then, in 1549 he became the Archdeacon of Carmarthen and Prebendary of Llangammarch.

Although Constantine was stripped of his registrarship and all his livings during Queen Mary's reign, he was back in favour by 1559, when he was made Archdeacon of Brecon, by Queen Elizabeth I. Despite causing the death of men at the stake, time seems to have expunged his guilt, and he too died in bed, aged sixty.

Stephen Vaughan, though betrayed by Constantine, was able to escape death, thanks to Cromwell's direct involvement. He was sent abroad, and apart from becoming a successful merchant, he acted as a diplomat for the king, and as an agent for Thomas Cromwell - demonstrating the truth of the old saying that there is no such thing as a free lunch.

Rafe Sadler married his Mistress Ellen Barré, only for the dead husband to turn up, some years later. It took an act of parliament to resolve the issue, and legitimise their many children.

Tom Howard's married life was turbulent, after he tried to throw over his loyal wife, and take on a younger lover. The duchess refused to go quietly, and gave her wayward husband plenty of grief. Both remained staunch Catholics, and Elizabeth was a close friend of Queen Katherine. She did, indeed, smuggle letters to the queen inside oranges.

The debasing of coinage was rife in Europe during this period, as was coin clipping - the art of paring slivers of silver or gold from coins. A currency survived on its reputation, and coins with short weight could damage an economy, if produced in great numbers. A later Master of the Mint, Sir Isaac Newton fought a running battle with counterfeiters, and introduced many clever safeguards to keep England's currency safe.

The Manor of the More really existed, and was thought to rival the greatest palaces in France and England for beauty, and opulence. Built by Cardinal Wolsey, it found its way into King Henry's hands after his fall, and was used for various things from treaty signings, to incarceration of the king's enemies. Eventually, it became too expensive to keep up, and fell into disrepair. Nothing now remains of this once great edifice.

Welcome to TightCircle Publications

Thank you for choosing this book from our catalogue of exclusive to Amazon titles. Here are some of our other titles, which may be of further reading interest. TightCircle is a small, independent publishers, and is supported entirely by customer sales, or rentals. If you like what you read, please tell your friends.

Towards Hell:1888 Year of the Ripper by Tessa Dale
Winter King by Anne Stevens
Sex, Secrets & Sensible Shoes by Mona French
The Black Jigsaw by Tessa Dale
The Chinese Puzzle by Tessa Dale
And Angels May Fall by Steven Teasdale
Sex, Murder & Killer Heels by Mona French
Killing Time by Tessa Dale
Midnight Queen by Anne Stevens
For Empire by Alex Destry
Crime in Time by Tessa Dale
Small Murders edited by C J Dowsing
The Soul Eater's Tale by Steven Teasdale
The Red Maze by Tessa Dale
Sex, Sonnets & a Cop Chick by Mona French
Violent Lives by Steven Teasdale
The Twice Hanged Man by Tessa Dale
The Condottiero by Anne Stevens

This book is dedicated to my life partner who acts as adviser, editor, proof reader, and supporter. My unending thanks, for your selflessness.

Made in the USA
San Bernardino, CA
23 February 2018